LENORE APPELHANS

LEVEL 2

Book 1 of THE MEMORY CHRONICLES

SIMON & SCHUSTER BFYR
NEW YORK LONDON TORONTO
SYDNEY NEW DELHI

SIMON & SCHUSTER BFYR
An imprint of Simon & Schuster Children's Publishing Division
1230 Avenue of the Americas, New York, New York 10020
This book is a work of fiction. Any references to historical events, real people, or real places are used fictitiously. Other names, characters, places, and events are products of the author's imagination, and any resemblance to actual events or places or persons, living or dead, is entirely coincidental.

For information about special discounts for bulk purchases, please contact Simon & Schuster Special Sales at 1-866-506-1949 or business@simonandschuster.com.
The Simon & Schuster Speakers Bureau can bring authors to your live event. For more information or to book an event, contact the Simon & Schuster Speakers Bureau at 1-866-248-3049 or visit our website at www.simonspeakers.com.
Book design by Lizzy Bromley
The text for this book is set in Janson.
Manufactured in the United States of America
10 9 8 7 6 5 4 3 2 1
Library of Congress Cataloging-in-Publication Data
Appelhans, Lenore.
Level 2 / Lenore Appelhans. — 1st ed.
p. cm.
Summary: Seventeen-year-old Felicia Ward is dead and spending her time in the hive reliving her happy memories—but when Julian, a dark memory from her past, breaks into the hive and demands that she come with him, she discovers that even the afterlife is more complicated and dangerous then she dreamed.
ISBN 978-1-4424-4185-9 (hardcover)
1. Future life—Juvenile fiction. 2. Death—Juvenile fiction. 3. Angels—Juvenile fiction. [1. Future life—Fiction. 2. Death—Fiction. 3. Angels—Fiction.] I. Title. II. Title: Level two.
PZ7.A6447Lev 2013
813.6—dc23
2012008501
ISBN 978-1-4424-4187-3 (eBook)
FIRST EDITION

FOR

DANIEL JENNEWEIN–

MY TOUGHEST CRITIC AND BIGGEST FAN

ACKNOWLEDGMENTS

MY DEEPEST THANKS:

To my editor, Alexandra Cooper—your insight brought this book to levels I never dreamed possible. To the entire Simon & Schuster team, especially Justin Chanda, Amy Rosenbaum, Anna McKean, and Lizzy Bromley. To my agent, Stephen Barbara—it's a privilege to have you and the Foundry team in my corner. To the very enthusiastic team at Usborne in the UK as well as my other foreign publishers for letting *Level 2* jet-set around the world.

To Ann Bonwill for brainstorming this book with me over tuna and onion pizza in Pompeii. To Lauren Oliver for the confidence boost. To SCBWI for resources and opportunities. To early readers of drafts and scenes, especially Jenny Bragdon for her liberal use of exclamation marks, Ana and Thea for asking the hard questions, and Kelly Jensen for insisting there be more feelings.

To my friends for their encouragement. Shout-outs to Kelly Billingsley and Rev. William Mullins for answering my questions, to my fellow book bloggers for challenging and enabling me, to Michelle Franz at Literary Logistics for helping spread the word, and to the Apocalypsies for the community and feedback, especially Heather Anastasiu, Tamara Ireland Stone, Jess Rothenberg, and Jodi Meadows.

To teachers who nurtured my interest in writing, languages, and travel—Bette Lorenzetti, Dr. Michael Seewer, Ellen Shelley, Marla Gamble, Dr. Rosemarie Lones, and Dr. Ronda Hall.

To Tori Amos for the music and the interview that got me thinking about bees and eternity.

To my family, especially my father for passing down a love of reading and book hoarding, my late mother for making me look up every unfamiliar vocabulary word in *Big Red* instead of just telling me what it meant, and my husband, Daniel—I'm so glad we're in this together.

CHAPTER 1

I'LL SLEEP WHEN I'M DEAD. I used to say it a lot. When my dad suggested I turn off the flashlight I thought I so expertly hid under my covers. That time youth pastor Joe told us to pipe down at the church lock-in. The balmy summer night I convinced Autumn to sneak out after midnight so we could dance in Nidda Park, arms outstretched to the stars. But then I died.

And now I can't sleep. Except, that is, when I access my memories of sleeping. You wouldn't believe how many times I've combed through the seventeen years and 364 days of my life, searching for those rare uninterrupted, nightmare-free stretches of slumber. Because sleep is my only real break from this endless reel of memories, both mine and those I've rented.

Naturally, I've compiled a top ten. Most of the list includes Neil, though I often revisit a memory of being cradled on my dad's chest as a baby. It makes me feel like nothing bad could ever happen to me.

His lullaby envelops me in such warmth, I can almost forget I'm trapped here in this pristine hive with a bunch of other drones. All my age, all from the United States, all females who died in accidents in the early twenty-first century. And all so addicted to their personal memory chambers, they barely ever venture out.

Not that I'm not. Addicted, I mean. It's just that everything's hazy when I'm out of my memory chamber. I don't even remember how I got here. And though I do retain names and faces and relevant details of my fellow inmates, I never seem to be able to hold on to much else. At most, there are snatches of my conversations with Beckah and Virginia, but these fade in and out of my consciousness like barely remembered dreams. The three of us are the only ones who spend time in the communal area at the center of the hive. And sometimes, before we are compelled to heed the siren call of our chambers, we sit awkwardly on the polished, blinding white floor that matches the color and texture of every surface in our godforsaken prison. We muse about what this place might be, if this is all we have to look forward to for the rest of eternity, and about how strange it is not to have to eat or drink, or sweat or pee.

But we rarely talk about our deaths. We don't remember much about them after all this time anyway. We try to keep it light, inconsequential. I suggest "movie nights," where the three of us pull up memories of the same film in our chambers and then get together to discuss the details until our thoughts are too cloudy to continue. Virginia never gives up in her attempts to teach us back handsprings and complicated lifts, but I don't mind because my body, entirely numb in this afterlife, doesn't feel the pain of always crashing solidly to the floor. Beckah prefers to chat about books and where on the network to find the best quality memory editions of her favorites.

That's what I plan to do now, to search again for a precise memory version of Thornton Wilder's *Our Town*. Back in high school it was one I skimmed, which means accessing my own memory wouldn't do much good. I've discovered it's one a lot of people skim, despite its relative brevity, because I've yet to find a deep, meaningful reading of it, and I've accessed at least two hundred copies by now.

But before I embark on my search, I decide to say hi to Neil.

I lie down in my airy chamber and fit my hands into the grooves at my sides, feeling a slight zing and a rush of endorphins as my skin connects. Above me the hologram interface lights up, and I use my index finger to scroll through my memory folders until I find one of my favorite memories of Neil. I push play, and I'm there.

Ward, Felicia. Memory #32105
Tags: Ohio, Neil, Hiking, Youth group, Favorite
Number of Views: 100,235
Owner Rating: 5 stars
User Rating: Not shared

It's one of those gorgeous spring evenings I can never get enough of, when the trees burst with fresh, impossibly green leaves and the air is fragrant with promise. I am nearing the end of a daylong hike with the girls from the church youth group, and I nod from time to time as if I'm listening to the chatter around me. The talking barely registers because my head swirls with impressions of last night. Of how close I sat to Neil in the back of the van on the way up here. How casually, and without looking at me, he shifted the coat on his lap until it spilled over onto mine. And then how, without missing a beat, he trailed his fingers down my forearm and let them rest on my wrist, as if to take my pulse. How awareness of my surroundings faded as I zoned in on the slightest movement of his hand inching forward, slowly, tantalizingly. How my skin tingled and my own hand ached to touch him back.

And I am going to see him again soon. Very soon.

"Felicia?" Savannah snaps her perfectly manicured fingers in my face. "Don't you think I'd make an ideal Esther? Pastor Joe says I'm too blond." She huffs, shaking her head so her long golden waves shimmer in the fading sunlight. "He says Esther should be played by someone with dark hair. Like you. But no one really knows what Esther looked like. It's all conjecture."

"Black wig," I manage to get out, my face flushing as I remember the intensity of Neil's gaze on me last night as we got out of the van, the last time I saw him before the girls and guys split off to our separate cabins.

"Are you getting sick?" Savannah recoils, and immediately reaches into her pink purse for her bottle of hand sanitizer. My nostrils fill with molecules of artificial peach. She doesn't wait for my answer but moves away from me, catching up with some of the others, leaving me trailing behind.

I pick up my pace when I see the lights of our cabins through the trees. My heart starts pounding, and I stuff my hands into the pockets of my hoodie. I look up, and I see him. He's at the edge of the fire pit, joking around with Pastor Joe and Andy as they light kindling, trying to get a fire going.

Neil looks up and sees me too. His blue eyes twinkle. His smile is so luminous and pure, it's like he's been saving it up his whole life just for me. Andy pokes him in the side with a twig and whispers something into Neil's ear that makes him blush. Neil punches him lightly on the arm, and Andy shakes his head, snapping the twig in half.

"Hi," I say when Neil approaches. My giddiness at being this close to him again bubbles up in my throat, and I giggle. I want to hug him. Really hug him. But not here. Not in front of Pastor Joe and Andy.

"Hey!" He reaches out and tugs playfully on the strings of my hoodie. "Want to go for a walk?"

I giggle again. "It's not like we haven't been walking all day." The guys group went hiking too but took a different trail. A more challenging trail.

"Oh." Neil blushes, his smile faltering, and he runs one of his hands through his brown curls. "You must be exhausted."

I am. I'm also parched, and sweaty. My shoes are covered in mud. "I'm okay." I sigh. I'd love to change outfits. "But maybe I'll go in and grab another bottle of water at least."

"No need." Neil's smile is back to full force. He leads me over to where he has stashed his backpack next to a tree, and he bends down to pull out a bottle of water. As I take it from him, my fingers brush against his, and the sensory memory of last night pulses through my body.

I lift the bottle up to my lips and watch how his gaze follows and lingers. He swallows, and I swallow. Our eyes meet.

I look away sharply, over at the fire pit, where the kindling is burning now and Pastor Joe gestures for Andy to give him one of the bigger logs. This is a mistake. I shouldn't be here, shouldn't encourage Neil's interest in me, no matter how much I want to. He's too good. And he deserves better.

"Maybe we should go help with the fire," I mumble. My eyes are stinging, and I squeeze them shut to keep angry tears from escaping. It's all so unfair. He probably thinks I'm like him, without a care in the world. But that couldn't be further from the truth.

I feel Neil's hand on my cheek as he turns my head back to face him. "Hey, what's wrong?"

I look up at him and am overwhelmed by the concern shining in his eyes. All the feelings I've been pushing down for the past months well up inside me. A couple of hot tears trickle down my face, and my nose starts to itch.

Neil takes my hand, deliberately this time, not caring who sees, and leads me into the darkening forest. We pick through the underbrush slowly, side by side, and with each step I feel better. Stronger. Safer. Finally I stop. Neil stops too and faces me. Even though he's only inches away, I can barely make out his outline. But I feel his warmth, hear his raspy breathing.

"Um, Neil, do you have a flashlight?" I whisper.

His breath tickles my ear. "A Boy Scout is always prepared." He takes my other hand and guides it down to the lower pocket of his cargo pants. "In there." His tone is innocent despite the bold gesture.

I'm a little taken aback, but I fumble around in his pocket and pull out a mini Maglite. I turn it on, and without letting go of Neil's hand, I twirl in a circle so beams of light bounce off the surrounding trees.

"We should go," I say. Then I turn the flashlight off and slip it back into Neil's pocket.

I step closer to him, and recklessness takes over. I reach up and touch his lower lip lightly with my finger, and I close my eyes—

A siren blares. Glass shards cut my face. Intense pain hammers me everywhere at once. One, two, three beats, and then I jerk my hands out of the grooves. I'm back in my memory chamber, almost surprised to see I'm unharmed.

Something's wrong. That's not at all how the night ended.

Voices buzz all around me, an unusual sound. I sit up to look over the ledge to investigate. The other drones are all doing the same.

"Did you feel that?" Virginia calls out. A chorus of yeses responds, and everyone makes their way down from their memory chambers, to meet in the middle.

I head over to where Virginia stands, and Beckah joins us.

"What just happened?" Beckah asks, shaking. She has a haunted look on her face, a look I see echoed on all the other faces.

A girl named Amber is pointing at something behind me. "Omigod!" she shrieks, excited. "There's a boy coming in through a door!"

Impossible. We haven't seen any boys here. Ever. I spin around, and my mouth drops open. Because I know this boy. And he's calling my name.

CHAPTER 2

"FELICIA!"

His deep voice echoes through the hive, and the drones go silent, looking over at me with open curiosity.

He's standing in some sort of rectangular doorway—one that has never existed before—and he looks uneasy, frantic even. From behind, an arm is pulling at his black, fitted T-shirt, and as I rush over, I try to catch a glimpse of his companion. But all I see through the door is more glaring whiteness.

"Listen." His voice is lower now that I'm near the doorway, his head turning and his eyes darting from me to whomever it is he's with, and back again. "I'll be coming for you. Soon. Be ready." He steps out, and the last I see of him is his black high-top Converse, halfway laced. There's a pounding sound, heavy footfalls, and the door slides closed.

Not even a second later I run my hands over the smooth wall the closing of the door left behind, feeling for a ridge, a hinge, a control panel. But there's nothing. Just like there was never anything to find the approximately one million times I've been over this wall before, searching for a way out. I beat my fists against it, and then turn and let myself slide down the wall, defeated. At least I know now for sure there's something more than this single hive. Which means Neil might be out there somewhere.

"Who was that?" asks Virginia. She crouches down, examining my face. Beckah hangs back a bit, staring at me in awe. The others crowd around, reaching out to press their own hands against the wall.

"That was Julian." I shake my head, still not quite believing it.

"Who's Julian?" Virginia probes. "You sure seem important to him."

"Very important," Beckah chimes in, tucking her petite frame in next to me. "He said he wants to take you away, but I know you wouldn't leave us."

"He's just someone I knew once." I look Virginia straight in the eye and do my best to sound dismissive so she won't pry. "I have no idea why he suddenly showed up after all this time." It doesn't make sense. Not that anything makes sense here.

I turn to Beckah and soften my tone. "Don't worry,

Beckah. I promise I won't leave you behind." And I mean it too. I'd go crazy if I didn't have her and Virginia with me.

Beckah lights up and reaches out to squeeze my hand. She's never given up her habit of touching us, despite our insensitivity to physical contact. "Thank you. You two are the best friends I've ever had," she says. I squeeze back.

"Well, he must be important to someone," Virginia says, clearly not yet ready to close the subject. "I mean, why does he get normal clothes while the rest of us are stuck with these shapeless white shifts? He even has hair." Virginia rubs her bald head. It's the same bald look we all have.

I laugh, the bitter sound of it strange on my lips. Leave it to Virginia, former head cheerleader, to ask hair and fashion questions. "At least you still have some color," I say. Virginia pushes up the long sleeves of her shift, proudly exposing more of her tawny skin. There are only two other girls in our hive who don't blend into the walls. The rest of us are so bleached out, we're like photographs that have been overexposed.

The other drones are starting to lose interest in the wall and in me. They drift back off in the direction of their chambers. The temporary excitement has been sucked out of the hive, leaving only the dull nothingness we're used to.

Virginia looks at the retreating drones with disdain and lowers herself to the floor with an exaggerated sigh. "Ugh. They're all so *boring*."

Beckah regards me solemnly. "Where would you even go if you could get out of here? Would you look for Neil?"

"Of course she would, silly," Virginia blurts before I can reply. "She talks about him all the time."

I untangle myself out of Beckah's grasp and cross my arms over my chest, imagining for a second they are Neil's arms wrapping me in a hug. "I really miss him."

"I wish I had the chance to have a boyfriend as nice as Neil," says Beckah. "Or any boyfriend, really." She picks at invisible lint on her shift.

"Eww . . . but what if you find him and he's, like, ninety years old?" teases Virginia. "Maybe it's better to stick with your memories." Of course Virginia has a point. We've been here so long, and it's entirely likely Neil lived to a ripe old age, that he got married and forgot all about me. It's too depressing to contemplate.

"I can't stand not knowing," I say, hugging myself tighter. "I need closure. To know how he lived. If he ever still thought of me. How he died."

Virginia and Beckah stiffen at the mention of death. "I really want you both to meet Neil," I say, hoping my enthusiasm will relax them again.

It works. Virginia winks at me. "Oh, but we have met him," she says.

She's referring to the fact that they've both rented some of my memories of Neil. I haven't shared the more intimate ones on the net, but if I could blush, I would. "I mean, for real."

I duck my head, but Beckah catches my chin with her steady fingers and lifts it so I'm staring into her faded blue irises. "I hope we find him, Felicia. You deserve to be happy."

Maybe I should tell her that happiness is not exactly what a girl with my checkered past deserves, but the words stick in my throat. A strange mist swirls around Beckah's head, causing her mouth to go slack, her eyes to go glassy. The mist seems to permeate the room and to sink into my skin, making my limbs feel heavy. I want nothing more than to lie down. The three of us pick ourselves up slowly and wander off to our separate chambers.

I climb in, my thoughts jumbled. What was it I wanted to do? Look for a book? No, something more urgent than that. The name tugs at the edge of my consciousness. Julian. I need to look for him. Figure out what he wants with me. Figure out if he can really get us out of here so I can look for Neil. Once I position my hands correctly, the familiar glow of the hologram screen greets me. I scroll through my Julian memories, so unvisited that I wouldn't be surprised to find them collecting cobwebs. I decide on our first meeting and push play.

Ward, Felicia. Memory #31125
Tags: Germany, Autumn, Julian, Sushi, The Three Seasons
Number of Views: 5
Owner Rating: Not rated
User Rating: Not shared

Autumn and I have commandeered a table at our favorite sushi restaurant near Eschenheimer Tor. We haven't been here long, but I've already downed my second cup of espresso, burning my tongue in the process. Autumn's not paying attention to me, or her steaming cup of green tea. She's got her notebook out and she's focused on the couple sitting next to us, who are arguing over who should pay the bill. As I tear open the paper covering my wooden chopsticks, I stifle a yawn.

"Should we get two orders of California rolls or one?" I ask Autumn. I split my chopsticks and place them carefully on my chopstick holder, a lacquered green stone.

Autumn lifts up her hand to shush me. She scrawls notes into her notebook with her purple glitter pen. The feathers on top of it bob back and forth, and I bite back my annoyance. After a few moments of harsh remarks in German, the woman next to us reaches into her purse, pulls out some euros, and slaps them into the black plastic folder provided with the bill. The couple gets up to leave. The woman strides to the door without a backward glance, and the man shuffles behind her. The door dings once, closes, and then dings again.

"How hungry are you?" I ask. Neither of us has bothered to open our menus. It's never a question of what we'll get, just how much.

"Let's do two orders," Autumn says. She stacks her menu on top of mine, and then tucks her notebook and pen back into her bag.

"So, what was that all about?"

"Something I learned from Mr. Bennett," she gushes. "Eavesdropping is the best way to develop an ear for authentic dialogue, which is going to help us so much with our novel."

For our latest in a string of half-completed writing projects, Autumn has come up with an idea for a book about three friends all fighting over the same guy. It's called *The Three Seasons* because each of the friends has a season as part of her name. Autumn will tackle two of the points of view: Autumn Hooper, "the long-suffering friend," and Chelsy Winters, "the mentally unstable one." Autumn has charged me with writing the point of view of Bethanne Summer Chandler, "the guy magnet." I think it's her passive-aggressive way of trying to tell me something.

I groan. "Why do we have to work on another novel? Can't we try a screenplay this time?"

"Maybe I'd rather be the cliché of the starving writer than the waitressing screenwriter." Autumn tucks an errant strand of her short blond hair behind her ear. "Movies are more your thing anyway. I'm not the one who spends my entire allowance on cinema tickets and downloads."

"I read as many novels as you do. Maybe more. I'm just not sure I want to write one. And I think you're so into this because you want to impress Mr. Bennett." I don't add that I doubt our tweed-wearing, classics-loving English teacher, as relatively young and sexy as he is, will be all that likely to praise our teen melodrama.

Autumn blushes. "Don't be a dream crusher," she retorts. "Have you even started on your first chapter yet?"

"Tell me again why I am involved in this project."

She goes into lecture mode. "You know it has always been our dream to be published by the time we're twenty. And I read online that multiple-point-of-view novels are hot right now. Finding the right voice for each character is essential."

I roll my eyes. "We made that pact when we were eight. How long are you going to torture me with it?"

"And, you owe me." Her tone hardens. "Everything's not always about you, you know."

"I know." I gulp. I suspect she's referring to my getting a highly coveted spot in Mr. Bennett's advanced writing seminar. She's the one who convinced me to go for it in the first place, and now she's angry that Mr. Bennett chose me over her, and that I refused to quit and let her take my place. I know I should give on this book project of hers, let her have her way for once, especially since she seems so envious of me sometimes. In the grand scheme of things, it's so minor. But the espresso has finally kicked in, and I feel jittery and argumentative. "Well, if we have to write something, couldn't it be a little more . . . epic?"

"C'mon, Felicia. We've discussed this." Her exasperation with me is loud and clear. "Mr. Bennett says it's important to focus on one project at a time." Autumn juts out her chin and fixes me with her steely gaze. "And besides, you need an awesome idea first. Do you have one of those?"

I take a deep breath, ready to fight this out if I have to. "I'm sure I could come up with one. How about . . ."

But my words die on my lips, because the door has

dinged again, and Autumn looks like she's been hit by lightning. She lunges at me and grabs my arm. "Dibs," she whispers under her breath, pinching me with her fingernails and shooting me a warning look. Then she pulls back with a radiant smile.

Though I want to tell her calling dibs doesn't magically make a person like you instead of someone else, I refrain. Instead I turn around to check out the latest object of Autumn's affection. My body stiffens with recognition. The boy walking in is achingly beautiful, too model perfect with his high cheekbones and strong jaw to be someone I'd know, but he looks familiar all the same. He scans the restaurant, reaching up casually to brush shaggy blond bangs across his forehead. When his dark eyes meet mine, the force makes me physically shrink back. He heads over to our table.

"*Ist hier frei?*" he asks in German. He pulls out the chair at the table next to us and sits down without waiting for an answer, never letting go of my gaze.

"Yes, this seat is free," Autumn answers in English, her voice tinged with a sweetness that makes me want to gag.

"Excellent," he says, easily switching to an English as unaccented as his German. "I knew today was my lucky day." He plucks one of our menus off our table with a large, pale hand and opens it. "What's good here, ladies?"

"The California rolls. That's what we're getting." Autumn leans over to point it out on the menu, though he doesn't stop staring directly into my eyes. "They make it with tamago here. Really tasty."

"Great." He snaps the menu closed and lets it fall onto his table. "I'll get those too, then." He waves his arm to summon the waitress. She comes over, and he finally breaks his eye contact, setting me free. I let out my breath. Had I been holding it the entire time?

Autumn addresses the stranger. "Is one order okay for you . . ." She trails off.

"Julian," he supplies, extending his hand in her direction, a charming smile on his lips.

"Autumn." She shakes his hand, lingering longer than strictly necessary before letting go. "And this is Felicia." She gestures at me as though I am no more than an afterthought.

I reach over to shake his hand too, to be polite, but my movement is jerky, and I knock the second menu to the floor.

I bend down to retrieve it at the same time as the waitress. She whisks it away, and as I straighten, Julian's hand grasps mine. His touch ignites a longing—and a pang of fear—that burns through my veins. I pull away instinctively.

"Hi." I look up at him through my long hair and then reach up with my hands to smooth it back into place. "Is it possible we've met before? Do I know you from somewhere?"

Julian chuckles. "Have you ever been to rural Kansas? The stretch of Highway 54 between Greensburg and Wichita?"

"No." So he's from Kansas? He doesn't look like a farm boy.

Autumn clears her throat and kicks me under the table. "Is one order enough for you, Julian?" Her eyes slide with naked admiration from his face down his imposing frame.

"Just a snack. One order is more than enough." He's tapping his foot, drawing my attention to his black Converse.

"We'll take three orders of California rolls," Autumn tells the waitress. The waitress nods and stalks off. They're never very talkative here.

Julian looks us over. "I take it you're Americans?"

"Our parents work for the U.S. State Department," I say. "You?"

"I'm taking a year off." He shifts in his chair and then rises. "We can shove these tables together and get a bit cozier." He pushes his table until it's lined up with ours, and then sits back down, satisfied. "Germany is my first stop. I want to explore the world, you know?" he says. "Been trapped way too long in one place."

"Well, join the State Department, then." Autumn laughs, a little too loudly. "We've been all over. Africa, Asia, South America."

"See, now that's impressive. To be so young and to have experienced so much already." He looks contemplative. "If you died right now, you'd still be so rich."

A shiver runs down my spine.

Autumn laughs again and places a hand on his arm flirtatiously. "Oh, we're not ready to kick the bucket yet, Julian. We still have to give you the grand tour of Frankfurt." She counts out the attractions of Germany's banking capital. "The Old Opera, the botanical garden, Nidda Park . . ." She pauses. "Well, anyway. There is a lot to see."

Julian cocks his head and regards us for a long moment.

"I'd be honored to have you two as my guides."

I shake off my dread and look over at Autumn. She's stretching like a bloom aching for the sun's attention. "We'd love to!" she squeals, bouncing in her chair, the color high on her cheeks. She bends over and extracts the feather pen from her bag again, and then offers it to him. "Write down your number for us."

He waves her pen away. "Actually, maybe we can meet here again tomorrow? Same time? I still need to get a phone."

"Right, of course." Autumn reaches down with one hand, takes out her pad, and places it on the table. She opens it up to one of the last pages and starts writing with her garish feathered pen, forming the loops of her name and her mobile phone number with a flourish. She sets down the pen and starts to rip out the page.

"Wait. Can you give me Felicia's number too?" Julian shrugs, and shuffles in his seat. "You never know. I may not be able to reach you."

"Uh . . . sure." She pauses. "Felicia? Is that okay with you?"

I don't know exactly why, but I don't want Julian to have my phone number. "Actually, my phone battery died. I have to get a new one," I lie. "Call Autumn for now."

Autumn grins. "That's right! No phone problems here!" She finishes ripping out the page and hands it to Julian. He nods, folds it, and shimmies it into the back pocket of his jeans.

There's an uncomfortable silence then, broken only by

the waitress returning with our tray of sushi. She places it on the table, and then distributes three tiny plates, one for each of us. I reach for the bottle of soy sauce as she walks away. I am in the middle of pouring when a flapping motion outside attracts my attention.

We all turn toward the window. "Whoa—what was that?" exclaims Autumn.

"Something must have spooked all those pigeons on that old medieval tower out front. I saw them earlier." Julian looks casually at his watch, and then gets up. "Sorry, ladies," he says, flashing us an apologetic smile. "Looks like I am going to have to cut our conversation short. Can we meet up tomorrow?"

"But what about your sushi?" Autumn bites her lip. "Can't you stay to finish it?"

"No, darling. Almost forgot about an appointment." He reaches into his back pocket. "How much do I owe you?"

"Don't worry about it." Autumn jumps to her feet. "We'll let you get the check next time."

"Good deal." He bends down and pecks Autumn on one cheek and then the other. "That is the custom here, right?"

"Right." Autumn giggles. "On your way to being a native already."

Julian crosses over to my side of the table, and I get up, too fast, knocking my forehead against his chin. He reaches out his hands to steady me, and I look up at him. He leans over and brushes his lips against the cheek that's hidden from Autumn's view. "See you soon," he whispers into my ear, and then pulls away abruptly. His promise thrills me as much as it frightens me.

He walks to the door. He pulls it open with one hand and waves to us with the other. And then he's gone.

"Oh, I'm in love!" Autumn crams a roll into her mouth and chews.

"What about Mr. Bennett?" I ask, settling back into my chair. I use my chopsticks to pick up a roll, but my throat feels dry. I put it back.

"Please!" Autumn slaps the table. "Seriously. You saw Julian. He's, like, everything I've ever wanted in a man."

"You don't know anything about him," I point out. "Except he's hot."

"Extremely hot," Autumn corrects. "And I'm meeting him again tomorrow!" She scoops up her bag, tosses her notepad into it, and pulls out her cell phone all in one smooth motion.

"Shall we take this to go?" Autumn asks. But she flags down the waitress for a box without waiting for my answer, and begins texting furiously. She's likely bragging to Nicole and her minions about her new conquest.

I slide the plate of sushi farther away from me and take a deep breath to fight the nausea rising up in my stomach. The feeling of déjà vu threatens to suffocate me.

I pull out of the memory, and then systematically revisit others from those early days of our acquaintance. There's the one when Autumn chatted animatedly for hours about

Frankfurt's history as we guided Julian around Old Town. I hung a couple of steps behind, trying to avoid his pointed looks. And then there's one from the week after that, when Autumn invited him to go with us to a classmate's party. She got drunk on white wine and the envious stares of all the girls, and some of the guys, in attendance. And of course, the day we met in Nidda Park for a picnic. Autumn tried to impress Julian by bringing a blanket and a vintage bottle of port, and clenched her teeth when Julian refused both and instead sprawled out on the freshly mown grass. I asked him when he planned to move on to his next adventure. He winked at me and said he was having too much fun with us.

I scroll down to the next Julian memory on my list, my finger hovering over the play button. A high-pitched wail sounds from below me, breaking my concentration. I sit up and peer out of my chamber just in time to see Virginia running up the stairs toward me.

"Come quick! It's Beckah. She keeps saying she's dying."

CHAPTER 3

I FOLLOW VIRGINIA to Beckah's memory chamber and have to push through the drones that have gathered there, like rubberneckers at a car wreck. Beckah's chamber is at ground level, so there are two exits—one at her feet next to the stairs and one from the side, facing into the hive. I bend down and peek in. Though her hands are no longer in her control grooves, Beckah's hologram screen is still on, blinking like an alarm in a way I've never seen before. Beckah's eyes are squeezed shut, and she's shaking her head back and forth, mumbling unintelligibly.

"Beckah? Can you hear me?" I caress her forehead, wishing my touch could be a comfort.

"She hasn't responded to any of us." Virginia bends

brought in three litters of kittens. Can you come help me?"

I nudge the puppy back into his cage and latch the door. As I head out to take care of the new arrivals, I smooth my blazer and brush away a small clump of dog hair.

But suddenly I'm back in my bedroom. The air is thick with smoke as I inch my hand up the door, feeling for the handle. I press my pillowcase over my mouth with my other hand, but it's not helping much. My breaths are shallow, but still I cough. When I finally find the handle, I snatch my hand away. It's burning. I have to find another way out. The window. "Help!" I try to scream as I crawl toward the window, but my voice is so weak. My strength is gone, and I crumple to the floor. "I'm dying! I'm dying."

But this is not me. I'm Felicia, not Beckah. As real as it feels, this is not my memory. I force my mind to push out of it and enter Beckah's console. I browse through her saved favorites until I find a memory of Beckah as a five-year-old sitting in the middle of a sunny meadow, plucking wildflowers and arranging them carefully in a basket.

I pull out of her grooves and then sit up to examine my hands. They feel raw and look oddly red. What's going on? I haven't been able to feel anything, except in my memories, until now, and pain is not exactly the sensation I'd choose for my first in an eternity.

"Are you okay in there?" asks Virginia.

I scoot out carefully, wincing each time I put weight on my hands. "I did it! I was inside Beckah's memories."

Only Virginia and Beckah remain in our common space. The other drones have moved back to their own chambers.

"Really? How?" Virginia looks from me to the semiconscious Beckah and back again. "That's impossible!"

"I honestly don't know. I imagined myself controlling her console, and then I was."

"What are you, some kind of telekinetic hacker prodigy?" Virginia appraises me as if seeing me for the first time.

"Actually . . ." I consider confiding in Virginia, but don't feel like getting into a bunch of lengthy stories about my shameful past. Not with everything that's going on. "It's nothing." I shrug as nonchalantly as possible.

She raises a nonexistent eyebrow but doesn't say anything.

"So anyway, I landed in this memory of her at the animal shelter, but then it, like, switched over to her death memory." I shudder. "Luckily, I was able to turn it off and go into one of her top tens. Maybe if we put her back in now, reliving it will calm her down."

"Let's do it." Virginia lifts Beckah's head from her lap and grabs under her shoulders as she raises herself from a sitting position.

I lift Beckah's legs at the same time Virginia lifts her torso. We stumble a bit, but get her back in and her hands settled into her grooves. She relaxes instantly, a smile forming on her lips.

"Wow. Impressive." Virginia straightens and nods in appreciation.

I raise my hand for a high five.

"Felicia! What's wrong with your hands? They're red!"

I groan. "I know. I burned them in Beckah's console. In the fire that killed her."

"Now, that's crazy." Virginia grabs my hands and turns them palm-up for inspection. "How can that happen? Things don't transfer from our memories. Because, believe me, if they did, I'd smell like Chanel No. 5 instead of a whole lot of nothing."

"Maybe I need to go on the network and try to find a memory of someone slathering themselves with burn cream." A smile tugs at the corners of my mouth. "I bet it doesn't smell too great, though."

"No. I bet not." Virginia taps her chin. "You said before you went into Beckah's console that a lot of weird stuff was going on, the system changing or something. What did you mean?"

"Have you forgotten the siren already? Julian showing up? Seeing a boy here for the first time ever definitely counts as weird."

Virginia narrows her eyes. "Oh, hell no! Now you're making stuff up."

Am I? My brain feels heavy, my thoughts murky. It's always like this when I'm out of my chamber for any length of time. "Julian was here. I'm sure of it."

Virginia chuckles. "Wishful thinking, sweets. But if a guy does ever come, send him my way. I could use a little man action."

"Trust me. If I wanted man action, I wouldn't get it

from Julian." The thought disgusts me. "You really don't remember he was here?"

"No. Because he wasn't," she says firmly. "Nobody has ever been here but us."

This place is starting to really creep me out. I stride over to the flat expanse of wall where I remember the door opening. Where Julian stood. I shudder.

"Where are you going?" Virginia follows me.

"There was a door. Right here." I pound the curved wall, drawing back as the sound echoes dully though the hive. "It was open and Julian stood right here."

"A door." Virginia looks at me like I am insane. "Really. I'm starting to think some of that smoke inhalation from Beckah's fire has given you hallucinations."

I bite back my frustration and push past her, returning to Beckah's chamber. "Let's just check on Beckah."

I peer into Beckah's chamber. Her eyes are open, staring at her lighted console, and her hands are folded across her chest. She looks peaceful. She looks dead. "Beckah?"

Beckah turns her head and looks at me. "Who are you?" she asks in a little girl voice. "Where's my mommy?"

I'm speechless. Virginia gasps behind me, and then she's beside me, reaching out to take Beckah's hands in hers. "Beck-ah!"

"You're not my mommy," says Beckah, pulling away. She scrambles as far from us as possible, which is not far. Then she pulls her legs to her chest and huddles against the smooth back wall of her chamber. "I want my mommy."

I exchange a look with Virginia, and we both straighten up at the same time. "Is this weird enough for you?" I whisper.

"But what's going on with Beckah?" Her eyes grow unnaturally wide. "Is this what is going to happen to us?"

"Maybe it's my fault. Maybe by programming a memory of five-year-old Beckah, I made her regress to that state?" I start to pace. It helps me fight through the sludge in my head so I can think. Ten long strides from Beckah's chamber to the erstwhile door. And ten long strides back. "Maybe I can get in there again and try to program something else?"

"Such as?" Virginia drops down to the stair closest to Beckah's chamber. "The day her momma left her? The day she got beat to a pulp by her stepdaddy because she didn't wash his dish fast enough?"

I stop in my tracks and glare at her. "No need to be sarcastic." Then I continue my pacing.

From what little I know of her life, Beckah didn't have a lot of good days, especially as she got older. And what was it going to help if I programmed in something from when she was seventeen and not five? She still wouldn't remember us, since she didn't know us while she was alive. At least if she were older, though, maybe she'd be more able to help herself. I know she's tougher than she looks.

"I can rent a comforting memory off the net for her," I say. "Calm her down."

"You know as well as I do that Beckah never has any credits. No one wants to rent her awful memories."

That's not entirely true. Beckah does sometimes get

good credits for her careful and thoughtful reads of classic and modern literature. In literary circles on the net she has some cache, especially because she was often patient enough to read entire books in one sitting. She's no S. K. Love, the top source for quantity and quality, but her memory editions get their fair share of rentals. The problem is, she spends whatever credits she gets as soon as they come in. I guess I might too if my life had been like hers.

"I can try transferring some of my credits to her." I amass way more credits than I can ever use. Turns out people here pay top credit for travel, and I did a lot of that in my short lifetime. It's the new experiences and sensations people clamor for, as everything familiar tends to produce a powerful state of ennui once you've done it enough.

"If that works, you can send some my way too." Virginia grins. "I'm getting critically low myself."

"Uh, yeah. I'll get right on that." I duck back down to check on Beckah. She's whimpering softly, chattering her teeth as if she were cold. Which she can't be. Either our afterlife bodies aren't sensitive enough to know the difference or the temperature stays a comfortable constant.

"Hey, Beckah. I'm going to bring you a kitty. Would you like that?" From the memory of hers I recently experienced, I know she has a soft spot for animals, so I figure a cat is a good bet.

Beckah nods slowly, her chin quivering. "I like kitties."

"That's great! Now, if you want your kitty, you're going to have to lie down again. Can you do that for me?"

She considers me for a moment and then nods again. "Okay." She crawls over and lies down in her grooves.

"Good girl. Now close your eyes. I'll be right back with your kitty, Beckah." I have the urge to tuck her in with a blanket and stroke her hair, but neither is possible, considering the lack of both. I cross my fingers that my plan will work. Perhaps I wasn't the best friend on Earth, but I want to be someone Beckah and Virginia can count on. I need to be.

I turn to Virginia. "Why don't you stay here and keep your eye on Beckah while I see what I can do from my chamber?"

Virginia gives me a mock salute. "Aye, aye, Captain."

I punch her lightly on the shoulder and then head back to my chamber. I pause to look around the hive—all the pod-like chambers are lit up as the drones shoot up on memories. Why is it that only Virginia and I care about what happens to Beckah? God knows we've all been here long enough to form a strong bond, and yet most of the drones have never shown the slightest bit of interest in getting to know one another. I've wanted to get out of here before, but now the tight quarters start to choke me. There has to be more to death than this.

I slide into my chamber and relax into my grooves, smiling as the warm glow of my hologram screen greets me. My body tingles in response to plugging in, like it always does. The pain in my hands is gone, replaced by tiny prickles of pleasure. The closest I can equate it to is slipping into impossibly warm bathwater filled with delicious spices on a chilly winter evening. Despite my chamber's cold, metallic appearance, it is a remarkably ergonomic setup. Whoever designed it—God? Angels? Evil overlords of death?—sure knew what they were doing.

The net architecture isn't the most sophisticated, but it has never been buggy until now. Its basic function is to allow you to access and rent out your memories as well as to rent the memories of others. When you access your own memories, you can tag them with labels. This is so you can find what you are looking for more easily but also so you can advertise your wares to others on the net. So for example, the succulent steak dinner I ate with my father at a Brazilian churrascaria in Buenos Aires when I accompanied him on one of his business trips, I labeled with "Dad," "best medium-well steak dinner ever," and "Argentina."

Obviously people want to make their memories sound as appealing as possible so that the memories will sell and garner them credits. This leads to a lot of "best ever" labels that are not at all accurate in their description. Fortunately, renters have the chance to give feedback using a star rating of one through five, five being the best and one the worst. My "best steak dinner ever" is currently rated a five, and it gets a lot of rentals, even though it costs more credits than a steak dinner rated a four (totally acceptable quality, in my opinion). People love a great steak—even, I suspect, those who were vegetarians in life. In any case, it's much more popular than my "best brussels sprouts ever." I wonder sometimes, though, does this collective rating of memories add value to our existence here? Do certain parts of people's pasts deserve to be remembered while others are forgotten?

The net is a sprawling place to surf, so once you find memories you enjoy and want to come back to, you can save them in a "favorites" folder for easier access. As long as you have the credits, the net helps a lot in quelling the boredom of our never-ending days. But it does have its limits. You can't access memories formed outside of your lifetime, so there are no journeys to the past and none to the future. I've tried to get around this so I can find out what happened to Neil, but I've had no success so far.

It's also not set up to "gift" credits or memories, but I've managed to crack the code and donate to other people before. Most simple would be to rent Beckah's memories to bestow credits on her account. I used to do this, but once I exhausted her book collection, my rentals were more charity driven than anything else. Since I don't want to take the time to rent a memory now—renting means playing back a memory immediately in its entirety—I opt for the hacker route.

I search through my database for a good cat memory to share. Usually when I feel like cuddling with a cat, I call up Neil's cat, Sugar. After school, and before Neil's parents got home from work, Neil and I used to take naps together in his room, though Neil insisted we keep the door open to keep him from acting on his impure thoughts. Sugar would join us, lying in the crook of my arm and purring like a motor. But sharing Sugar would mean sharing Neil, and I don't want to risk that, just in case the system is really messed up and I can't get my memory back.

I decide to share one of Zamora. She was the sweet-natured stray that visited us during one of our stays in Washington, D.C., between country assignments. My mother wouldn't let us keep her officially since we traveled too much to be responsible pet owners, but she did buy cat food for her, so I considered her our cat.

I pick one to transfer to Beckah's account, a warm summer morning when Zamora was stretched out on my lap while I watched cartoons. It's a long shot, but I try to copy and paste and drag and drop. Both methods produce error messages. I'm going to have to go in the back way and code my own path, something I don't like to do because it reminds me too much of my sins. There's a tiny button at the top of the screen, and I push it for three long beats with short pauses in between, a trick I discovered accidentally a while back. The screen fills with code, and I rearrange it, trying out various combinations and switching back to the home screen to see if it works. Finally I see the "In use" designation and give myself a virtual pat on the back.

I hop out of my chamber to report back to Virginia, but she's not there. Alarmed, I rush down the stairs and over to Beckah's chamber and look in.

It's empty. Beckah is gone.

CHAPTER 4

MY SCREAM attracts the attention of Virginia and the other drones. Virginia rushes over. The other drones do not.

"Why did you leave Beckah all alone? She's gone!" I try not to sound judgmental, but I can't help it.

"What are you talking about?" asks Virginia, genuine confusion on her face. "Who's Beckah?"

Her words hit me hard, and I stare at her, openmouthed. This cannot be happening. If Virginia still remembers me but doesn't remember Beckah, then whoever controls this place not only removed Beckah physically from her chamber, they must have deleted her from the net altogether. But why do I still remember her?

"Who was in this chamber if it wasn't Beckah?"

Virginia scrutinizes the empty chamber and then scrunches up her face at me as if I am asking a trick question. "Uhhh . . . that chamber has always been empty."

I cross my arms over my chest. "Seems pretty wasteful," I say, my tone betraying my impatience.

"You look stressed out, Felicia." Virginia puts her arm around me and knocks her hip against mine. "Can I suggest renting a couple of my rocking parties to cheer you up? I could use the credits, and I know you're good for them."

"I'm not in the mood, thanks." I extract myself from her embrace and stalk back to my chamber. How is it that Virginia can remember me but not the three of us together?

"Suit yourself!" She hums a Pink song. Loudly. Once I get to my stairs, I turn and catch her swaying to the beat of her music with her eyes half-closed. Totally blissed out.

I couldn't have dreamed what happened in Beckah's chamber. I'm not going crazy. I'm not.

I slam myself into my chamber and pull up my console. The memory I shared with Beckah is no longer displaying "In use." Instead there is a flickering "Error" message. I access my labels cloud and scan it for "Beckah." Nothing. Same in my book favorites. All of Beckah's editions are gone. Wiped from the net as if they never existed.

I'm stunned. All this time, I've known I'm dead—at least what people still on Earth think of as dead—but I've never felt completely dead, because I obviously still exist in this place, whatever it is, and I can access my life anytime. It never ever occurred to me I could be so easily erased.

I heard somewhere once that people never truly die while people on Earth still remember them. As long as a person is in someone else's thoughts, a part of them lives on. Does that mean that everyone who once knew Beckah is now dead too? Is that why she is gone from here? But surely everyone who once knew me must be dead too, considering I've been here for what seems like lifetimes upon lifetimes.

Has Beckah ceased to exist? Or has she moved on to another plane? Up until the last six months of my life, I had little interest in church and religion, but I knew enough about heaven that I'm pretty sure this can't be it. Could it be some sort of purgatory? Or even hell?

I get the impulse to hear Pastor Joe's sermon about heaven, to see if it might give me some clue as to where we are and where Beckah might now have gone. He preached it the first Sunday I attended Central Christian with my grandmother, after being banished by Mother for being a security risk to her job. It was also the first time I met Neil.

I search through my folders until I find it, and I'm in.

Ward, Felicia. Memory #31655
Tags: Ohio, Neil, Heaven, Amazing singing voice, Church
Number of Views: 2,918
Owner Rating: 4.5 stars
User Rating: 4 stars

The bitter January wind whirls brittle leaves around the shiny black leather pumps Grammy insisted a proper young lady should wear to church, and it whips at my shin-length skirt. I have one hand at my throat, clutching the cashmere of my Burberry scarf, a relic from a time when I could actually sort of afford one. I'm glad Grammy doesn't consider plaid as unladylike as flats and as sinful as skirts that fall above the knee.

My other arm is linked with Grammy's, and we are inching up the stairs that lead to the grand front doors of Central Christian Chapel. When I saw the handicap accessible ramp leading into the back door, I nudged her in that direction, but this is another comfort Grammy deems improper. She'll come in the front entrance or she'll stay home.

Once we finally reach the door, I push it open, only to be greeted by a wildly overenthusiastic girl my age.

"Good morning, Mrs. Ward!" She rigorously shakes Grammy's hand and then mauls me with a hug. "You must be Felicia! Your grandmother has told us so much about you." She pulls back and beams at me, seemingly unfazed by my stiff posture and deer-in-headlights expression. "Come, we'll have Mr. Eaton escort your grandmother to her usual pew, and you'll sit with all of us up front."

"Good morning, Savannah," Grammy says. I expect her to make a stand, but she nods primly and gestures at an elderly gentleman who must be Mr. Eaton. "Enjoy the sermon, Felicia. I'll see you at the end of the service."

"I'll introduce her to the whole group," Savannah says. My insides clench at the thought of meeting so many new people. She prods me in the side with her pink crystal-encrusted Bible. "Let's go! We want to make sure we get seats on the left side. It has the best view. You'll see."

Since Grammy has clearly dismissed me, I follow Savannah, wondering what kind of view she could be talking about. There are moderately impressive stained-glass windows along both sides of the chapel, depicting angels and people from biblical stories, but I can't see that the ones on the left, which appear to be mainly from the Old Testament, are any more worth viewing than the New Testament scenes on the right side. The space behind the pulpit is sparsely decorated. There's a cross over the baptistery and two doors, one on either side, that lead to the two sets of steps flanking the chancel. An upright piano and a scattering of empty chairs occupy the left side of the chancel, a single half pew the right. All in all, it's a spare building, a pale imitation of the richly adorned cathedrals of Europe.

"Here we are." Savannah stops short of the pew in the second row and gestures as if presenting me my prize winnings on a game show. "The best seats in the house."

I shrug off my coat and fold it into my lap as I sit down, hugging it to me in an attempt to keep the intoxicating effects of Savannah's bubbly energy cocktail from spilling over and soaking into my pores. Savannah sits beside me, unzipping but not bothering to remove her jacket. "I'd keep that close." She pats my coat. "It does tend to get drafty in here."

"Thanks for the tip." I hope I don't sound as crabby as I feel.

If I do, Savannah doesn't remark on it. She points out various people to me and feeds me tidbits about their small-town lives, barely taking breaths between her exclamations. Soon enough a group of girls files in from the other side of the pew and squishes in next to me. Savannah introduces us. Their waves and greetings seem muted after Savannah's, though they are still far peppier than I am used to this early on a Sunday morning.

The girl to my right adjusts her glasses and then reaches over me to squeeze Savannah's arm. "How was your date last night?" she whispers loudly.

Savannah flutters her eyelids and takes a deep breath. "Let's pretend it never happened."

Glasses Girl pulls back and nudges me in the ribs with her elbow. "What about you, Felicia? Do you have a boyfriend?"

The word "boyfriend" dredges up thoughts of Julian. Not that he was really my boyfriend, or that I'll ever see him again. "No." I don't feel the need to elaborate.

Thankfully, Glasses Girl turns away and starts up a hushed conversation with the other girls. Savannah checks her watch and tells me the service is starting.

As if on cue, the door to the right of the pulpit opens, revealing an ancient woman who hobbles in and sits at the piano. She arranges her sheet music and perches a pair of bifocals on her nose. Other musicians trickle in and find their seats. I feel Savannah tense beside me, and there is a collective holding of breath. Then an unassuming young man with unruly brown curls enters, guitar in hand, and closes the door behind him. The congregation breathes out in what seems like a mix of relief and anticipation. I half expect them to start clapping.

As the band launches into a hymn I don't recognize, the young man makes his way over to the pulpit, swings the guitar strap over his shoulder, and starts strumming. He looks heavenward and sings in a pure, rich baritone. The effect on the crowd is immediate. Savannah and the other girls gaze at him with rapt expressions. He's incredible, even to someone like me, who, thanks to my father's work as a composer, has attended countless concerts by world-class singers.

It's both the emotion in his voice and the words he sings that penetrate me to my core. "*Blessed be the tie that binds . . . When we asunder part, / It gives us inward pain; / But we shall still be joined in heart, / And hope to meet again.*" Too soon the hymn is over, and there are tears brimming in my eyes. I hastily wipe them away with the end of my scarf, hoping no one has seen.

The young man backs away from the pulpit and sits in the last empty chair on the far left. An older man in a suit advances reverently to the microphone. "That's my dad," Savannah breathes into my ear. "He's chairman of the deacons." Her intrusion startles me, but she seems oblivious.

"Thank you, Neil." After a pause Savannah's father makes some church-related announcements, asks for prayer requests, and gives a report of Reverend Lewis's adventures in East Africa, where he's on his month-long mission.

Pretending to pay attention, I study Neil from the corner of my eye. Objectively he's not the type who would usually turn my head. He's cute enough, in an earnest, squeaky-clean kind of way, if a bit on the skinny side—but nowhere near as striking as Julian. He's clearly focused on what Savannah's father is saying, and rewards his clunky attempts at jokes with generous, dimpled smiles.

"Let us now go to the Lord in prayer," says Savannah's father.

All heads bow around me as he begins to pray. Neil is totally immersed in the act of talking to God, eyes squeezed shut and lips mumbling. It's such a raw, personal moment that I have to avert my gaze. I study my hands, noticing the chip in my nail polish on my ring finger. Grammy will be apoplectic if she sees.

"Let us all stand and raise our voices in praise of Him!" Savannah's father relinquishes his place at the pulpit, and Neil bounds up, guitar ready to rock. The congregation stands as the band plays an up-tempo tune. Everyone seems to know the words but me.

"Are the words printed in those?" I ask Savannah, indicating the leather-bound volumes on the back of each pew.

She giggles. "No," she whispers into my ear, and pulls out papers from her purse. "We're too modern here for those old things. Here's a bulletin."

I check the song text and sing along, grudgingly at first. The energy in the room is infectious, and soon I can't help but smile as my voice lifts praises upward.

In the middle of the fourth song, Savannah peels off her jacket and lets it fall onto the pew behind her. She pulls her hair together over one shoulder and smiles brightly at me. "If anything can lift your spirits, it's Neil Corbet and the Central Christian Worship Band."

The final song is a slow, meditative number, and everyone, including Neil, closes their eyes for this one. Again I feel like I've interrupted a private moment, so I close my eyes too and let the congregation's voices wash over me. Neil's voice soars above them all, and a wave of happiness, so rare these days, spreads through my body.

The music stops. The spell broken, we all sit down again. The worship band members put their instruments down in their chairs and make their way to seats saved for them in the audience. I can't help but notice that Neil eschews the front rows for a place toward the back next to a couple who could be his parents.

Savannah's father returns to the pulpit and introduces Pastor Joe, the youth pastor, as the one who will deliver the sermon today in Reverend Lewis's absence.

Pastor Joe takes the stage. He's in his midthirties, casually dressed in khakis and a sweater, with thinning reddish hair and a ruddy complexion. He has a serious look about him, but his first words surprise me: "Is heaven boring? Are we just going to sing and listen to angels strum harps all day, every day for the rest of eternity?"

The youth group around me titters.

"Some people say that if that's all heaven is, then they'd

rather take their chances in hell. They say unrepentant sinners have all the fun, which we know not to be the case. Now, I'm not going to tell you all the reasons you don't want to be in hell. Instead I'm going to tell you why you do want to go to heaven.

"Revelation chapter seven, verse sixteen tells us that in heaven, 'Never again will they hunger; never again will they thirst. The sun will not beat upon them, nor any scorching heat.' Folks, that means there is no more suffering in heaven. We can lay down our burdens at the foot of the Lord."

Pastor Joe goes on with his sermon, but I let my mind wander, catching only bits and pieces: ". . . where moth and rust do not destroy—God's city is adorned with jewels and its streets are paved in gold—for I go to prepare a place for you . . ."

He speaks for a good forty minutes, so long that even Savannah's attention wanes. She's doodling hearts in the church bulletin around the notes she's taken on the sermon.

Finally Pastor Joe leads us in the final prayer and dismisses us.

Savannah folds her papers into her Bible and gathers up her jacket and mittens. We both stand, and Savannah pulls me into the aisle.

"Doesn't Neil have the best voice?" she says as we join the crowd making its way to the front exit. "We keep telling him he needs to try out for one of those talent shows on TV."

"He does." I unfold my coat and put it on, debating whether I should ask Savannah to tell me more about Neil. I know she must have the scoop.

But before I can decide what, if anything, to ask, Savannah does a scan of the sanctuary and breaks out in a flurry of spastic waving. She touches my arm. "It was such a pleasure to chat with you!" And then she rushes off, pushing through the few people behind us, back toward the pulpit, where her friends stand.

I continue my slow march toward the doors and shake my head at Savannah's use of the word "chat." "Monologue" is more like it. And though I'm relieved to be released from her constant barrage of information, I can't deny that it was nice to have someone treat me like I'm a normal human being rather than a social pariah.

There's a tap on my shoulder. It's Neil.

"Felicia?" There is a note of uncertainty in his voice, though I instantly thrill at the way he says my name. It has never sounded so beautiful.

"Neil?" I phrase it as a question, though obviously I know it's him.

He relaxes and smiles warmly. "I see my reputation precedes me! Excellent."

"You're only the shining star of the world-class Central Christian Worship Band," I say.

"You liked it?" He seems surprised but pleased. "Your grandmother tells me you play piano. You might have noticed we can use some fresh blood." He's right about that.

No one in the band other than Neil looks a day under fifty.

"You want me to try out?" I purse my lips, a pound irritated but a pinch grateful that Grammy has apparently been talking me up.

"You wouldn't have to try out." His tone is casual, inviting. "I've heard some of your recordings, and someone with your talent is welcome to join anytime. Mrs. Fogarty and her arthritic fingers would thank you."

"It's nice of you to think of me." I look down and busy myself by buttoning up my coat. I fiddle with the top button that always gives me trouble. "But I don't play anymore." I can't even look at the piano without thinking about how horribly I let down my father.

Neil doesn't say anything, but I see a flash of concern play across his features. "I don't know if I should say anything, but—"

"You shouldn't," I blurt, cutting him off.

Neil seems to consider this a minute, and then pats my shoulder carefully, as if I might shatter and spread my shards all over the holy house of God. "It was great to finally meet you."

Grammy calls my name. I nod curtly at Neil and trudge over to where Grammy is standing with Mr. Eaton. As I guide Grammy back out the door toward her old Crown Victoria station wagon, I risk a peek over my shoulder and see Neil through the open door, still in the same spot, watching me with a bemused smile. And I have to smile too.

I surface from the memory and am met by Julian's stare. He's standing on the stair outside my chamber.

"Time to go." He says it softly, as if he regrets waking me.

I lift myself up on my elbows. Seeing him here overwhelms me. What if he's the one who took Beckah? He had access to her, after all. "What are you doing here? Do you know where Beckah is?"

"No time for questions. We need your help." He offers his hand to help me out of my chamber, but I slap it away and climb out.

"Why do you think I'd ever want to help you out?" I challenge.

"Because," he says with an infuriating grin, "I know where you can find Neil."

CHAPTER 5

HE KNOWS WHERE NEIL IS? My desire to see Neil again wells up inside me, a deep ache that breaks through the fog. At this point I'd do almost anything to find him, to find out if he survived, even hang out with Julian. But—

"Wait. How do you know about Neil? I didn't even meet him until I moved to Ohio." Every part of my brain is on alert. "Did you follow me back to the States, hoping you could get me into even more trouble?"

Julian laughs. "You think I'm a stalker now?"

"Let's just say it wouldn't surprise me."

He narrows his eyes. "When I was on the mainframe, I looked up what you have been accessing."

"But how—"

"You're not the only hacker in the universe, you know. You've been viewing lots of memories of Neil. And not so many memories of me." He clicks his tongue with disapproval. "Should I be jealous?"

"Ugh, why would I want to revisit the worst parts of my whole life?" I scowl at him. Jerk.

He grabs my wrist, a little too hard. His touch jolts me, sending shock waves down my spine. How can I be feeling something from someone's touch? Are the rules changing?

"Listen. We don't have much time. If they've taken your friend, then they're onto us. You're no longer safe here. We need to go. Now." He pulls me down the stairs and toward the door.

I pull back. "Since when do you care about my safety?"

He grimaces but still doesn't let go of my arm. His touch is starting to make me feel light-headed, drunk, pliable. "I know you're angry. You have every right to be after what happened." His voice softens, making him sound almost vulnerable. Almost. "I know I may not have been that trustworthy in the past. But I need you to trust me now. We have to go."

A loud blast knocks me to the floor, facedown, taking Julian down with me.

"Felicia!" Julian swears and immediately goes into action mode, jumping up, flipping me over, hooking his arms under my armpits, and pulling me toward the wall. As he drags me, I am horrified to see that the blast targeted my memory chamber. Its once smooth planes are ragged, flames licking at what was my refuge for so long.

Julian taps out a series of knocks against the wall with his foot, like Morse code, and a door appears and slides open. As he swings me clear of the door, I see the drones streaming from their chambers and into the common area.

"Felicia!" It's Virginia, and she's sprinting, knocking over any drone that gets in her way. But before she can make the door, it slides closed, and the last thing I see is her anguished face.

"Virginia!" I choke out a sob, and kick at the door with the side of my leg.

Julian slaps my face. It stings. "Can you walk?"

"Open the door back up," I plead, my face throbbing. "We need to get Virginia! We can't leave her in there."

Julian's face looms large above mine. His golden hair frames his forehead and cheekbones like a halo, but his expression is anything but angelic. "Can. You. Walk." He enunciates every word. It's not a request. It's an order.

I'm dumbfounded, but I nod. Julian grunts and hoists me to a standing position. I fall against his chest, and he puts his hands on my arms to steady me. Warmth spreads through my veins, and my skin tingles. It's the same sensation I get from my chamber, only amplified. It's so out of place, and yet, I'm euphoric, so dizzy with feeling that I want to cry out. I hate my body for responding to Julian when my soul wants only Neil. I close my eyes, and with all my strength I back away, breaking off the contact. The effect is like being thrown into a cold pool of water and all too quickly going numb. I want to reach for him again. But I don't. I won't.

When I open my eyes, Julian is looking at me curiously, and his expression has softened. "No need to worry about your friends. The guardians of this place aren't after them. They'll simply extinguish the fire and pump in their doping gas, and no one in there will even remember it happened."

"Guardians? Doping gas?" I ask dumbly. I feel like a computer whose circuits have overloaded.

"Unless you want to end up as charred as your chamber, I don't have time to explain." He reaches for me, but I step away from his grasp. I'm not letting him touch me again.

"I see you're fit." He barks out a laugh. "Let's go."

My only real choice is to follow Julian. Even if I could somehow get back into my hive, my memory chamber is ruined. And I have no idea how to navigate the outside on my own. "You really know where Neil is?" I ask him, trying to keep the desperation out of my voice.

"Yes."

"Then lead the way."

His lips twist into a satisfied smirk. Not his best look. "Stay close behind me, and let me know when you start to feel woozy. We'll stop and find a place for you to plug in."

He takes off running the corridor at a brisk pace, and I run after him, my bare feet slapping on the polished pathway. I make sure to leave a few strides between us.

Pushing down my fear and confusion, I register the grand scale of our surroundings for the first time. On either side of us are seemingly never-ending rows of identical hives. Each individual hive is shaped like a traditional

English skep, the kind beekeepers used to weave from straw to house their bee colonies. Taken together, the hives look like mountains of neatly arranged plastic eggs pressed up against one another, half buried. The ceiling, if there is one, is high enough that I can't see it. Just as inside the hive, every surface, including the pathway beneath us, is a blinding, pristine white. If anything, it's even brighter out here—so bright that everything blurs around the edges. I'm struck by the utterly eerie foreignness of it all. I almost feel like I'm a lab rat in some futuristic sci-fi maze.

It's strange to run in the afterlife. Because I breathe only out of habit and not out of necessity, I don't have to worry about what lying around so much has done to my conditioning. It's liberating. Like the first turn on the track, when you still feel invincible.

"What did you mean when you said I should tell you when I feel woozy?" I call out to Julian.

He slows enough so we can run side by side. "You're an addict. And you don't want to go cold turkey with this drug. We will have to wean you off it little by little. Put your hacking skills to good use."

So we are being drugged. That explains why we're all so lethargic. "Who is drugging us? And why?" Though I'm less than thrilled it's Julian, it's nice to finally be around someone who might have some answers about this place. He must have some good connections if he knows so much.

Julian shoots me a sidelong glance as if contemplating how much he should tell me. "It's a long story, and we shouldn't be talking out in the open like this. We don't want to attract unwanted attention."

As if to prove his point, a low buzzing sound comes up behind us, rapidly getting louder, like a plane coming in for a landing. Julian shoves me into the V-shaped recess between two hives. He clamps his hand over my mouth and whispers into my ear. "Scanner drone."

I wrestle away from his hand but stay in the shadows with him. I'm grateful for his protection, but he still has a long way to go before he'll have my trust. We stand there as a bee roughly the size of my head lazily zigzags down the corridor, about six feet above us. Every few yards it emits a quick scan of yellowish light from its undersides, a jarring splash of color in such a white environment.

After a few minutes Julian decides it is all clear, and we set off again. We don't talk, though I really have to bite my tongue to keep from asking him a million questions, including what the heck that yellow light is for. The scenery is monotonous, but I start to detect a pattern. The corridor we're in is about the width of two lanes on the highway, and at regular intervals we cross over intersections with corridors of similar width that run perpendicular to ours. I count as we go along and discover that each block is made up of one hundred hives. The counting keeps my mind occupied, but soon enough I lose focus and my legs sputter like a car running out of gas.

Julian notices I've dropped off, and he stops, glancing around as if to get his bearings. I don't know how he can tell where we are, if he can. Everything looks exactly the same to me. "We'll stop here," he says.

He motions for me to follow him to the nearest hive, and he does his little tapping trick again, only this time with his fist. A door slides open, and we hop in before it slides closed again. The interior of this hive is like mine, only this one is half-empty.

"We're in luck," Julian says. "It's much less hassle when you don't have to deal with all the addicts."

"It's not our fault." I bristle. "Can you please stop calling us addicts?"

"Whatever." Julian rolls his eyes. "Pick out your suite, *tout de suite*." He chuckles at his lame joke, and it's my turn to employ the eye roll.

"Too bad you died before you could have kids, Julian. You have great dad jokes." I pause, and despite the smog clogging my entire being, a vivid picture of twisted steel and shattered glass flashes uncomfortably through my mind. "How did you die anyway?"

Julian draws back, his lips pressed together in a thin line. "I don't want to talk about it."

"Okay. Then can you tell me what that yellow light was? Coming from the scanner drone?"

"I could," he says in an exaggerated way that implies he won't.

"Julian . . ." I'd like to slap him, but it'd mean touching him.

"Chill." Julian tilts back his head and gives me a lazy smile. My insides flip-flop despite my anger. "If you get caught in that yellow light, you'll get picked up by the guardians. They don't exactly like people running around outside the hives."

"I won't get caught, then," I mumble. What else did I want to ask him? Questions pop into my head, but as soon as I almost have my tongue around one, another question crowds it out. The drugs make my thoughts as slippery as stones in a river.

I plop myself into the nearest empty chamber and fit my hands into the grooves. At first nothing happens, but I wiggle my fingers and concentrate on imagining my files and folders. The screen chugs slowly to life, loading strange code and symbols. Then I feel it, the delicious tingles and the sweet clarity of mind that comes when I plug in. Everything is there, exactly the way I left it. The error message on the cat memory I shared with Beckah pops up again.

"Did it work?" Julian pokes his head in.

I nod, and Julian reaches in and laces his fingers through mine. I try to jerk my hand away, but he's superstrong. "Enjoy the memory" is the last thing I hear him say.

Ward, Felicia. Memory #31233
Tags: Germany, Julian, AFN, Rainy day
Number of Views: 3
Owner Rating: Not rated
User Rating: Not shared

I'm sitting on the sofa in the living room, sipping coffee I poached from Dad's luxury stash, flipping through the American Forces Network programming. I could watch something on German TV, but I don't make a habit of taxing my brain when I have a welcome break from Mother. Besides, I find the public service announcements, which AFN broadcasts in lieu of commercials, strangely entertaining. The bulk of subscribers to AFN are military abroad, so there are spots on being suspicious of strangers, keeping your uniform spiffy, and picking up toys left on your stairs so your family doesn't trip and die.

Rain is coming down outside in sheets, pattering so hard against the windows that they rattle. I used to revel in weather like this. But in Frankfurt it seems like most days are overcast with intermittent showers, as opposed to our last assignment in Nairobi, Kenya, where sunny skies were the norm.

Sun wasn't the only advantage of being stationed in Africa. In Kenya we lived in a mansion with help (cook, maid, driver, and two very necessary security guards). Here we live in a three-bedroom apartment in a claustrophobic community populated solely by other consulate staff and the hordes of diseased bunnies that pollute our lawns, so separate from the rest of the city that we might as well be in America.

But Frankfurt beats Nairobi for safety. Nairobi is called "Nairobbery" by the expats who live there, and I experienced the high crime rate firsthand on the eve of my thirteenth birthday when I made the mistake of running into a dark alley by myself. I've had nightmares ever since. The nightmares were so bad in those early days, I awoke screaming, blubbering incoherently about some man who was coming to take me away. Dad was always the one who'd come in and try to soothe me back to sleep with his gentle tenor. Because Mother, of course, needed to be well rested for her long days at the office serving our country.

Now that Mother has been promoted to American Citizens Services chief, she's working even longer hours and traveling more. She may not be interested in my maintaining my sanity, but she's religious about my maintaining my 4.0 GPA and padding my applications with extracurriculars so I can get into an Ivy League. If I don't have homework, piano practice, or one of my other activities, Mother gives me Foreign Service practice tests to improve my general knowledge. It's exhausting. Fortunately, Mother will not be back until late tonight, thanks to some embassy function in Berlin. Unfortunately, Dad has been in Papua New Guinea for weeks now researching a tribe that makes music with conch shells. I wish he were here. He'd know what to do about my nightmares getting worse again lately.

I'm contemplating whipping up a prepackaged mashed potatoes snack, when the doorbell rings. I spring off the sofa and hurry to the entryway, where I press the buzzer and check my reflection in the mirror. I open the door. It's Julian, drenched, teeth chattering.

"Can I come in?"

I'm not supposed to let boys into the apartment when Mother and Dad are away, but Julian looks so pitiful, I usher him in. "How'd you know where I live?"

"I ran into Nicole earlier. You know, from that party a couple of weeks ago? She told me." He's shivering in his thin jacket and rubbing his arms.

"Autumn's not here," I tell him. Autumn has been smug, bragging about Julian hanging out with her practically every day for the past two weeks, so I assumed they were on their way to being a couple.

He shrugs. "I know."

"I'll get you some towels." I head across the living room toward the hall bathroom.

I open the linen closet in the bathroom and pull out a couple of faded beach towels. As I shut the closet door, I catch Julian's reflection in the mirror affixed to the outside of the door. I jump.

"Oh, hey—sorry I scared you," he purrs into my ear. He's right behind me, too close for comfort. I realize I don't know anything about him. Not even his last name.

I turn quickly, knocking my elbow into one of the shelves. Julian has discarded his light jacket, and I'm suddenly all too aware of his body. I scan the thin, white T-shirt clinging to his well-built chest. "Uh . . . I think my dad has some sweats that might fit you, if you want to get out of those wet clothes."

"It's really sweet of you to think of my welfare," he says. But when I try to move past him, he blocks my path. My heart hammers in my chest. Fear? Exhilaration? I don't quite know. On my second attempt he lets me by. I rush into my parents' room, extract an old GWU sweatshirt and some gray sweatpants, and toss them into the bathroom. He catches them, and I pull the door shut.

I pace the living room, berating myself. I shouldn't have let him in, shouldn't have given him my dad's clothes. Now he'll have to stay at least until his clothes are dry—half an hour. What if Mother finds out from one of our nosy neighbors? What if Autumn finds out and gets upset? It's not like she has to be afraid I'm going to make a play for Julian, but since her family's arrival in Germany, only two months after my family moved here, she has seemed so insecure about boys.

The bathroom door creaks open and Julian emerges, toweling his hair casually. I brush past him, scoop up his wet T-shirt and jeans, and carry them through the living and dining rooms into the kitchen, where the dryer is. I set the cycle, throw in the clothes and a dryer sheet, and slam the door. I hit the start button, and the dryer rumbles to life.

I take a deep breath and march out to meet Julian. He's made himself comfortable on the sofa. And turned off the TV. It's presumptuous of him, and it rubs me the wrong way. "It'll run half an hour, and then you can go."

He arches his eyebrow. "But what if it's still raining?"

"I'll loan you an umbrella."

He laughs. "Nicole said you were uptight!"

"Nicole? Who cares what Nicole thinks?" I sputter. "I'm not uptight. I'm conscientious. There's a difference."

Julian pats the sofa next to him. A dare. I sit down, closer to the armrest than him, my posture rigid.

He grins and shakes his head. "You are uptight! Look at you. Too uptight to play poker, I bet."

"I've played it. I'm a total card shark. Watch out!" I make claws with my fingers and give him my scariest look.

"You really need to work on your bluff." Damn.

"Whatever." I sink back into the cushion and concentrate on watching the raindrops hurl themselves against the window, desperate to break through.

"If you have a pack of cards, I can teach you," he offers.

"First tell me your last name."

"Jones." It rolls off his tongue easily.

I get up and go over to the cabinet next to the piano, where we keep our games. I rummage through it. "No cards. But I have . . . Skip-Bo . . . Yahtzee . . . and Sorry."

"Never heard of strip Skip-Bo." He shakes his head slowly in mock dismay.

Ugh. He thinks he's so charming. I throw the Skip-Bo deck at him, missing widely. The box falls harmlessly on the area rug under the coffee table.

He puts his hands up in surrender. "Kidding! We can play Yahtzee, then. At least it has dice."

So we play Yahtzee. I win every time, racking up Yahtzees like my fingers are telling the dice exactly how to roll.

"You could be a Yahtzee shark." He stretches his arms out and takes a deep breath. "It's not as sexy as a poker shark, but it's a step in the right direction, I guess."

The dryer buzzes loudly. "Looks like it's time for you to get going, Julian."

"Wait, why not make a wager? We play one more game, and if you win again, I leave without putting up a fight."

"And you won't mention to Autumn you were here today?" My gut tells me she wouldn't understand that today has been totally innocent.

He raises one eyebrow. "No."

"Good. And if you win?" I grin as I knock the dice around in my hand. "Not that you have any chance of that."

He touches my hand, stilling it. "If I win, which we all know is unlikely . . ." He pauses for dramatic effect. "I get to kiss you."

Kiss me? Is he serious? Suddenly his hand feels too hot on mine. There are a thousand reasons why we shouldn't kiss, but now that he's brought it up, it's all I can think about.

As if reading my mind, Julian leans over and softly brushes my hair behind my ear. I'm hypnotized, drawn in by the dark blue depths of his eyes. His hand slides behind my neck, and he inches closer until his face is the tiniest sliver away from mine. I part my lips, my entire body tense and waiting.

He pulls away, and I deflate, coughing to mask my confusion. I don't want him to know how much he's thrown me off balance. "Well, okay, then. Since you won't win anyway, it's a deal."

We play. This time, however, I'm just not getting the Yahtzees. I'm rolling well, but then, so is he. Finally, only the Yahtzee row is left for the both of us. If I get a Yahtzee or neither of us does, I win.

I go first, but the Yahtzee is not in the cards. Now it's up to Julian to win or lose.

Julian takes the dice from me. "Can you blow on them for luck?"

"Luck for me? Or luck for you?" I ask him, tapping my foot. What's happening to me? Am I flirting?

"I would like to think my luck is your luck too." His voice is soft, like a sigh, and he looks down at the dice as if they hold his future within them. It's like getting a glimpse of a whole different person.

I chuckle weakly and blow a short puff of air onto the dice, playing along. It seems to reenergize him.

"Let's do this!" He winds up his arm as if he's about to pitch a baseball, and lets the dice fly onto the table. A Yahtzee—all sixes. I can't believe it.

Julian stands solemnly and pulls me to my feet. He closes the gap between us until I'm pressed against his chest and he's kissing my neck. I don't resist, though I know I should. "I have wanted to do this since forever," he moans into my ear.

He tilts my head up and kisses me full on the lips. I sink to the sofa, and he moves with me, never breaking contact, deepening the kiss, running his hands expertly up and down my back. My traitorous body arches toward his as he guides it so that we're lying side by side, entwined in each other's arms. I'm so wrapped up in the sensation of Julian's kiss that I purposely ignore the rapidly fading daylight outside. Ignore the fact that it has long since stopped raining.

Finally we break apart. My lips feel raw, bruised. "Wow. So, um . . . you can get your clothes out of the dryer now." I stumble up off the sofa, disoriented. How could I have let this happen? "I can make some spaghetti."

Julian stretches out like a satisfied cat. "Thanks for the offer, but I'd better go. You know, before it starts raining again."

He changes back into his clothes, and I let him kiss me again by the door. "I hope we can do this again sometime," he says as he leaves. I stand in the doorway, rooted to the spot, half-delirious with joy, half-racked with guilt. I can hardly believe Julian has so much power over me that he's transformed me into someone who'd betray her best friend.

As I exit from the memory, I can still feel the weight of his lips on mine. It's revolting. I charge out of the chamber, ready to yell at him for forcing me to relive that particular memory. The kiss that set off a terrible chain of events I'd rather not think about.

But he's not here. He's not in the center area, and unless he changed into a white shift, he's not in any of the other chambers either. I take a peek into the closest occupied chamber and see the face of a little boy who seems to be about six years old. I bend down to get a closer look, and cover my mouth in shock. The little boy is strapped in.

CHAPTER 6

THE BOY'S EYES ARE WIDE OPEN, but he doesn't react to me, even when I wave my hand in front of his face. His hologram screen casts a strong, unbroken light over his small body, which is taut against its restraints. That familiar glow has never looked so sinister to me.

I dash from chamber to chamber. They are all the same—occupied by young children who have no chance to get up and move about. It's perhaps a small freedom, considering we're all locked in hives, but when I try to imagine being strapped in, I start to panic.

I return to the boy and poke around the bonds at his ankles, wrists, and chest, looking for clasps or some way to remove them. Though the boy doesn't stir, his eyes tick back and forth like a metronome, as if in a deep REM sleep. Finding no way to release him, I sink to the floor. What kind of people would do this to children?

I hug myself into a ball and wish I could weep. I want so badly for the tears to come. For my life that was cut short. For the ocean of loneliness in my heart when I think of Neil and my family and friends. And to express my rage at my unseen jailers. For locking me in a prison all this time, cut off from everything except my memories. For drugging me. For taking Beckah. For destroying my chamber. And for their cruelty to this boy and all the others like him.

I'm so wrapped up in my grief that I block out everything else. I imagine I'm at home in my bed—not the one in Frankfurt that holds too many nightmares but the one with my first grown-up mattress and the frilly pink bedspread, before sleep became something I preferred to avoid. I can almost feel the bedspread's satiny softness against my cheek.

"I see you've figured out materialization." Julian prods my side with his foot. "Way to go."

"What are you talking about?" I sniffle, and wipe away tears and snot with the sleeve of my shift.

"You're crying." He says it so matter-of-factly, it takes me a few seconds to catch his meaning. I stare at my now soiled sleeve and touch my face gingerly with my fingers. It's puffy and wet. I'm crying. I'm crying!

"But how? I've never been able to before." And I've tried. I attempt to stand up, but my limbs flop like jellyfish and refuse to obey. I collapse against the base of the chamber I recently occupied. The one where Julian forced me to relive our first kiss. I glare at him with all the energy I have left.

"Careful. This whole crying indulgence has already drained you of the bit of power you were able to siphon off for yourself. Now you have to plug in again to recharge." He curses under his breath. "This puts us behind schedule."

He approaches me with purpose, but also caution, as if cornering a skittish animal. "Let me help you back in."

"Wait." I beg him with my eyes. "Talk to me for a minute. Please."

He regards me for a few beats, then nods and sits cross-legged on the floor in front of me, his posture so perfect and his body so balanced that he resembles a yoga master. Or a statue of a yoga master.

"You're starting to be able to change the code of this dimension. We call it materialization. It's a good sign. It means you're strong. It means I was right to come and find you."

The confusion I feel must show, because Julian immediately elaborates. "You've never been able to cry before because it's not part of the program." He sounds bored and annoyed, as if he's told me this a thousand times and I just haven't been paying attention. "Whenever you plug in to your chamber, you let the program feed off your energy and your power. That you could cry now means you were able to reclaim some of your power for yourself. You can wield that power to hack the system. You can change things to the way you like them."

"I'd like to set these kids free," I rasp.

Julian shakes his head. "That would take a lot more power than you have at the moment. Besides, the guardians here have an excellent reason for keeping these kids strapped in."

"You're defending them?" I'm incredulous. I suspected Julian was heartless. But this is madness.

"I'm not defending them." He raises his voice just enough that I know I've hit a nerve. "I'm merely pointing out the obvious. They're too young. These kids don't have the capacity to plug themselves in and roam the net. They go through the memories of their lives in sequential order, over and over again. It is not like they are suffering. They have no idea they are here."

"But they shouldn't be locked up by themselves," I say. "They should be with their parents. So they can be held and know they're loved."

"Everyone needs that." He shifts his weight forward, and reaches out as if to caress me, but I flinch. Bare my teeth.

"Don't! Just don't." How dare he? Does he think if he touches me, I'll give in? Tell him it's okay that he's a monster?

He puts out his hands in a gesture of surrender and rocks back into his rigid pose. "Okay, calm down. I will not touch you unless you ask." His eyes glint with mischief. "Unless you beg."

I choose to ignore this additional provocation, and

change the subject. "Materialization. Is that why you have hair and eyebrows and normal clothes?"

"Exactly!" Julian smacks his hand on the floor, startling me. "Now you're getting it." He winks. "Watch this."

Julian shimmers before my eyes, and his T-shirt and jeans ensemble is replaced with my dad's GWU sweatshirt and jogging pants. "What do you think?"

I shudder. "Ugh! No! Anything but that."

He grins wickedly. "If you say so . . ." He shimmers again and is left in nothing but a Speedo, smooth chest and washboard abs glistening with water droplets as if he's just stepped from a pool.

"Julian!" I gag. "Stop fooling around."

"Fine," he says, his tone now serious. He shimmers again and materializes back into his normal outfit. "I see you're still uptight."

"I'm not uptight," I protest.

"Yeah, I know. You're conscientious." We trade venomous stares. "Is this little powwow done? Can I help you plug in so we can get on with it?" He says it like he's a babysitter and I'm his bratty charge who has stayed up long after her bedtime.

"Can you tell me one more thing before you do?" I don't wait for him to answer but press forward. "Why can't I ever seem to remember much that goes on here? Is it the drugs you were talking about?" I feel unbalanced, unmoored. Must be withdrawal symptoms.

"Good guess. You've heard of the Lethe?"

Lethe. It sounds familiar, but I'm not recalling its significance. Not that I'm going to let Julian know that. "The Lethe. Sure. What about it?"

"The guardians use a derivative of the water from the Lethe to hinder people from remembering much. It keeps everyone from getting too attached and from forming plans. And it makes the memory chambers all that more attractive and addictive . . . Hey, are you okay?" His eyes widen in alarm.

My body is shaking convulsively. "Nooooo . . ." My voice is no louder than a whimper.

Without asking like he claimed he would, Julian scoops me up in his arms and transfers me quickly to the chamber. He places my hands into the grooves, and I feel better the instant my finger pads connect. This time he doesn't force anything on me but retracts his hands politely. I don't care about Julian anymore, though, because the sensation of being in the chamber is so ambrosial, it crowds out everything else. But I've held on to one word. "Lethe." I languidly pull up my tags and find one mention of "Lethe." I surge in.

Ward, Felicia. Memory #31725
Tags: Ohio, Neil, School, Mythology, Lethe
Number of Views: 98
Owner Rating: 3 stars
User Rating: 2 stars

The bell signaling the start of fifth period echoes through the deserted hallway as I unfold my new schedule in front of my locker. Late again. But I don't care. In my whole school career, up until today, I was never late once. Never allowed myself that sort of slipup. Being on time, sitting in the front row, writing copious notes, none of it matters anymore. I have one semester before I graduate, but I'm merely going through the motions. All my dreams, if they really were my dreams at all—of getting into an Ivy League school, of being a diplomat or a politician or secretary of state—are impossibly out of reach now. I still need to put in a minimum of effort to graduate, but my fire to succeed, to exceed expectations, has been irreparably extinguished.

I take a deep breath, slam my locker shut, and drag myself toward Mythology, room 112, Mrs. Keats. The door is still open when I get there, so I slip in and scan the room for an empty seat. I see a familiar face. Neil. He smiles and waves me over, but before I can claim the seat next to him, Mrs. Keats asks for my schedule.

"Ah, Felicia Ward." She reads my name off the now crumpled sheet of paper. "Nice of you to finally join us. We were expecting you more than a week ago."

My classmates laugh. I clear my throat and offer a mumbled apology but no explanation. Mrs. Keats dismisses me with a sigh, handing back my schedule. I beeline to the back of the class and sit next to Neil.

"You weren't at church on Sunday," Neil says. "We missed you."

"Grammy wasn't feeling well. I didn't want to leave her."

"Can we get started now?" Mrs. Keats raises her voice to silence the smattering of conversations still in progress. "Thank you."

I turn my attention away from Neil and do my best to focus on what Mrs. Keats is saying.

"If you did your reading last night like you were supposed to, you know we are going to talk about the underworld today. Now, in Greek mythology the underworld wasn't hell. It was a place all souls went to when they died." Mrs. Keats goes on, detailing the various realms of the underworld: the pit of Tartarus, the Elysian Fields, and the rest of the land of the dead, which was ruled by Hades. Occasionally I halfheartedly scrawl a key word into my wire-bound notebook.

Soon she's waxing poetic about the five rivers of the underworld: the Styx, the Acheron, the Kokytos, the Phlegethon, and the Lethe.

"Who can tell me what the purpose of the Lethe was? Alyssa?"

A pert, pretty girl in the front row answers, and I can tell she's the type who always raises her hand. Who is always right. I can tell because she's the girl I used to be. "The Lethe was the river of forgetfulness," she trills. "Dead souls drank from it to forget the worries of their earthly life. It was ruled by the goddess Lethe, who offered oblivion."

Lethe. I write it down. Underline it. Circle it. Stab at it with my fluorescent orange highlighter.

"And the Phlegethon?" Mrs. Keats asks.

Alyssa again. "The river of fire. Dead souls who swam there boiled with rage."

"Well, I am pleased to see at least one of you came prepared," grouses our teacher.

She goes on with her lesson, peppering her lecture of the rites and traditions of the underworld with occasional questions, the majority skillfully answered by Alyssa. But I allow my mind to wander, to daydream about what it would be like to lie down on the banks of the Lethe and drink just enough to make me forget about the past few months. The thought is undeniably appealing.

The bell pierces through my daydream, and students stream out of the classroom in a cacophony of slammed books and displaced desks.

Neil hovers over me. "Which way are you going?" he asks.

I consult my schedule as I stand up. "Physics. Room 163. Mr. Howe."

"That's in the science wing, near the auditorium. I can walk you. We have choir practice there today." He grips his binder tightly as we exit the classroom and enter the mob of fellow students hurrying to their next class. "In the auditorium, I mean. Not the science wing."

I have to laugh. "I'm sure you could raise all those formaldehyde frogs from the dead with your singing voice. It'd be quite a sight to see."

Neil ducks his head, blushing. "I'm better at raising spirits than souls," he jokes.

"Do frogs even have souls?" I look up at him. "Do you find frogs in the underworld taking sips of the Lethe to forget all those times they ate rotten flies or fell off their lily pads?"

"I don't know, but it seems like a good question to ask Pastor Joe. We could ask him together," he suggests shyly. "You know, if you're there next Sunday."

"We'll see how Grammy feels. Dad's looking into getting her a part-time nurse, but it's so expensive. . . ." I trail off. "She is ninety-one years old, after all. She's going to have some bad days."

"Ninety-one! I never realized."

"Don't worry. No one ever thinks she's that old. My dad was a late-in-life miracle." I look away, pick up my pace as we round a corner. "And I was a late-in-life accident," I say bitterly, under my breath, my mother's ultimate rejection slashing at me all over again.

Neil matches me footstep for footstep, but he stays silent, as if allowing me to compose myself. Either he doesn't know what to say or he's perceptive enough not to say it. As we walk, he's greeted by classmates and teachers, and he has a smile for everyone. By the time we reach my physics classroom, the hallway has cleared, leaving only a few stragglers.

I try to put on a cheerful expression to mask my distress. "Thanks for walking with me."

Neil doesn't seem to buy my sudden brightness. "Look . . . I know we just met, but if you ever need someone to talk to . . ." His eyes shine with sincerity, warmth, kindness. All those sentiments I haven't gotten nearly enough of lately.

I take a deep breath and ask him the question foremost on my mind right now. "Do you think it's weird to want a little taste of the Lethe? Just enough to go back to a time when things were less complicated?"

"Well, I don't think it's *that* weird. I mean, everyone has bad experiences, right? We've all done things we wish we hadn't." He shifts his weight from one leg to the other. "I don't think I could go through with it, though. Because, you know . . . even those things—maybe even especially those things—make us who we are."

The school bell rings. I'm late again. Six for six today. And not only that, I've let my new lack of ambition for being on time affect Neil, too. "Uh, sorry for making you late."

"Hey, no big deal. Choir can't start without me anyway." From anyone else that statement might sound cocky, but not from Neil. He even seems slightly embarrassed.

A man who must be Mr. Howe approaches, looking as though he's eager to close the door and get started. "I better go in," I say to Neil.

He gives me half a wave and heads off down the hallway.

Mr. Howe takes my schedule and indicates that I should sit down. I do, once again in the back row.

My new physics teacher starts his lecture, but I find it hard to concentrate on elementary particles and instead ponder what Neil has said about not wanting to forget his troubles. He seemed sincere, but then, the couple times

I've talked to him, he's never been less than peaceful and content. It's hard to imagine he's ever gone through something terrible. I'm sure if he had, if he truly knew what pain was, he'd want a gulp of the Lethe water.

I cross my arms on the desk in front of me and lay my head down. In the dark cocoon of my arms, I close my eyes. But the familiar flashes of my bed drenched in blood force me to sit up again. My stomach rumbles, and I raise my hand for a hall pass. Mr. Howe grouches, but I don't care. I rush to the restroom and make it just in time to throw up today's lunch of ham sandwich and blueberry muffin into the toilet.

I hear a whapping noise and look up with a start. I'm no longer in the girl's restroom, puking out my guts. I am in the memory chamber, and Julian has a pair of drumsticks he's beating on the overhang above me.

When he sees my eyes have opened, he tosses the drumsticks and they disappear into thin air. "Great! You're up. You look refreshed. Time to get moving."

I slide out of the chamber and examine the sleeve of my shift. It's clean and pressed, without the merest hint of my recent bout of tears. Damn, these chambers are better than a dry cleaning service. "I'm ready."

Julian gives me a once-over and then does his tapping trick at the wall to make the door open. I'm going to have to get him to teach me that. He peers into the corridor and then motions for me to follow him.

Our journey is almost identical to the one we took

before. Same monotonous scenery of hive after hive. Same wall of silence between us. The only difference is that now we have to keep ducking into alcoves to avoid the scanner drones, which come two or three at a time.

Finally I falter, and Julian scouts out the nearest hive while I work at staying upright. "That one is full." He checks out several more, shaking his head each time he emerges. "They're all full. We'll have to do this the hard way."

He pounds out his secret code on one of the hives to make the door open and leads me inside. A quick scan reveals that all the chambers are indeed full, and the figures inside are much larger than what I am used to seeing.

Julian chooses one nearest the door at ground level and shakes the shoulders of its occupant. "We'll need this chamber for a while, sir," he says in a commanding but pleasant voice.

A man scuttles out, startled. I gasp when I see him. Could it be?

But no, the man is not my father, though he does bear a rather striking resemblance to him.

"What are you up to, mate?" The man sways to and fro as if inebriated.

"This." Julian raises his fist and punches him in the face.

CHAPTER 7

THE MAN THUDS TO THE FLOOR, out cold. Julian drags him to the other side of the hive, depositing him there in distaste.

When I get over my shock and find my voice, I yell at Julian. "What did you do that for?"

"Now he can't refuse you his chamber," Julian says, crossing his arms over his chest.

"But how can hitting him cause him to lose consciousness? I thought that couldn't happen here."

Julian shrugs. "He believed it could happen. You needed a place to plug in. So plug in."

I shake my head weakly in disgust and crawl into the now vacated chamber while I still have the energy to do so without Julian's assistance. Seeing the man makes me yearn to see my dad again. I fiddle with the man's settings until I can load my own, and on a whim decide to revisit the last trip I took with Dad. I flex my fingers, and then I'm in.

Ward, Felicia. Memory #31272
Tags: Turkey, Dad, Scary storm, Musical goats
Number of Views: 3,024
Owner Rating: 4.5 stars
User Rating: 2.5 stars

The ancient Peugeot we've hired chugs and bumps up the winding road at such a slow speed that I want to scream. We've been in the car for hours, and there's nothing for me to do other than check periodically if my cell phone has reception (it never does), stare out at the scraggly trees, and think about all the fun I could be having if only Dad had trusted me to stay alone over fall break.

In the front seat Dad talks to our driver and translator, a squat man with a tendency to grunt and grin a mouthful of gold. They converse in a mishmash of broken Turkish and English, and any attempt I make to decipher what they're saying over the roar of the motor results in a headache. I zone out and absently doodle Julian's name in the dusty glass of the windowpane and cross it out again until my finger is caked with grime.

"Are we almost there?" It may be the fortieth time I've asked since we left Istanbul this morning at the crack of dawn. We have stopped several times to stretch our legs and gas up the car, most recently an hour ago in the outskirts of Ordu, but I'm itching to finally be free of this metal cage on wheels.

Dad turns his head and winks at me. "Azrak says to be patient. A fine assortment of goat cheeses awaits us in the next village."

I groan. It is Dad's preoccupation with goats, specifically a musically inclined herd here somewhere in the wilds of the North Turkish coast, that ruined my plans to alternately avoid Autumn so I could sneak around with Julian, and to spend time with Autumn to reassure her that nothing is going on. Because Mother was sent to Montenegro for two weeks to help them sort out their passport office, Dad insisted I come with him on his research trip. Or as I like to refer to it, his wild goat chase.

As I stretch out my arms, the charm bracelet Autumn sent me for Christmas last year comes free from under the sleeve of my fleece jacket. I twist my wrist and watch as the charms catch the rays of the midafternoon sunlight. The tiny piano charm I bought myself, but I fixate on the other two, both dolphins, Autumn's favorite animal. When she gave me the bracelet, she said the dolphins reminded her of us, two faithful friends since childhood adrift in an ocean of constant change. I tuck the bracelet back under my sleeve.

The road is getting bumpier now, if that's even possible. Dad throws worried glances behind him, but I know he's not nearly as concerned about my bruised tailbone as he is that his precious recording equipment in the trunk might get damaged. He confers with Azrak, and the car slows to a crawl.

Finally we arrive at a village. Azrak parks in front of a crumbling concrete building, and both he and Dad jump out. Azrak opens my door for me, and I mumble polite thanks as I step out onto the dirt road. A group of young boys kicking a half-deflated soccer ball gawk at us and then break out into cherubic smiles as they hold out their grubby hands.

"You have candy?" Azrak asks me.

"No." I scowl.

He shouts something at the boys in Turkish and they scatter, the biggest one taking the soccer ball with him.

"We'll get some supplies here in Cam Basi before we go set up camp," Dad says, brushing off his khakis with the backs of his hands. "Azrak assures me the goatherd I'm seeking has been spotted around these parts. It's not too much farther now."

I grimace and follow Dad and Azrak into the building. One side is lined with stalls where women in a sea of colorful headscarves sell everything from rolls of fresh cheese to sheep heads with their eyes gouged out. The rest of the room is a makeshift café with groups of men huddled around tables playing backgammon, smoking cigarettes, and drinking tea. I'm a million miles away from where I want to be.

Dad and Azrak are already haggling over some flat bread. I tap Dad on the shoulder and tell him I'll wait outside.

When I emerge from the stuffy building, I take a deep breath of the cool mountain air and shiver. I imagine I can smell the Black Sea, though I can't. Not really. If it weren't October already, I might have sold Dad on a side trip to a beach, though he's not one for passive activities like lying out. He'd likely insist on building sand castles and embarrassing me.

I walk down the road a bit, past homes that look like no more than huts. The enticing scent of spiced meat on the grill emanating through the wooden slats makes my stomach rumble. At the end of the row, I turn and walk back toward the car. The wind is starting to pick up, carrying with it bits of torn paper and withered leaves.

I'm in time to slide into the car and help Azrak arrange our purchases in the backseat next to me. I peek into one of the plastic bags and am greeted by a pair of fat trout, their slack mouths gaping.

"You didn't buy a sheep head, did you, Dad?"

He smacks his forehead in mock horror. "Oh, no! I forgot the sheep head. Maybe we can get one on the way back?" he teases. He leans over the seat back and makes as if to tickle me, but I dodge his wriggling fingers. Azrak starts the car, and we're off.

The ride is short, as promised, and in no longer than twenty minutes, we're standing in front of a ruin of a house with one door falling off its hinges, and no roof.

"This is where we're staying the night?" I ask, incredulous.

Azrak grunts something unintelligible and begins unpacking a tarp from the trunk.

Dad rubs my shoulders. "It's just for tonight, sweet pea. Can you help me look for rocks we can use to secure the tarp?"

"Fine," I grumble, ducking out of his grasp and walking in the opposite direction. I shield my eyes with my hand and squint into my surroundings. The landscape is breathtaking. Rugged and lonely with vast swaths of tall, tangled grass. A sob builds in my chest, and I don't quite know why.

I wander around, kicking at the grass until I find a sizeable stone that looks like it will do. I haul it back to our "shelter" and add it to the pile my industrious father has already gathered. "That's enough, I think," he says.

While he and Azrak work on the roof, I carry in the food, the cooking equipment, and our sleeping bags. I leave Dad's precious cargo in the trunk. It will be safer there. I rustle through the bags and break off a chunk of bread, which I top with the moist, crumbly cheese. It tastes amazing, salty and tangy on my tongue. Before I know it, I've devoured a whole round of bread and cheese.

When Dad and Azrak finally finish securing the tarp, I'm sitting against the wall on my sleeping bag with a copy of *Our Town*. We're discussing it in class when I get back.

"Ah, *Our Town*." Dad takes the copy from my hands and flips through it, scanning the pages as if he's looking for something in particular. My bookmark flutters to the floor. "'*Do any human beings ever realize life while they live it?—every, every minute?*'" he reads. "Such a powerful line."

"Hey!" My frustration with having to overnight here in the middle of nowhere like squatters reaches a fever pitch and I erupt, snatching the book from his hands. "I'm not even that far yet. And you've lost my place."

Dad startles at my outburst and backs away without another word. He and Azrak go outside and busy themselves with building a campfire to prepare the trout. They offer me some when it is flayed and cooked, but I refuse.

The tarp above us flaps, and the wind whistles through the gaps between the rocks. "Storm coming," Azrak wheezes. He belches loudly and then burrows into his sleeping bag headfirst. He doesn't even remove his shoes.

Dad and I both take off our shoes and then shimmy into our sleeping bags. Feetfirst. I arrange my pillow so it cradles my neck, and I stare up at the undulating motion of the flimsy tarp. I cross my fingers that it doesn't start raining.

Dad keeps clearing his throat next to me, and I know he wants to say something.

I throw him a bone. "So, has Azrak ever seen these famous goats of yours?"

Dad exhales loudly. "He hasn't, but we talked to some people from the village who have. They say they've never heard anything like it."

"How does it work?"

"Seems this goat herder was once a blacksmith. For fun he forged a whole octave of bells to put on his goats. And he is training them to run in some sort of order, so it's like they're playing a musical piece. Once I heard about it, I knew I had to see it. And record it."

"How random." I'm unconvinced this is worth missing out on what's happening back home. These days spent in a dump, listening to the muffled snores of a Turkish man, are days I'll never get back.

"Look, Felicia . . . I know you didn't want to come . . ."

"No, I didn't."

". . . but I couldn't leave you at home by yourself. You're seventeen."

"Seventeen is old enough," I grumble. "Nicole's parents let her stay at home alone." I know it's a weak argument, especially since Nicole's exploits while her parents are out of town are so legendary, I'm sure even my father has heard about them.

"You used to love coming on these trips with me." His voice is full of emotion. "I know it might not seem like it now, but there's more to life than parties and studying. The point is to keep trying new things, meeting new people, visiting new places. Once you settle into a rut, no matter how fun that rut may seem, you stagnate. You might as well be dead."

I snort. "We will be dead if those rocks fall on our heads."

"Good night, sweet pea. Try to get some sleep."

And I do try to sleep. But I lie awake with my eyes squeezed shut for a long time, unsettled by the storm and afraid my nightmares will be extra fierce in this strange place. They've been more vivid lately, interspersed with flashes of bright light, and I've been getting less and less sleep because of them.

Dad wakes me, so I guess I must have fallen asleep at some point during the night. He puts a hunk of bread in my hand and starts to whistle. "Roll up your sleeping bag, sweet pea! The goats are on the move!"

I rise groggily, squinting in the bright sunlight, and gather up all my belongings to meet him at the car. I can think of better ways to spend my morning than lugging around my dad's crap. He trades me the camping gear for his audio equipment. "Do you see them?" He points beyond the hut. "There on the crest of that hill. We have to hurry."

He sets off, and Azrak and I follow. All the while, I keep my eyes on the herd of goats. They munch grass in the morning sunlight, and the bells tinkle as they move.

Once we're in recording range, Dad sets up his equipment. Just in time too, because the goatherd bellows at the goats, and they prance and buck all around him. The sight alone of this orderly chaos is enough to transfix me, but the eerie, discordant melody of the bells has me rooted to the spot. It's far from perfect, but I can understand now why Dad wanted to see them.

Dad's face is flushed and there are tears shining in his eyes. "See, sweet pea. What did I tell you? These are the moments that make life worth living. These are the moments I try to capture and convey when I compose."

I close the distance between us and slip my hand into his. The rest of the world fades away, and it's just me and my dad, watching one of the most bizarre and beautiful spectacles I'll probably ever see.

I surface then, the strange music still clanging in my ears.

"The nice gentleman wants his chamber back," Julian says. "Can you restore his settings before you get out?"

I do what Julian asked and wiggle out of the chamber. The man Julian punched is standing behind him, rhythmically rubbing his jaw.

"Thank you, sir," Julian says as if dismissing him.

The man shuffles back into his chamber without another glance at us.

Julian heads for the expanse of wall that hides the door. "We need to go."

I still have so many questions. "But . . ."

"Let's go." His tone, impatient and vaguely menacing, leaves no room for discussion. It doesn't seem worth it to fight him now, so I follow him out of the hive.

We're back on the run. As I fall in behind him, I wonder how long we're going to have to traverse this expanse, this seemingly never-ending colony of hives, in order to find Neil. To keep frustration at bay I play a game. For every hive we pass along the corridor, I guess what types of people might be trapped there. That hive on the right could be full of former circus clowns. The one on the left teems with vicious gangsters. When I run out of easy descriptors, I start to make up individual histories. The clown who, because he refused to take off his red nose, was killed in Pamplona. The gangster who gave up his family for true love but was tracked down years later and was sent to sleep with the fishes.

I'm surprised by how long I'm able to stay clearheaded outside my chamber. Should I tell Julian? Or is it better if I pretend I'm foggier than I am? It's not that I'm scared of Julian exactly, but it seems wise to tread carefully around him.

The hives start to rumble, and the path roils and cracks, throwing me to my knees. There's a flickering, too, like the electricity is on the fritz. It lasts only a few seconds and then everything is calm again.

Julian pulls me up and points at a mass of the scanner drones—at least ten—bearing down on us. "We have to take cover. Now!" Julian opens the door to the nearest hive, and we fling ourselves through.

"Whoa! Close call." In relief I smile up at Julian, but the smile dies on my lips. With a grim expression he swivels me around to face the communal area of the hive. It's not empty. It's full of burly men, fuming with anger. And all their eyes are on us.

CHAPTER 8

THE DOOR SEALS SHUT BEHIND ME. I claw at it in desperation. I have to get out of here.

"Stay calm," Julian whispers into my ear, pulling me away from the wall, closer to his side. "They can't hurt you unless you believe they can."

Julian's words barely register. As the beady-eyed pack approaches, the leader snarls and I cower.

"You two responsible for the banging in my head?" He lunges at me and wraps his meaty arm around my neck, pressing me up against his chest. "Make it stop!" he howls at Julian. "Or I'll off your little girlie here."

He squeezes me so hard that if I depended on a windpipe to keep air flowing to my lungs, I'd be passed out by now. I tense, too terrified to even struggle. This can't be happening again.

Julian holds his hands out to the leader in a pacifying gesture. It goes ignored. Instead a hulking brute with a long scar along his forehead rushes at him, fists swinging. He lands a punch on Julian's face, right at the cheekbone. It knocks Julian off balance enough for a comparatively scrawny man to bound over and shove him easily to the floor. This riles the rest of the group up into a frenzy. They press in and egg on the attack.

My panic escalates. Can they rip us apart? What happens if they do? Can you die when you're already dead? I sure don't want to find out. And definitely not like this.

I can't even see Julian anymore, he's so surrounded by the writhing mass of men. A misty fog seeps from the wall of the hive, blurring the scene even more. Dark thoughts hover and jab at the edge of my mind, like a swarm of stinging wasps, telling me to give up. To give in.

But then Julian roars. He rises and spins like a tornado in slow motion, flinging the scarred hulk away from him and into the crowd. He elbows anyone who blocks his path as he makes his way over to where I stand, still in the vise-like grip of the leader.

Julian leaps at us, and at the same time, I feel the man slacken against me and loosen his hold. As I begin to keel over, Julian catches me and kisses me full on the lips. His touch distracts me momentarily from everything else. It quells the dark thoughts in my head. Heat rises in my chest, replacing the panic and hopelessness. I'm dimly aware of our attackers lumbering away.

I can't surrender to Julian. I push against him roughly, and he releases me, making my body go cold and my head fuzzy. The noise comes back, a low level buzzing that gets louder as it swirls around my thoughts, pricking and probing for a way in. "Stay alert!" Julian barks into my face. "Focus your mind on me. You are stronger than them!"

I peer at him drowsily, taking in his distressed jeans and his shredded shirt on the way up to his face. His jaw is clenched and his eyes are mere slits. "What do you mean?" I slur.

He shakes me. "The doping gas is trying to invade your mind. You don't have to let it in."

The doping gas. I remember then where I am, what I have to fight for. I close my eyes and concentrate on driving the dark thoughts away, on building a wall to keep them out. They screech and groan as I beat them back, a hideous din. I lay the final brick that completes my defenses, and I'm rewarded with the sound of silence. I fall into Julian's arms, fully spent.

He cradles me against his broad chest. The raw edges of his tattered shirt tickle my cheek, and the heat of his skin sears my own. "You did it," he says with awe. "You beat the gas. It took everything you had, but you did it."

I remember our attackers then, and my eyes pop open. "Are they gone? Those men?"

Julian cranes his neck, back and forth in a fluid motion. "None in sight. And there's even a chamber free," he says. "Why are you so afraid of them, anyway?" He carries me up the stairs to a chamber. "They're only simple drones. And after the recent system-wide malfunction, the guardians have reprogrammed the hives to release doping gas every time they register a group disturbance, and sometimes even when a group is only hanging out. It calms them and sends them back to their chambers."

"But how do you know that?" I shudder. "Sorry. It's just . . . I hate crowds. Brings back bad memories."

"It's okay. I understand." Julian sets me in the chamber, and I scoot back so I can lie down. "About the doping gas," he says, "I'm deducing, based on reports we've had from other rebel cells, that they are reprogramming. This is the first time I've seen it for myself."

"How come it didn't affect you at all?" I ask, positioning my hands into the grooves.

He shrugs. "I've been out and about a long time. The doping gas can't touch me."

The screen takes its time loading, and as it does, I let my eyes flick over to Julian's face. I expect to see concern or pity, but instead I see cunning. Triumph. It gives me the sickening feeling that he's using me. So unlike Neil. With my last ounce of energy, I pull up my Neil tags and pick one at random. I press it, and I'm in.

Ward, Felicia. Memory #31938
Tags: Ohio, Neil, Youth group, Underground church
Number of Views: 7,098
Owner Rating: 4 stars
User Rating: 3.5 stars

I slam the door of Grammy's car and survey the parking lot before me. It's packed with vehicles, indicating a good turnout for the church lock-in. Even though I'd gotten used to the youth group over the past two and a half months of Sunday church services and Wednesday prayer meetings, I still hadn't wanted to come. But Grammy needed to go in overnight for some tests at the hospital, and she insisted, told me she made sure Pastor Joe would keep an eye on me.

I rub my hands together and then pull the info flyer from the pocket of my fleece. I probably should have worn gloves, but the budding trees and flowers in Grammy's front yard had fooled me into thinking that winter was long past. The flyer instructs me to meet the group in the fellowship hall, so I bypass the dark, forlorn chapel and head toward the bright lights of the building twenty yards to its right.

As I enter the foyer, Savannah rushes up and hands me a cardboard medallion hanging from a loop of yarn. It looks like something a child might make. "Put this around your neck!" She's so keyed up, I think her eyes might pop out of her head.

When I take the medallion from her, she slides my overnight bag from my shoulder and slings it over into the corner onto a jumbled pile of coats and backpacks. "What's this for?" I slip it over my head.

"You'll find out soon enough!"

We stop by the registration table, manned by several adults I recognize from services. A woman looks up at me. "Felicia! So glad you could make it." She marks off her list and nods. "Your grandmother sent in your payment last week, so you're all covered."

As Savannah pulls me into the fellowship hall, I try to push down the simmering anger in the pit of my stomach. Did Grammy really need to stay overnight for those tests, or was it a ploy to get me here? And why is she spending money we don't have? I am fed up with her interfering.

The large open room is full of teens clustered in groups, sitting on the carpeted floor. Most are balancing paper plates stacked with chips and cookies, and paper cups filled with punch. Savannah skips the snack table and leads me over to her friends, sprawled out right in the center of everyone. As I pick my way uneasily through the crowd, I scan faces, looking for Neil. He hasn't been at many church activities lately, and I register his absence now with strong disappointment. I reluctantly admit to myself that I so readily accepted Grammy's excuse because I hoped he'd be here tonight. The realization makes me feel hot and itchy, but it doesn't mean I *like* him. It just means I like being around him. I plop myself down next to Savannah once we reach her circle, and smile tightly at the girls when they greet me.

A trumpet sounds, and a column of boys dressed as

Roman soldiers marches in the front doors and stands at attention in a single file formation. Neil's best friend, Andy, drags in a prisoner by a short length of rope, a prisoner whose head is obscured by a burlap sack. The room erupts in excited bursts of chatter when Pastor Joe enters and moves toward the prisoner. We all stand up, trying to get a better view of the proceedings.

Pastor Joe pulls the sack off with a flourish. It's Neil. Despite his flushed cheeks and tousled hair, he holds his head high, defiant. I squeeze my arms around myself to steady my jangled nerves. He is here after all.

Pastor Joe clears his throat. "It's the first century AD. The Romans are cracking down on Christians. You are not allowed to gather for worship. You are not allowed to profess your faith. If you do, and are caught, you will be dragged to jail and interrogated. Like this man was." He jabs his finger at Neil, who makes a show of struggling in his bonds. Andy pulls the rope tighter, causing Neil to stumble against him. "He claims to be your leader and has been accused of organizing a secret gathering of Christians somewhere in this compound. We will make an example of him and throw him to the lions!"

The crowd gasps as two soldiers salute Pastor Joe and lead Neil off. But before they can get far, four women dressed as angels glide in the front entrance and form a barrier between Neil and the soldiers. One of the angels unties the rope. Neil faces us, his eyes pleading. "Find me! I will tell you the truth. And the truth will set you free." Then he sprints toward us, and we part to make a path for him. He pushes through the back doors and disappears into the depths of the building, which I know to be lined with small classrooms.

Both Pastor Joe and the soldiers appear to be under a temporary spell. One of the angels addresses us. "By the power of God, we will hold back your Roman persecutors for five minutes. This will give you a head start to try to find your leader, who will be at the location of the secret meeting. If you are stopped by a Roman soldier, they will ask if you are a Christian. If you say yes, they will take you to jail."

The angel reaches out and takes the hand of one of the audience members, pulling him to her side. She fingers the medallion around his neck. "Each of you has been given a medallion. Open it in private and read the clues it gives you. Good luck. Go!" The angels surround Pastor Joe and the soldiers. The audience jostles around me, and I take deep, measured breaths to stay calm and tell myself that no one here wants to hurt me. They stream toward the back doors, stuffing cookies into their mouths and sloshing down punch. The trash cans near the exit are overflowing with paper debris by the time Savannah and I reach them.

I look over at Savannah. Her eyes are glittering. "I love underground church! We can't let them catch us, Felicia. Last time, they dunked us face-first in grape jelly, and it took me forever to wash it out of my hair."

Once through the doors, we're at a crossroads of sorts. We could go down the hallway to our right or forge on ahead.

"This building is not that big," I say. "It can't be too hard for them to find us."

Though most of the crowd goes straight, Savannah and a couple of her gang veer right. "Looks can be deceiving," Savannah asserts. The girls around us giggle. I'm embarrassed that I've never bothered to learn their names.

We run, our pounding footfalls echoing through the hallway until we hit a dead end. Savannah opens the door on the left, and we follow her into a dark room. She flips on the light switch, and I see a set of stairs leading down.

"This is one of the entrances to the underground tunnels," Glasses Girl explains to me. "They were built as part of the Underground Railroad to help hide escaped slaves. One passage leads to the chapel. Others lead to the kindergarten, to the gym, to the pastor's house, and to the administration building."

I'm impressed. This does make the game infinitely more exciting.

"Listen, girls—we have to find the secret meeting place before the Romans find us." Savannah scrunches up her face in thought. "So, there are five passageways and five of us, right? I say we each scope out one of them and then meet back here. The one who finds Neil can lead the rest of us to him."

Glasses Girl speaks up. "But if we find the secret meeting place, they won't let us leave again. It's too dangerous!"

Savannah scoffs. "Don't actually go in. Peek in and come back."

She assigns the girls their routes, and they dash off.

Then she turns to me. "The easiest to find is the gym." We take the stairs down together, and at the bottom she points out a narrow passage to our right. "Keep going straight. You'll know it when you see it!" She squeezes my arm. "Don't forget to read what your medallion says. And keep it to yourself. Don't even tell me, because some of the Christians are Romans in disguise. Got that?"

"See you back here?"

"Yes." She grins. "Well, unless I get caught."

Savannah heads the opposite way, and I peer down the passage I am to take. It's narrow and dimly lit. Judging from the amount of spiderwebs, it's not used often, or maintained well.

I close my eyes for a minute and remind myself I'm playing a game. I'm in Ohio, not Nairobi. Once I've gained enough courage, I walk briskly down the chilly passage and ascend the stairway at the end. The door at the top is closed, and I bite down my panic as I turn the handle. Fortunately, it creaks open.

I peek into a cavernous gym. It's dark, but there is a soft glow of a candle coming from behind stacks of thick blue mats on the far side. Could this be the secret meeting place? Or is it a trap? I tiptoe as carefully as I can across the gym, but a squeak of my tennis shoe betrays me.

"Who's there?" calls out a voice in a stage whisper. I see a familiar head of curls pop up behind the mats.

"Neil?"

Neil stands up all the way and waves me over. "Felicia!" He looks down at his watch. "Seven minutes, forty-five seconds. That must be a new record. How'd you find me?"

Once I am behind his barricade, he sits down on a low pile of mats shoved haphazardly against the wall. The candlelight flickers, and I'm suddenly aware we're alone together—really alone—for the first time. "Oh . . . Savannah sent me down this hidden tunnel." I perch next to him, careful to leave a respectable amount of space between us. "Now I have to go back and get her. Let her know I found the secret meeting place."

He shakes his head. "You can't. Against the rules."

"What are you going to do if I try to go? Handcuff me to a mat?" I run my fingers over the mat's surface. It's rougher than I expected.

He leans over toward me on his elbow and looks at me gravely. "If I have to . . . ," he says in a low voice. But then he straightens and laughs, diffusing the tension. "What does your medallion say?"

I finger the medallion around my neck. With my thumbnail I scrape along the edge to loosen the tape and unfold it. I have to squint to read it. Underneath a password are the following words:

YOU ARE THE CHOSEN ONE.
IF THE ROMANS CATCH YOU,
THEY WIN THE GAME.

"It says not to get caught," I tell Neil, remembering Savannah's warning. "I have to go back, you know. I promised Savannah." And I want my promises to mean something.

He sighs. "Since I don't have a pair of handcuffs handy, I guess I can't stop you. But I have to lock the door you came through. It's too dangerous, open like that."

"But isn't this a safe house? I didn't think the Romans could get to us once we're here."

"They can—if they can get in. That's why there are angels guarding the main doors. They only let you in if you have the right password."

"Right, but they won't see me if I come back through the tunnel. Couldn't you let me back in?"

"But how do I know it's you?"

I shrug my shoulders. "I don't know. Can't we make up a secret knock or something?"

"Good idea." Neil starts tapping on the mat, sometimes with the flat of his palm, which makes a long sound and sometimes with his fist, which makes a short sound. "So try this." He slaps the mat three times with his palm, taps twice with his fist and then slaps one final time with his palm. "Long, long, long. Short, short, long. Morse code for *O* and *U*. 'Open up.'" He grins. "Spelling out 'open' would be too long."

"Where'd you learn Morse code?" I'm sure he has a nerdy explanation.

"In Eagle Scouts. For my signaling merit badge." Yep, nerdy.

"I was a Girl Scout for a year. Juniors. In fourth grade. I got a badge for selling the most cookies."

"Just a year?"

"Yeah, I got kicked out," I admit. "My mother was scandalized." It makes me almost nostalgic now to think back to a time when getting asked not to return to Girl Scouts was the blackest mark on my record.

"Kicked out, huh?" He looks like he doesn't believe me.

"The troop leader's daughter told her mom that I stole her boyfriend. So . . ."

"Did you?"

"No way! I only said, like, two words to him when I stopped by his house to deliver his family's cookie order." I start to giggle, the absurdity of this conversation getting the better of me. "Apparently, afterward he told her I was cute."

"Such a heartbreaker." He says it softly, seriously.

I sober, fast, and change the subject. "So like this." I tap out our new secret knock. Long, long, long. Short, short, long.

"That's it."

"Then I guess I'm ready." I stand up.

"I guess you are." He stands up too.

We walk in silence across the gym and then stand in front of the open door to the tunnel. But once I see it stretch out before me, I find I don't want to leave Neil.

"Why haven't you been at church much lately?" I blurt, trying to stall the inevitable.

Neil grins. "Play practice at school. We're doing *Our Town*."

"Seriously?" I guess I shouldn't be too surprised. It's a popular work.

"Why?" He laughs. "You thought I'd only do musicals, right? I do sing one song at least."

"No, it's not that. We read *Our Town* last semester. At my old school." I omit the abysmal grade I got on my paper. "Which part did you get?"

"George Gibbs." He pulls at the collar of his polo shirt.

Sounds about right. I wonder who gets to play Emily. Who gets to kiss him. "That scene at the end, where George lies down on Emily's grave . . . it's tragic."

"It is." His gaze roams over to the flickering candlelight and then to the front doors of the gym. "But the part that always gets me is when ghost Emily chooses to relive her twelfth birthday."

"Yeah, that was so . . . emotional." I regret not reading the play more closely. If I had, I would know what he's talking about and be able to answer more intelligently. No better time to get going, I guess. Sighing, I step into the tunnel. "Well, see you back here in a few."

"Don't get caught," he tells me, reaching out his hand. My breath catches in my throat, thinking he's going to touch me, but he grabs the doorknob to shut the door behind me. The lock clicks.

I run back to our meeting place, my heart beating wildly in my chest. Glasses Girl and the other two are there, though Savannah is not. I tell them I've found Neil, and we wait. The minutes tick by, and I wonder if I made the right decision to come back. Occasionally we hear shouting, but no one comes our way.

Finally Savannah shows up, smiling and puffing her hair. We celebrate not being jailed and jellied. I lead them back, perform my secret knock, and Neil lets us in.

We sit on the mats, laughing and talking. Once in a while the main doors open and others come join us. Then Pastor Joe comes in to tell us the game is over. The soldiers, including Andy, march in behind him, looking dejected. The chosen one was never caught, and the Christians win this round. I cheer as loud as anyone else.

We spread our sleeping bags onto the mats in the gym, and although we're told to pipe down, the room never gets totally quiet. We're too pumped up.

A knocking sound. Long, long, long. Short, short, long. My eyes pop open, and a hologram screen shines above me.

"Where is she?" It's a melodic voice, but demanding and cold. I freeze.

"She's up there, powering up in a chamber," Julian answers nonchalantly. I must not be in danger. Relaxing slightly, I shift my position in the console so I can spy on the new arrival.

Tall and imposing, she's as striking as a runway model. Her pink hair is cropped in a pixie cut, and she's wearing a strapless, sliced-up silver ball gown over a pair of skinny black jeans and six-inch silver stiletto boots. "Get her down. You've been due back for more than a week. Eli wants to prepare phase three." Her words are sometimes a little too clipped, sometimes a little too slurred, an accent that sounds vaguely Scandinavian. Icelandic maybe.

Julian starts up the stairs, but I slip out by myself and gingerly make my way over to the top step. I feel so underdressed in my plain white shift, though I guess nothing I could conjure up from my earthly wardrobe would rival this girl's funky elegance. Might as well not even try. Probably don't have enough power yet anyway.

"You must be Felicia," she purrs up at me, her voice as soothing as honey. She saunters over and drapes her arm around Julian. "I'm Mira, a friend of Julian's. Are you ready to go?"

Mira's presence raises a ton more questions, and her unexpected friendliness gives me the courage to ask one. "I've been wondering something."

"Yes?" Mira narrows her violet eyes and retracts her arm. Her shift in demeanor is dramatic.

"How did you and Julian get out of your hives? I tried forever to get out, and I never found a way."

Mira and Julian exchange a significant look.

"We were recruited by the rebellion, the angel underground," Mira says.

"Angels?" I gape at her. "Wait . . . so angels are fighting the guardians who are enslaving us here?"

Mira laughs. It's like the tinkling of a thousand tiny bells. "Julian, dear . . . how much have you told her?"

"Not much." His answer is gruff.

"I can see that." Mira gestures at me to come closer. I descend until I am standing on the second stair from the bottom and looking straight into her eyes.

"Forget everything you have heard about angels. That they are some kind of celestial beings who only want the best for you, who want to protect you. True—some are like that. Like the rebels." She reaches out and takes my hand, guiding me down the last two steps.

"But then there's the Morati." She says it sadly, like a lament. "Enemies of good, unhappy with the job God gave them as guardians of this realm. And they want you."

CHAPTER 9

"ME? WHAT DO THEY WANT WITH ME?" My body wobbles, and I might fall if not for Mira's hand on my wrist.

Mira tosses her head, and her chandelier earrings sparkle wildly. "By 'you,' of course I mean 'us.' The rebels and their recruits." She releases me and opens her arms wide, as if she's about to give me a welcoming hug. "You are one of us now."

It's all too much to take in. Julian and Mira want me to join a rebellion? Against angels? How can she possibly think we have any chance against celestial beings that must be immensely powerful? I drop like a stone, my butt thudding against the stair.

Mira crosses her arms and frowns at me through her impossibly thick eyelashes. "I thought you said she was strong."

"She is strong," Julian insists. "She fought off the doping gas."

"Did she now? That *is* good news."

"Thank you." My courage swells a bit at the sudden admiration in her voice, though her mercurial moods are starting to give me whiplash.

"I am not going to lie to you." Mira's feet shimmer as her voice hardens, and she shrinks five inches. The stiletto boots have morphed into sleek black running shoes. "The Morati do not tolerate resistance. They seek to silence us while they prepare to wage their war against heaven. We were a mere thorn in their sides, but as our ranks grow, I think we stand a chance to end their tyranny and return balance to Level Two." She grimaces. "But we have to outsmart them first."

"Balance? Level Two?" What in the world is she talking about?

"Think of this place as a waiting room. Earth, what we call Level One, is about creating and forming memories. And this waiting room, Level Two, is about processing those memories, sifting through them to find the meaning of your time on Earth. To come to terms with it so you can move on."

A mix of anxiety and excitement gnaws my insides. Though I'm not sure I want to know the answer, I go ahead and say what's on the tip of my tongue. "So there *is* something more than this. A Level Three?"

"Ah . . . that is the eternal question, is it not? What comes next?" She regards me coolly, as if trying to decide how much to tell me. She gathers the long strips of her skirt around her and sits next to me on the stair.

"What we know is that humans move on from here, but angels don't. The Morati have recently gathered enough power to travel back and forth to Earth, but whatever comes next eludes them. It infuriates them to have to help humans reach a higher plane where they themselves are not allowed."

Julian starts tapping his foot and lets out an exasperated sigh.

"Am I boring you, Julian?" Mira asks, saccharine sweet.

"The scanner drones seem to be multiplying by the minute out there. I'm worried that if we don't get going soon, there'll be a higher chance we'll get caught."

Mira's haughty look in response says it all: At that moment Julian might as well be a spider skittering across the runway while she's strutting it. But then she feigns a yawn and glances around the hive. "I'm bored of this place anyway."

She snaps her fingers, and a motorcycle helmet appears on her head, already fastened on her chin. She strides across the hive, pulling on elbow-length leather gloves in two smooth motions. "Fix your shirt, Julian. You look like you're posing for the cover of a romance novel about pirates." She snaps her fingers again, and a Ducati appears by her side.

Julian doesn't bat an eye, as if he's immune to her barbs, but I have to stifle a laugh. Julian doesn't like to look foolish, and despite everything I've been through so far, I'm still able to find it funny that Mira can put him in his place.

He shimmers, and his shredded shirt is as good as new. "A motorcycle?" he scoffs. "The idea is not to draw attention to ourselves. You rev up that thing, and you'll attract whole swarms of scanner drones."

"Oh, please! They're not programmed to pick up anything but voices. And they can only do *that* at the quadrant range."

"That's true as far as we know, but do we really want to risk it with all the system changes we've seen recently?" Julian presses his lips into a thin line and stares her down.

"Fine." She pouts. "But I am not running." She hovers her gloved hands over the Ducati, and it transforms into a skateboard. "Time to go." She expertly mounts and propels herself toward the door. She taps out the code that opens the door, pops the tail of the board to attain air, and sails through the opening.

"Show-off," Julian mutters. But his bemused half grin tells me he at least partially enjoys her antics.

Though Mira's level of materialization ability is impressive, I'm not sure I want to go with her back to the rebels' hideout. I don't care about being recruited, and I certainly don't want to fight a war. I just want to find Neil. "Uh, we're not really going with her, are we?"

Julian puckers his mouth as if he didn't expect me to make trouble, and the door slides closed, separating us from Mira. "Look, you have two main objectives right now. Avoid the Morati and build your strength. Even if you don't want to join our fight, we can protect you while you detox."

"But what about Neil—"

The side of his face twitches. "Do you honestly think you'll be any help to Neil in your current condition?"

Julian has a point. To have a realistic chance of getting Neil out of his hive—and I assume he's in a hive somewhere—I need to be at my strongest. It makes sense to stick with the rebels for now, even if I don't especially want to.

The door slides back open, and Mira peers in. "Hello? Can we go?"

I bite inside of my cheek and sigh. "Yeah, okay."

We fall into place behind Mira. As usual, our journey is silent except for the dull thuds of our feet hitting the ground and now the low hum of Mira's wheels. I'm left again to my own whirring thoughts, a barrage of questions that fight for dominance.

I never considered that angels could be the enemy here, though it does now seem like a logical deduction. I guess I had always heard some were cast out of heaven and became demons, followers of Satan that ruled hell and roamed the Earth, tempting mankind. Or maybe this is hell?

But that can't be right. Mira called it a waiting room, a second level after Earth, not hell. I try to recall any angel lore having to do with evil angels in purgatory or afterlife realms other than heaven or hell, but I can't. I've never missed the Internet more. Without it I'm dependent on Julian and Mira and their capricious whims, like a starving person begging for crumbs. And of course it's also possible they're feeding me lies. I'd be a fool to trust Julian completely again. But until I know more, until I get stronger, I'm at their mercy. Because, who am I kidding? What choice do I have? I'd be lost out here in this unchanging landscape of bulbous hives.

We run on and on. I concentrate on putting one foot in

front of the other, even though I'd almost rather hide out in some random hive, plug in, and let my mind sink into a blissful oblivion of memories. It's tempting. But the thought of seeing Neil again for real tempts me more. Even though I have no idea how we'd fare if I did find him. Could we avoid the Morati by ourselves? Or would we still need to use Julian as a guide?

Maybe I really could be of some use to the rebel mission to overthrow the Morati and restore peace. Give all those children who are strapped into chambers a chance to laugh and play. Give everyone a chance to move on.

And maybe, should we somehow succeed, I might be granted a second chance. Not at an earthly life. As far as I know, no human comes back from the grave. But maybe I could see Autumn again. And my dad. Mend things with them. Tell them how sorry I am for the way things turned out. That I was such a rotten friend and daughter.

Mira and Julian stop suddenly, and I crash into them, catching my foot on the axle of her skateboard and causing it to pitch forward. Mira dismounts effortlessly, but the force throws me sideways, and I stumble but right myself before falling.

Mira twitches her nose, and the offending board vanishes, along with her helmet and gloves. She approaches the nearest hive, smoothes down strands of her hair with her long fingers, and raps on the wall. The door slides open, and she enters without a backward glance.

Julian offers his arm to me, as if he's my escort to a fancy ball, but I reject it. He shrugs and goes in too. I step over the threshold behind him and am amazed by the scene that greets me.

Furniture and rugs are scattered throughout the common area, giving the hive a surprisingly cozy vibe. A plush sofa, the color of ripe eggplant. Two overstuffed armchairs. A high-backed chaise longue. I'll be able to detox in comfort, that's for sure.

On the left-hand curve of the hive, there is the typical stacked set of memory chambers and one stairway going up. On the right-hand curve the wall is smooth, as if the memory chambers have been sandblasted away. Straight ahead hangs a golden swath of velvet material, gathered in a way that reminds me of a curtain in a theater. In front of that there is a bank of computer equipment. Cables snake out in all directions, some hooked into the memory chambers, others lifeless and frayed. A dark-haired boy hunches over the computers, totally immersed in his work.

"Any updates, Eli?" Mira asks as she kicks off her shoes. She arranges the throw pillows on the chaise longue and curls up on it, the ragged silver strips of her silk voile gown fluttering around her.

Eli swivels in his stool and regards me with a mix of curiosity and detachment, as if I'm a scientific specimen to be pressed onto a slide and studied. Like Julian and Mira, he's unusually attractive, with high cheekbones and a perfectly symmetrical face. Even his severe military buzz cut and thick-framed eyeglasses can't diminish his looks.

He turns back to his computers. "I ran more phase two ops.

Subjects overloaded and are bound to be picked up."

"Overloaded? What does that mean?" I ask. My hands start to tremble, a first sign I'll have to return to a chamber soon.

Eli clacks at his keyboards, ignoring me.

"I'd try again in quadrant ninety-nine," Mira says. "Perhaps the more active subjects are better equipped to deal with your ops."

A tremor runs through me, and I stagger over to a chair.

"I think it is time to show Felicia to her chamber. She must be simply exhausted after our long journey." Mira's exaggerated politeness doesn't ring true. I'm sure she just wants to be rid of me so she can discuss whatever phase two is in peace. But I don't argue. I'm far too shaky for that.

Julian unhooks some cables from the chamber nearest the floor and gestures for me to get in. I do, eagerly, sighing with relief when the fizzy champagne feeling rushes through me. I know what memory I need to visit. I mess around with the settings of the chamber until my folders load, and I dive in.

Ward, Felicia. Memory #31300
Tags: Germany, Autumn, Julian, Hacking
Number of Views: 3
Owner Rating: Not rated
User Rating: Not shared

"Why do you organize all your books by color?" asks Julian. He's lounging on my bed, clearly bored of watching me type for the past half hour.

"If you can't stop distracting me, I'm going to have to ask you to leave," I scold. "Just because you're done with school doesn't mean I can blow everything off." Without taking my eyes from the screen, I reach for my cup of coffee and try to take a sip, but discover it's empty. I let it clatter back onto my desk with a sigh.

He grumbles and bounces on the bed, making the springs groan. My *Our Town* essay is going to suck. And not only because I'm hyperaware of Julian's presence, but also because my brain is too jumbled to write coherent arguments.

He jumps up and throws open my closet. "Ha! Exactly what I suspected! All your clothes are organized by color too." Before I can stop him, he's at my dresser, opening the top drawer, revealing my rainbow of accessories.

"And you even sort your socks." From the middle he pulls out a green pair, rolled neatly into a ball, and tosses it at my head playfully.

I catch it. "Fine. I'll take a break." I try to get past him so I can put my socks back, but he stops me by brushing his lips against mine. As the kiss deepens, I let the socks drop to the floor.

My cell phone rings. I pull away from Julian reluctantly and answer it. It's my mother, telling me she'll be late again tonight. I assure her it's fine.

"By the way, I bought my plane ticket today," says Julian when I hang up. "I am going to Angkor Wat. Like you recommended."

My heart sinks. But it soars, too. I always knew

this—whatever this is—would be short-term. Even shorter term than most of my relationships. As much as I've become addicted to his lips and hands all over my body, it will be a relief to stop lying to Autumn.

"Oh?" I say. "I hope you're waiting until after November fifteenth. Nicole throws a killer birthday party. Or so I hear." I don't know why I'm even telling Julian this, since I'm hardly a fan of Nicole or big parties in general.

"I forgot about that, but I can change my ticket." He sits down at my laptop. "May I?"

"Of course." I watch him as he types a long series of numbers into my browser and pulls up the website for TransAsiatic Airlines, though it doesn't look like a normal consumer site but more like a client interface. "Don't you have to pay a penalty to change? Maybe it's not worth it."

"Pay? No. It costs the airlines nothing to make changes." He inserts a USB drive into a free slot and copies a program onto my desktop.

"So, what do you do instead?" I ask, wary. Is he about to do something illegal on my computer than can be traced back to me? "Or do I not want to know?"

"See this?" he asks, indicating the window on the screen. "This is a spoof I made of TransAsiatic's remote access VPN. Fortunately for us, their security is crap. The program I loaded onto your laptop uses brute force to crack the passwords so the tunnel endpoints authenticate." He brings up his password program, and I watch in fascination as it runs through alphanumeric sequences. "There we go."

Once he's in, he zooms through a myriad of booking screens and pop-ups, inputting information when prompted. I get the feeling he's done this before, and it freaks me out. "I am now leaving on November eighteenth. I upgraded myself to first class while I was at it."

"But that's against the law!"

"No need to be so uptight."

"I'm serious, Julian. What if I get in trouble for this? I mean, you put a hacker program on my computer. My mother could lose her security clearance and get kicked out of the Foreign Service!" And then she would kill me. If that could prove her loyalty to her job and convince them to take her back.

"No one will notice. Trust me. First class on that flight is practically empty. All those seats won't sell in the next month. I am already on the plane—might as well fly in style. It makes no difference to them."

I'm glad he gets to stay a couple of days more, but doubts prickle my skin. "You're absolutely sure they can't trace any of this to me?"

Thunder claps across Julian's features, and I flinch. But as quickly as the storm clouds gathered, they part, and Julian beams at me in a way that makes me crave his approval.

I say, "It's pretty cool you can get into their system like that."

"Let me teach you a few tricks." He says it casually, as if hacking is no big deal. "Untraceable, of course."

"I don't know . . ."

The door buzzes.

I look at my clock. "Shit! It's six already. That's Autumn."

"Should I slip out your window?" He asks it blandly, as if it wouldn't bother him to have Autumn catch him here.

"Better not. Someone might see you. It will look even more suspicious that way."

I walk to the door like I'm going to my own execution. I make up and reject excuses as I go. This is bad. Julian hangs behind in the living room.

I buzz Autumn in and open the door.

"Hey!" She bounds up the stairs, her cheeks red from the cold, her hands full of paper. "Are you finished with your essay yet? I brought you a few more chapters of our book to go over."

"Uh, no. Not yet."

Autumn hands me the pages, hole-punched and tied with purple satin ribbon. She walks in. I take a deep breath. I might as well get it over with. "Julian came over to use my computer . . ."

"Hey!" Julian greets her warmly with a hug. "We still on for the movies tonight?" Somehow it doesn't seem fair that I'm the one who has to sneak around while Autumn gets to go out on the town with him.

If Autumn is surprised to see him here, she covers it well. She smiles. "Of course."

"Great. Pick you up at seven thirty." He puts on his jacket, kisses me perfunctorily on both cheeks, and then heads out the door with a wave.

Autumn watches him go with a sigh. "I'm going to be so bummed when he leaves."

Now's probably not the best time to tell her he has booked a ticket already.

"So, what did you two talk about?" she asks once we reach my room. As she flops herself down onto my bed, I notice the pair of socks still on the floor where I dropped them. I kick them under my dresser while I deposit her manuscript on top of it.

"Not much," I say. I hate that lying comes so easily to me. "A little about Nicole's big birthday bash." I reach for a bottle of nail polish. Scarlet. The perfect color for someone like me.

"She better invite me this year," Autumn says. Nicole is notorious for inviting a bunch of guys to her parties but only a select group of girls. And every girl at our school hopes to make the cut.

"Can you hand me the nail polish remover?" I point it out to her on the night table on the other side of my bed. She rolls over and picks it up along with a bag of cotton balls.

"And don't worry." I take my supplies from her. "She'll want Julian to go, so she has to invite you." Rather than crowd Autumn on my bed, I sit on the floor and begin to rub off my pink polish. The sharp scent of ammonia fills the room.

She bites her lip at my mention of Julian. "Did he say anything about me?"

"Um . . . sure. He said you were going to the movies

tonight." Another lie. Julian never said a word about Autumn. He never does when we're alone together.

"Maybe tonight's the night he'll finally kiss me for real!" Autumn squeals. "He's such a gentleman. He says the physical stuff should wait until a couple gets to know each other better. But, God! I've been waiting, like, a month already."

Ugh. Now I feel even worse. Because I'm happy he hasn't kissed her. I open the bottle of scarlet and paint my thumbnail first.

"You know, when I first saw Julian was here, I got a little scared," she confides. "I thought maybe he decided he liked you better."

He does, but she doesn't need to know that. "Nothing to worry about here." And soon there won't be, because he's leaving. Then we can put this unpleasant chapter of our friendship behind us. Right hand polished, I move on to the nails on my left hand.

"I trust you," she says. I can tell deep down that she knows she shouldn't. But she does anyway. Because she has an enormous capacity for self-delusion. For overlooking the obvious even when it is slapping her in the face. It makes me want to pinch her. To violently rip her out of her cocoon of obliviousness.

Our eyes lock for a long moment. I break off first, screwing the cap back on the nail polish and then standing up. "My essay's not going to write itself," I say, turning toward my desk. I don't want her here anymore. In moments like this I wonder whether we are bound together by true feelings of kinship or if we've merely clung to each other these past ten years out of obligation, fear, or lack of other prospects. Her huge doll collection made her the ideal friend back when we first met at our post in Ecuador and at our subsequent stint back in D.C., but since we both got to Frankfurt a year ago last summer, after four years apart, I'm starting to think maybe I've outgrown her. That's what moving so often can do to you. It makes you continually question your place in the world, and seek out those few who understand what you're going through.

Autumn hops off my bed and pulls my arm so I'm facing her. "You're so pale. And those bags under your eyes! You need to get more sleep."

"I'm fine." I wriggle my arm forcefully from her grasp, careful not to smear my polish. I sit at my laptop and start typing, hoping she'll take the hint and leave me alone. If she hangs around much longer, I might scream.

"Okay, then," she says over my shoulder, her voice tinged with hurt. "I guess I better get ready for my date. Hopefully I'll have something to report tomorrow."

"Hopefully," I mutter as convincingly as I can manage.

After Autumn lets herself out, I squeeze my eyes shut in frustration and slam my palm down on my laptop. It clicks closed with a loud pop.

My eyes flutter open, and I sit up with a start. I'm back in the hive, and everything's quiet.

I exit the chamber. Mira and Julian occupy the armchairs, and Eli remains riveted by his screens.

"Have a seat," Mira says. "Eli is configuring and testing different parameters. And I am positively dying of boredom."

"Can you die?" I sink into the sofa, enjoying the way the silken fabric caresses my skin. "I mean, we are already dead."

"I wouldn't call it dying, exactly." Mira purses her lips, as if talking about death is too distasteful a topic. "If something should befall you here, you would cycle through again. Get resorted. You would lose all memory of what happened to you here before—not that it matters to most people, since they don't retain much anyway. But if it happened to you . . ."

Eli butts in loudly, without turning. "It wouldn't be convenient to our plans right now. So please, try not to get yourself killed."

"Don't worry about that." Not that I care about their plans, but if I'm resorted, I won't know that there's a way out of the hives. And that would be a huge personal setback. "Did Beckah get resorted? I can't access any of her memories anymore."

"And Beckah is . . . ?" Mira looks up at the ceiling, and I get the distinct feeling she's not interested in talking about anything other than the rebellion.

"She's my friend," I say. "She disappeared from my hive."

Mira ignores my sharp tone. "If she had been resorted, you could access her memories. She is more likely in the isolation plains."

"Isolation?" I ask, goose bumps rising in my soul.

"It's for anyone who might mess up the equilibrium of the net," Julian explains. "Like, they don't want people renting the memories of murderers slashing up their victims."

I squirm in my chair. "Are the victims there?"

Julian shakes his head. "No. For whatever reason, it seems murder victims skip Level Two entirely. Who knows where they end up."

"But why would Beckah be there?" I press.

"Was she insane? Violent?" Mira narrows her eyes, as if judging me for being friends with such a person. "The Morati prefer to avoid placing people in isolation, because those people don't supply the net. And the Morati need all the energy they can get if they're to break into heaven."

I gasp. "What? *That's* why they aren't helping us move on? Because they are harvesting our energy?" It sounds like something straight out of *The Matrix*.

"The Morati tried for centuries to escape this realm, without success. And then one day they broke through the divide between here and Earth and were able to go back. They figure the more people they hold here, the more power they possess, the better the chance they have of reaching the next level." She sits up, and leans toward me. "You want to know the craziest part? In the beginning people plugged themselves in voluntarily!"

"But why?" I can't imagine choosing to lock myself away like that.

"Originally Level Two was designed so that in order to access memories, people touched each other's palms.

But this method allowed them access only to the types of memories you're supposed to relive in order to move on. The Morati offered a system where you could choose which memories you access. Your memories, your neighbor's memories, strangers' memories. People loved having millions and millions of memories at their fingertips."

"We can't access memories of the Romans, or the Pilgrims or Civil War soldiers. Why not?" I ask.

"People who lived before your lifetime had long moved on by the time the Morati put the net in place. They probably wouldn't have understood how to use it anyway," says Mira, settling back into her chair.

"So," Mira continues, "the Morati made the net even more attractive by creating credits as currency to appeal to humanity's basic greed. People become so absorbed in amassing fortunes and chasing down the ultimate highs, they forget they are supposed to be concentrating on moving on."

"So why isn't the underground helping people cross over? That could reduce the Morati's power."

"It could," Julian says, "but people access only their happy memories. Or rent the enjoyable moments of others. Not what they need to confront to move on." He stands up and moves closer until he's towering over me. "You were no different, Felicia."

Julian's right, of course. I did skip over everything unpleasant. I didn't want to face my pain. My weaknesses. My fear. But his patronizing tone annoys me. "Still sore that

I spent all my time on the net with Neil instead of with you?"

To my surprise Julian folds his arms across his chest and squeezes his hands until his knuckles are white. Is he *jealous*? I can't fathom it. After all, he's the one who ditched me.

Mira squints at him and suppresses a smile. "To move on you must embrace both the good and the bad parts of yourself. And you have to stop pining for earthly pursuits." She shoots me an especially pointed look. "And people you left behind."

"What do you mean?" I ask, though I suspect I know what she's insinuating.

But Julian's the one to rub it in. "To move on, you'll have to give up Neil."

CHAPTER 10

"GIVE UP NEIL?" I ask, stiffening. How can I possibly give him up before I even find him again? It's so unthinkable, it's absurd. "Are you saying I shouldn't keep searching for him? You do know where he is, right?"

Julian doesn't answer me. He stalks across the hive and slams out the code that opens the door. Long, long, long. Short, short, long. Where have I heard that before? I rack my brain, and it dawns on me. It's the Morse code Neil showed me. Why in the world are they using it here? Does it work for every door?

Mira simply shrugs, seemingly not surprised by Julian's exit. "Don't worry. There's not some rule that you have to give him up immediately. And in any case, it's totally up to you when you move on. It's hardly surprising you're not ready yet."

"Better for us," Eli says. He removes his glasses, folds them carefully, and tucks them into his shirt pocket. I know it must be an affectation, because there's no way he needs to wear glasses. At least, my formerly blurry eyesight is perfect now, so his must be too. It makes me prickle with dislike for him.

"Right." Mira rises and puts her hand on Eli's shoulder, as if to underscore her solidarity with him. "We do hope you'll join our cause first."

"What is it exactly you want me to do?" I ask, wary.

Eli rubs his temples in a circular motion. "We need a more targeted approach."

"What do you suggest?" Mira sits back down, giving Eli her full attention.

"Felicia is an especially active subject." He talks like I'm not even in the room. "If we map her brain waves, we can run the search parameters to find other subjects like her. That might reduce our failure rate."

Mira looks pleased by his suggestion. "I think we should try it."

"Wait—don't I have any say in the matter?" I ask, indignant. "And why do you need to find more people like me?"

Eli picks up one of the cables attached to his bank of computers. He attaches small white circles to the frayed ends of the cable and then approaches me. "Keep still." With precision and speed he presses the patches to my forehead. His eyes are cold, his face utterly expressionless, like a robot. "Go to your chamber. Access a memory."

I'm so tired of blindly doing what I'm told. Running around with Julian. Coming to this hideout. And now going to my chamber just because Eli wants me to. I back away from him, reaching up and pulling the cable so the patches snap off my forehead one by one. "Not until you tell me what's going on." I let the cable drop to the floor. "And why you keep failing."

Eli's anger is as quick as the flame of a blowtorch, but then he catches himself. "We can hold you down if we have to," he says.

"Oh, Eli!" Mira laughs her full-on tinkling-of-bells laugh. "I think she deserves to know what she's getting herself into." She springs out of her chair and pounces on Eli, exaggeratedly pinching his cheek. She retrieves the cable and hands it to him.

He takes it and examines the patches for damage. He removes a ripped one and replaces it, stonily silent.

Mira speaks instead. "This is a numbers game. We need more support if we are going to go up against the Morati. We need new recruits. With your help we can find the high potentials and ask them to join our cause."

"But why only me?" I ask, gesturing in a wide arc at all the hive's empty chambers. "Wouldn't you be more successful if you had more help?"

"We keep our cells small, so if one is captured, it's not a fatal loss," Mira explains. "The other cells have their own recruits."

It sounds reasonable. I'm not sure why Eli feels the need to be so supersecretive about all of this. "Okay. So all

I'm doing is accessing a memory, right?" I step toward Eli with a resigned sigh.

"Glad to have you on board," Eli says. His curt delivery is coated with the tiniest sliver of sarcasm. He may allow himself to show an emotion yet.

Once he has reattached the patches, he accompanies me to my chamber, holding the cable like a nurse might hold an IV for a patient at the hospital. I climb in, careful not to make any sudden movements that could pop a patch.

"Make sure you access something emotionally compelling. It will improve the quality of the scan," says Mira. "May I suggest a memory of Neil?"

Just to spite her I almost decide to access something excruciatingly boring. Such as one of the many times I was packed like a suitcase into a dilapidated bus or pickup truck and made to ride for hours through third-world landscapes of dust and poverty on one of my parents' trips.

But my need to spend time with Neil wins out, and I slip into one of my well-worn memories of him.

Ward, Felicia. Memory #32019
Tags: Ohio, Neil, Queen bees
Number of Views: 3,000
Owner Rating: 4 stars
User Rating: Not shared

The doorbell rings, echoing through the silent house. That must be Neil. I take a deep breath and put down the scissors and the insert from the paper I was clipping coupons from. I scan Grammy's sleeping face in relief. The bell didn't wake her, so I won't either. God knows she's earned her rest.

After I tuck the afghan tighter around her legs, I give her a quick kiss on her forehead.

I slip my shoes on by the door. When I open it, Neil smiles in greeting. Damp curls cling to his forehead and to the collar of his jacket. He smells like soap and licorice. My heart flutters in my chest. "Ready?" he asks.

"Thanks for helping out," I say as we walk toward his car. He comes around with me to the passenger side and opens my door. Based on my experience with him so far, this sort of old-fashioned gesture probably shouldn't surprise me, but it does. No other boy has ever bothered.

Neil gets in and fastens his seat belt. He turns his key in the ignition, and the car rumbles to life.

I latch my seat belt too. "I don't know why Uncle John thinks I can still do this. I haven't been around his bees in years." Probably hoping I'll get stung a bunch of times. A way to punish me for sullying the family name.

Neil moves the car into drive and then grips the steering wheel at ten and two. "Don't worry. Andy and I worked with a colony for part of my environmental science merit badge last year. His uncle is a beekeeper too."

"Right," I say, rolling my eyes. "Boy Scout stuff again."

Neil bristles at my mocking. "Boy Scouts have really helped me find my way," he says, hitting the left turn signal and the brakes at the same time.

I gulp. Now Neil probably thinks I'm rude. I need to say something nice. Something to steer this conversation down more pleasant avenues. Because despite my destructive tendencies of late, I don't want to crash and burn. Not with Neil.

"I think it's great," I say. I mean it too. "You're a man of many talents."

"Yeah?" he says, sounding not entirely convinced. "Most girls like you think Boy Scouts is a one-way ticket to dorktown." He leans forward to check traffic from the right.

"Girls like me?"

"You know . . ." He turns his head away from me as he steers the car into traffic. "Pretty girls."

It catches me so off guard, a hot blush blooms in my chest and rapidly spreads up my neck and across my face. I know I'm attractive, physically at least. Plenty of people have told me that through the years. Little does Neil know how ugly I am on the inside. He can't see the scars.

I decide it's best to ignore his comment. Change the subject. "So John lives off Route Four. It's only a couple miles."

"I know where he lives." He sounds irritated. "This is a small town."

"It is. Definitely the smallest I've ever been stuck in," I say under my breath.

Neil's usually so open and so good at coaxing me out of my dark moods. But today he's guarded and quiet. He doesn't even look over at me during the drive, making what is in reality only a few minutes seem like an eternity.

When he stops the car in Uncle John's driveway, I get out and take big gulps of the spring air. I walk to the gate and open it with the key Grammy gave me. "The boxes are along the back fence."

Neil follows me. "So John just wants us to make sure the hives don't swarm? Or do we have to put on new supers, too?"

"He doesn't think any of the supers will be fully capped with honey yet. But if they are, we can take them off and leave them on top of the hives."

"Sure. Standard procedure."

"He said the suits are in here." I stop at the shed and throw open the doors. Two shiny white beekeeper suits lie draped over a chair next to a narrow table covered with supplies.

Without saying a word Neil lifts one of the suits high enough that I can duck under it and shimmy in. Once I adjust the suit around me, I hold the other one up as high as I can for him.

As his head emerges from the wide-necked shapeless tunic, I have to laugh. He adjusts the wide-brimmed-hat part of the unwieldy suit over his drying curls, and gives me one of his devastating dimpled smiles through the black mesh netting meant to protect his face. Soon we are both doubled over clutching our sides, laughing uncontrollably. It's when I grab on to his sleeve for support that he quickly sobers and straightens.

"You know, beekeeping is a serious business," he scolds. Do I detect a teasing note in his voice? I'm not sure.

"Uh . . . yeah. I know." I take a pair of pink rubber gloves from the table and pull them on.

Instead of reaching for a pair of gloves for himself, Neil picks up a plastic bottle and squirts his hands with the contents. "Vinegar," he says, like he anticipates me asking him to explain his odd behavior. "It repels the bees, and it's easier to extract the frames with your bare hands. At least, I think so." He points at the long row of vinegar bottles and chuckles. "And apparently your uncle thinks so too."

"Must be a new obsession of his, then." I run my hand along the bottles. "He always wore gloves when I used to come here with Grammy."

"Gloves are perfectly acceptable."

I pull off my gloves. "Squirt me."

He raises an eyebrow. "You sure?"

I'm not at all sure. "Totally."

He douses my hands with the vinegar, and I rub them together. "Too bad we don't have olive oil. We could make a salad dressing." Ouch. Lame joke. So lame, Neil acts like he doesn't hear.

We waddle across the yard to the rectangular wooden hutches where the bees are housed. It looks like a bunch of boxes stacked upon one another. They're utilitarian and not the slightest bit romantic. The front of each box features a carving of a skep, the traditional cone-shaped beehive design. I trace the carving with my finger, wishing skeps hadn't been outlawed. I know it's for the health of the bees, but still. "Beehives used to be so much prettier."

At the nearest box I hang back and let Neil inspect the individual frames. He pulls them out and scans them with practiced precision. Once I feel like I've had enough of a refresher course, I move to the far end and start inspecting too. Bees trickle out of the boxes, and buzz about the frames, but they don't attack us.

"No swarm cells I could see," Neil says after he has looked through his boxes. "You?"

"Didn't see any either."

"The supers are fine too. It's really too early in the season for there to be much honey anyway."

"Yeah. Hey, did you ever notice how bees fly in figure eights?" I ask as we return to the shed. "I mean, not always. But sometimes. I wonder why."

"I asked Andy's father about that once. He said the scout bees do it to communicate certain things to other bees, like if they've found a new food source or a new place to live. I've heard Pastor Joe say it means bees have a connection to the eternal. You know, because a figure eight is a symbol for eternity."

It's funny to hear him talking so seriously while he shuffles around in the baggy suit. I have to stifle a laugh. "I've heard that."

Back at the shed we struggle out of the suits.

There's a loud buzzing sound close to my ear. I move to swat the bee away from me, but it zips past my eye and stings me on the temple. It burns like fire. "Ow!"

I close my eyes tight, grit my teeth, and take deep breaths. Neil takes my chin firmly in his hand. "Hold still. I'll get the stinger out."

I peek one eye open. Neil's face fills my field of vision, and his nearness distracts me from the pain. He squints his eyes until they crinkle, and his perfectly straight, perfectly white front teeth bite his lower lip. A lower lip that's slightly fuller than his upper lip, and suddenly incredibly tempting. "Got it." He puts down the tweezers, but he doesn't back away.

I raise my hand toward my face, but he catches my arm in midair. "No rubbing. Let me put some baking soda and vinegar on it. For the pain. It works."

I stare at his hand around my wrist.

He blushes and drops my arm like a hot potato. "Sorry about that."

"No, it's fine. Fix me up."

Neil reaches behind him for a box of baking soda, opens it, and pours some out into his hand. He drizzles a bit of vinegar onto it and rubs the two ingredients into a paste. Then he pats my temple with the mixture. The pain recedes into a dull throb.

"You're right. It feels much better now." Everything feels better when I'm around Neil.

He searches my face carefully with his eyes, and then bites his lip again. "Can I ask you something?" His expression radiates hope.

I freeze. Is he going to ask to kiss me? It's the gentlemanly thing to do, I suppose, but it seems like odd timing, considering I've been stung by a bee and I have baking soda all over my face. If he does want to kiss me, I wish he'd just do it. Because if he asks me, I know I'll be disciplined enough to say no. For his sake. I mean, the perfect choirboy with someone like me? I'd feel too guilty.

"Ask away."

"Are you going on the camping trip next weekend with the youth group?"

I can't believe it. He gets all serious and googly-eyed to ask me if I'm going to a church function? "No. Can't. I have to stay with Grammy. Besides, we can't really afford it."

"Are you sure? We'd all love for you to come." He smiles shyly. "I'd love for you to come."

Not many people these days seem to do more than tolerate my presence, let alone sincerely seem to want me to be around. Grammy puts on a good show, but I've heard her early-morning hand-wringing with my dad on the phone about how I've disappointed everyone. How I won't touch the piano. How I hardly eat anything. And speaking of my dad . . . I can hear the hurt in his voice during our strained conversations. It's more than I can bear.

I take a deep breath, making my decision—for better or worse. "Okay, then. I'd love to come. Grammy willing, of course." I'll find some way to pay for it.

"That's wonderful!" He pulls me into a spontaneous hug, and at first it doesn't faze me. After all, hugs and handshakes and welcoming smiles are like hyperinflationary currency to church people—produced so freely that they're not worth much. But as his warmth soaks into me, and he hugs me tighter, I find myself hoping he'll never let go. I close my eyes and press my cheek against his, skin on skin.

The moment is interrupted by a slow clapping, and my skin goes cold. I open my eyes. Mira hovers above me. "Excellent! That was a real showstopper."

I rip the patches off my forehead and throw the cable as far as I can, which isn't far. "Were you snooping in on my memories?" I ask.

"Does it look like I have access to the mainframe in this hovel?" Mira asks. "I saw the pictures from your brain scan. Seemed quite active. Highly emotional."

"We've identified twenty-two further high potentials in quadrant ninety-nine," Eli reports from his station. "One of them is from Felicia's hive. A subject called Virginia Burrell."

CHAPTER 11

I BOUNCE OUT OF MY CHAMBER. Finally some progress. "Virginia's my friend! Are we going to go pick her up?"

Eli grunts. "No." He pores over some printouts, his pencil scritching and scratching as he makes calculations.

Mira shoots me a sympathetic look. "We'll look for her later. Right now we need to move on to another hideout," she says. "You've already plugged in here twice."

"I've been scrambling the signal. They can't tell where she's plugged in," Eli argues. "And I'm too busy to move again."

"Safety first, Eli. You know that." She waves her hand, and everything except the chair Eli is sitting in disappears. Even his pencil. "Let's go."

Eli looks so lost without his tech, I have to cover my amusement with a question. "How do you know where to go when you're out there? Everything looks the same to me."

Eli whirls around in his chair and stomps his boots down, startling me. "Don't you ever stop asking questions?" His voice is low and measured, but his tone is so dismissive that defiance rises within me, unbidden and unstoppable.

"Look," I say, my voice rising, "I didn't ask to join your team. You asked me. The least you can do is show me some respect."

Eli raises his hand, palm facing me, and closes his eyes. He begins to chant in a language I don't understand, but it has the practiced melody of an incantation. A whoosh of air pounds me into the wall. I hit the floor and gasp. He's thrown me across the room, without even touching me.

He opens his eyes and smiles tightly. "When you can do that, that's when I will show you respect."

I stumble into a standing position and rub my wrist. What's his problem? "Teach me, then," I growl.

"All in due time," Mira says, ever the peacemaker. She sweeps over to Eli and pulls him from his chair. "The faster we get going, the faster you can get back to work." She turns to me. "And don't mind Eli. I think the pressure of leading this rebellion has gotten to him."

She taps the wall so the door opens—Neil's code again. She gestures for us to follow her. I look back into the hide-out one last time. Eli's chair is still spinning.

"What about Julian?" I whisper as I fall in step behind Mira.

"He'll catch up with us. He's out on a mission to try to gather more recruits."

We've run past only about fifty hives of the sector block when I hear the unmistakable buzzing of the scanner drones. I expect Mira and Eli will have us duck into another hive, but Mira surprises me. She conjures and hurls a hooked rope up at the junction where two hives connect, and then pulls on it to test if the hook is secure. She bounds up the rope until she's kneeling on a ledge and reaching out her arms toward me.

I gape at her and the rope. Does she expect me to climb up too? The buzzing gets louder. My hands start to tremble. I can't do it. Eli throws me upward with a rush of air. It's enough for Mira to grab on to my shift and pull me onto the ledge with her. Eli leaps up too, bringing the rope with him.

From our vantage point between the hives, we watch the scanner drones zigzag below us, flashing their yellow light as they seek out anomalies. As they pass, I count them. Twenty-four. More than double the last time.

Once they're gone, Eli throws the rope off to the other side and scrambles down. Mira touches the rope, and it stiffens into a pole, taut and slippery enough for me to slide down into a corridor that's only as wide as an alleyway. When we're all back on the ground, Eli leads us down the alley until we hit a main corridor. We're one hive away from the main corridor where we escaped the drones—and the only corridor I've been in so far—so I make a right turn toward it. But

Mira takes hold of my arm and leads me to the left. We pass ninety-nine hives before we reach the next junction, each with a narrow alley in between, and I finally get a better idea of the geography of this place. Each sector is one hundred hives wide and one hundred hives long. As we run, instead of barreling along in a straight shot like usual, we make a lot of left and right turns at the sector boundaries. At first I try to keep track of where we're going, but as the turns add up, I give up. It's too much.

Finally Mira stops in front of a hive, taps on the outside wall using Neil's code, and ushers me in when the door opens. As soon as we enter, she twirls her index finger, and the interior of the hive is instantly decorated to match our previous hideout. Right down to Eli's pencil that clatters to the floor. He strides across to pick it up and checks if his papers are in order. He nods, seemingly satisfied, and settles into the sofa at the same time that Mira positions herself in the armchair facing him. I sit next to Eli on the sofa.

"I've never seen so many scanner drones flying together before," Mira says. "Used to be you could go weeks without seeing a single one. The Morati must be stepping up production because they feel threatened."

"They should feel threatened." Eli cocks his head and looks at me thoughtfully. "To answer your question from before we left the hive, we locate one another by scanning for signature brain waves. After all this time, I merely have to think of Mira, and I know where she is. I can communicate with her too. Like telepathy." He glances over at Mira, and she smiles indulgently.

So he finally deigns to answer my question. Nice. "No matter how far away?" I try to keep the eagerness from my voice. This might be a way for me to find Neil on my own. And Virginia and Beckah. And everyone else.

"As long as she has not left Level Two, I can find her. And that goes for anyone I have a close relationship with or come in physical contact with." He reaches out and puts his hand on my knee, his expression vaguely menacing. "Now I can find you, too. And eventually, when you've mastered the skill, you can find me."

"Uh . . . great," I say, scooting away from his hand. It drops onto the sofa between us with a thud. "Can't the Morati pick up on all this scanning and communicating?"

"At the same time you send out the signal, you need to block it from everyone but the intended recipient." He acts like this is self-explanatory.

Why does he always feel the need to chastise me? He had to ask questions once too. "So . . . how do I find people?"

Mira answers. "The farther away a person is, the more power or connection it takes to find them. That's why you need to start out with someone easy. Someone you have known your whole life who you care about deeply."

Someone I have known my whole life rules out Neil. "My dad." The last time I saw him, when he dropped me off at Grammy's, his expression drooped at half-mast as he drove away.

"Yes. A good person to start with," she says.

I bite my lip. "Do you think he's out there somewhere?"

My heart fills with hope that I might see him again. If I can find him, then I'll know it works. That I have a chance to connect with Neil again.

"Even if he is, you might not find him on your first try," warns Eli. "Or even your thirtieth try. These things take time."

"What do I need to do?"

"First access a memory of you two together. And then, with that scene fresh in your mind, you reach out to him."

"I'll try." It sounds easy enough. A bubble of joy rises up within me, and I leap across the floor like a ballet dancer, not caring that Mira and Eli are watching. Then I settle myself into the chamber and debate about which memory of my father I should pull up. The water balloon fight that had us soaked and silly during carnival in the Ecuadorian city of Guaranda? Dad conducting one of his own symphonies while I accompanied the orchestra on piano in front of the Japanese president? Or a quieter, more recent moment? I decide on the latter and go in.

Ward, Felicia. Memory #31373
Tags: Germany, Dad, Heart-to-heart
Number of Views: 73
Owner Rating: Not rated
User Rating: Not shared

I swish through the revolving doors and pull my rain-drizzled hair into a low ponytail as I head to the elevators.

Because dad's office is on the fourth floor, I usually take the stairs. But today I'm not feeling up to it. I push the call button, and the doors ding open. Three yawns later I'm in front of Dad's door, rattling the knob. It's locked. I rustle though the pocket of my rain slicker and pull out my key ring, a rubber puffin declaring I ♥ ICELAND. I insert Dad's key and let myself in.

Dad's office suffers from split personality disorder. Most of it is sleek and modern—sharp angles of high-end recording equipment mingle with neat stacks of paper printouts of Dad's scores. But then there's what I call the cozy corner, ruled over by an ancient leather sofa with the texture of butter. Next to it is a vintage wood-paneled radio, topped with a record player. Vinyls of everything from Bach to The National lie strewn in haphazard piles. I pull *High Violet* from its sleeve and put it on, setting the needle toward the middle so I can hear the song "Bloodbuzz Ohio."

The drumbeat at the beginning instantly lightens my mood. I shuck my coat and boots and sit cross-legged on the sofa, waiting for Dad to arrive. I pull my cell phone out of the pocket of my jeans to check the time. 4:05 p.m. He said to meet at four, but then, Dad's usually late. Mother always says he operates on Dad Standard Time, a full hour later than atomic time.

After the record winds down, Dad swoops in the door, his arms full of shopping bags. "You're here!" He's out of breath, probably from taking the stairs. "Can you help me with these?"

I take two of the bags from him and drag them over to his tiny kitchenette. "And put on some espresso while you're over there."

Once I place the bags on the counter, I dig out a packet of ground coffee from Café Wacker. I measure out the grounds and turn on Dad's impressive coffee machine. "How about a ristretto instead?"

Dad laughs at our private joke. "A ristretto is the purest shot of coffee in the world," he mimics Porter Huntley's stuffy accent perfectly, and I dissolve into giggles.

Porter was attached to the British embassy in Nairobi, so we often saw him at official parties and functions. Dad found him arrogant and insufferable, especially his insistence on testing the quality of the waitstaff by ordering a ristretto, and Dad never passed up an opportunity to mock him.

After the machine sputters out Dad's shot, I set it to brew again to pull my own espresso. I place Dad's glass on his desk. "How's the ultra fabulous goat symphony coming along?"

"Making fun of goats again? Goats discovered coffee, you know." He downs his shot, smacks his lips. "If it weren't for a ninth-century Ethiopian goatherd named Kaldi noticing that his goats were extra peppy after munching on a certain berry, you wouldn't have the chance to sneak sips of coffee whenever possible."

I retrieve my espresso and drink it with relish in front of him. Such bravado would not go unpunished by Mother, who is convinced coffee will stunt my growth, but Dad lets a lot of things slide. Plus, I think he secretly likes it that I've turned into such a connoisseur, like him.

He smiles ruefully, pulls a penciled-in score from the shelf, and sets it on the piano. "Could you play the first few measures for me?"

I sit down on the bench, brushing my fingers over the keys as I scan over the notes Dad has written for the piano part. Like most of his music, it starts off pleasing and harmonic, utilizing safe major chord structure. But already by the end of the second line, the notes become dissonant and foreign. Dad always says it's his way of waking up the listener. It works too.

As I play, he stands right behind me, his foot tapping against the wooden leg of the bench. It's his usual modus operandi, but today it annoys me. I lose my concentration and flub up a full measure, and am not able to pull it together again. I can't do this anymore. Can't go on pretending everything is normal when I feel like my head could explode any minute. "Damn, Dad. Back off, okay?"

He shuffles backward, and the once light, playful atmosphere turns tense. I stomp my foot, slam down the cover of the piano, and retreat to the sofa to sulk.

Dad makes a show of being busy at his desk, probably thinking his difficult teenage daughter just needs her space. But really I crave his reassurance. Too bad it's something I'm too stubborn to admit out loud.

I stare at him, willing him with all my being to put

down his papers and ask me what's wrong.

Surprisingly, it works. "What's wrong, sweet pea?" he asks finally, resting his chin on his knuckles and giving me the perfect concerned-father look.

"Nothing. I'm fine."

He gets up, comes over to me. "Can I sit down?"

"It's your sofa," I say, more sharply than intended. Why can't I make it easy for myself to get what I want? What is wrong with me?

"You seem on edge today," he says, stating the obvious. "You haven't been like this since . . ." His eyes flicker with realization. "Are your nightmares getting worse again? Is that it?"

As an answer I hang my head and cover my eyes with my palms, using my fingers to rub my scalp.

"I'm so sorry." He puts his arm around me and pulls me close. I tense at first, but then let him draw me fully into his embrace. He kisses my forehead. "I really thought moving away from Kenya did the trick. You were doing better for so long."

"I feel like I'm falling apart," I say. "To try to avoid the nightmares, I resist sleeping until I collapse. I'm sucking down ten cups of coffee to keep awake every day. I'm annoyed by everything Autumn says. And my grades . . ." I lift my head and look at him with pleading eyes. "Don't tell Mother . . . but I got a C minus on my *Our Town* essay."

He sighs deeply. He's not happy about my news, but he can take it. "You know, your mother wasn't always such an ironfisted taskmaster."

"Oh, no. . . ." I groan and cover my ears with my hands. "This isn't your speech about how Mother used to be such a free spirit, is it? And how I should cut her some slack?"

He chuckles and starts rubbing my shoulders, humming the Irish lullaby that always soothed me as a child. I let him massage me, and after a few moments I drop my hands into my lap.

"Okay," I say grudgingly, blowing out my breath to show him how truly exasperating he is most of the time. "Tell me the story. I know you are dying to."

He shifts his position on the sofa so he's looking at me. "Your mother and I got to know each other in the malaria ward in Dakar. But that's not the first time I saw her."

"It wasn't?" I sit up straighter. Of course I knew the story of how they met in Senegal. I'd heard a thousand times how they were the only foreign patients in the whole hospital. But I hadn't heard about a prior sighting. Interesting.

"Word came to the rural mission school where I taught that a white woman had arrived with the peace corps for an agriculture project a few villages over. And, of course, I was curious." He grins ruefully. "But I had a lot of responsibilities at the mission, and no mode of transportation, so I sort of forgot about her."

He pauses for such a long time, I think he has decided not to tell me after all. "And then?" I prod.

"About a month later we had a special delivery. Someone in Dakar decided to donate a bunch of used bicycles to the kids at the mission, and there was a lone adult-size bike in the shipment too. Since I was by far the youngest teacher on staff, they let me have it.

"Saturday came, and I rushed off on my new bike in search of adventure. Naturally I got lost." He laughs. It's a well-known fact that Dad has no sense of direction. "As dusk was falling, I happened upon a village. Her village, as it turns out." He pops his knuckles. It makes me flinch.

"I heard singing. She had this lilting, otherworldly voice, your mother. I didn't want to disturb her, so I hid behind a hut and observed her."

I interrupt, "You mean you spied on her!"

He slaps the top of my head affectionately. "You see why I've never told you this part before?"

"Sorry. Please do go on, sir," I say, in my best imitation of Porter's haughty British accent.

"So there I am crouching behind this hut, utterly hypnotized by her song. And then she began to dance. And she was so free. So unburdened. Like she could take flight any second. Yes, I was a goner." He smiles at the memory.

"That vision of her awoke something in me. Something restless and wild. And I knew when we ended up next to each other at the hospital in Dakar, fate had brought us together."

"I wish I could've known her like that," I say wistfully. I've known her only as an uptight disciplinarian who constantly judges me.

"Maybe you will someday, sweet pea. Maybe you will." He has this faraway look in his eyes, as if he wishes she were still such a free spirit instead of the hardened career woman she's become. He gets up, goes over to the piano, and lifts the lid up, his smile full of encouragement. "Do you want to give it another try?" He wants me to be a full-time concert pianist someday, but we both know Mother would never allow it. Despite my talent, and Dad's place in the classical music world, she has made it clear that playing piano professionally is out of the question. Though her ambition for me to be like her chafes, and I truly love the instrument, I've never been all that jazzed about the rigorous practice a musical career would demand.

"Is it okay if I don't?" I stretch out my cramped limbs and lie down on the sofa, its buttery softness caressing my cheek. "I'd really, really like to take a nap."

"Of course!" He looks pleased as he sorts through his piles of records. He selects one, and soon enough I hear the dulcet strains of Brahms. "Sweet dreams, honey."

And for the first time in a long time, I drift off to sleep with a smile.

When I awaken and see the hologram screen flickering above me, I squeeze my eyes shut again. It always feels so real, reliving these memories. Realer than this place. Normally I come out of my memories in a sort of daze, able to savor the sensations of my life on Earth for a few precious seconds. But no matter how hard I try to hold on to them, these moments slip away, leaving me hollowed out and hungry for more. In Level Two, time is a never-ending burden. In my memories time is weightless and there's never enough.

I sit up and pinch my arms, digging in my fingernails, hoping to draw some blood. Because maybe I'm not dead. Maybe I'm dreaming all of this. Maybe I am living my nightmares. But no blood comes.

I shake off my disappointment and try reaching out to my father with my mind. I gather all my strength and pour it into one thought: Dad smiling at me proudly.

As if I've developed radar, I sense hives and their occupants. But I don't recognize anyone. And I know instinctively I haven't been able to reach far enough.

I shift in my chamber, and I am about to get out, when I hear a tapping followed by Mira's voice. I freeze and close my eyes again, in case they look over at me.

"Have you run phase two ops on any of our new high potentials?" Her heels tap against the floor.

"I did a small sample. They overloaded too." Phase two ops? Overloaded? I may not know what they're talking about, but it's clear it isn't good. Maybe it's related to their failure rate.

"That's disappointing. Did you try the friend?"

"No, I'm saving her for last."

Are they talking about running ops on Virginia? But they can't be. Mira said that we could try to pick her up.

There's another set of taps followed by Mira's laughter. "Well, look who decided to join us again."

"Maybe we should just leave them alone," says Julian. His voice is close.

"And let the Morati keep using them as batteries? Somehow I doubt God will be handing out rewards for that," Mira scoffs. "Especially not if the Morati succeed in breaking through."

"But they do look so peaceful like this." He reaches out and touches my lips. I snap open my eyes.

He draws back his hand as quickly as if he had touched a hot poker, and backs away. "Aaah, you're awake."

I slide out of my chamber and salute them. "Drugged-up battery reporting for duty."

Julian looks at me sympathetically. "You're beating it, you know. Soon the Morati won't be able to use you anymore."

"Maybe, but everyone else is still addicted."

"That's why we're hacking the system, blasting people with scenes from their deaths. Forcing them out of their drowsy numbness," Eli says.

I must not have heard him correctly, because what I think Eli just said can't be possible. "Wait . . . you don't mean the rebels are responsible for the chambers malfunctioning?"

Mira raises one perfectly arched eyebrow. "Of course. What did you think?"

I'm stunned for a single instant, and then my long simmering anger boils over. "I thought . . . ," I choke, trying to get the words out, "all these bad things—the malfunctions, Beckah disappearing—were happening because of the Morati. But I was wrong, wasn't I? You don't care who you hurt! You're no better than terrorists!"

I get up and back away, needing to gain as much distance as I can. It's imperative that I find Virginia before they do. If they hurt Beckah, they'll have no problem hurting Virginia, too. Or Neil. Or anyone I care about. Or even me.

I don't know who scares me more—the Morati or my supposed allies.

CHAPTER 12

I TURN ON MY HEEL and make a break for the door. Praying it works for me, I pound out Neil's code to open the hive door. Long, long, long. Short, short, long. And I'm out.

I'm so disoriented by the sudden view of the looming white hives, I forget which way we arrived. But right now I need to run. All I know is that Virginia needs me. And I don't let my friends down.

I haven't gotten far when something slams into me from behind. As I tumble, I'm twisted upward, and I land on top of a human form. The tingling sensation tells me it must be Julian, and I try to fight my way out of his grasp. But he's too strong.

"Felicia! Calm down!"

I let my body go slack, and he loosens his grip. I roll off him and jump to my feet, pulling successfully away.

"Don't bother running again," Julian warns as he gets up, his eyes flashing. "What were you thinking? You're too weak yet to get far on your own. You can't even evade me!"

I throw my arms up. "I knew you were up to no good! How could I be stupid enough to trust you again?"

"Okay, so maybe I left some of the details out—"

"Some?" I hiss. "Like you don't care who gets hurt as long as you get your way?"

"Keep your voice down."

I step forward, closer to him than is comfortable, but I want him to feel the full force of my rage. "I am done with you." I only barely restrain myself from spitting in his face. And then I walk away.

"You can't do this." Julian changes tactics now, a pleading note in his voice. "Going out on your own—against the Morati—it's suicide! If they catch you, you'll find out there are worse things than death."

I turn and face him. He looks wild. Desperate. "Is that what Beckah found out? Please, just give it up." I run.

"I won't." He runs beside me. "I can't."

I stop, and he stops too. His expression is so wrecked, a sliver of doubt creeps in. Is it possible he does have my best interests at heart?

"Why did you get involved with the rebels?"

He shakes his head wearily. "Look, I know some of the rebels' methods may seem questionable."

"Questionable?" I sputter. "That's an understatement."

"But honestly there are only two sides here: the rebels and the Morati. I know what side I'd rather be on. Do you?"

"How can you even ask that?" I curl my lips with disgust and start running again.

He catches up to me in a flash and spins me around. "You're going the wrong way."

There's a cracking sound. A few white pebbles trickle down the nearest hive and scatter in front of my feet.

Julian scoops them up and squeezes them to dust in his fist. "Ahh . . . you see? This is another sign that the Morati are weakening. Eli's ops must be more successful than he thinks."

"Better beam him that message," I say angrily.

"What do you mean?"

"I know you can communicate telepathically with them. Eli told me about him and Mira."

He shushes me. "We have to keep quiet. We're lucky we haven't attracted any drones."

"Then I'd better get going."

"Listen, yes we communicate telepathically. We have to. It's not like there's wireless reception here." He extends his hands to me, palms up. "I'm sorry about your friend. You could make a difference, you know. If you stick around, maybe no one else needs to get hurt."

And for once he really does sound sorry. "Can I go pick up Virginia? Make sure she's safe?"

"It's not up to me . . ."

I push him and set off again.

He catches my wrist. "But we'll talk to Eli."

He's right about the rebels being the lesser of the two evils. At this point, while I'm still so weak, I need allies, even if I don't agree with their tactics. Once I'm stronger, if it seems like Virginia is in imminent danger or if I get a good opportunity to slip out, I can always leave. I yearn to break away and never look back, but instead I nod at him grudgingly, and we walk back to the rebels' hideout.

Creatures of habit, Eli sits at his workstation and Mira lounges on the sofa in a body-hugging pink leather catsuit that matches her hair. They both greet my return with stony-faced silence, as if they can't quite believe I'm not 100 percent supportive of their plans.

Guess it's up to me to break the ice. "Tell me this. How do you live with yourselves? How can you justify torturing innocent people with memories of their deaths?"

Mira pats the space next to her on the sofa, an invitation to sit down, which I ignore. "You know the story of the fall? When Lucifer was thrown out of heaven?"

"Yes, because Lucifer wanted to be more powerful than God."

She smirks. "Is that what they're teaching kids these days?" She reaches behind her for a pillow and then curls herself around it. "When God created Adam in his own image, some angels felt threatened. Though Lucifer and his minions vehemently refused to serve Adam, most angels, including the archangels, voiced their unwavering support for God. But then there were still others who hesitated and said nothing. So what happened?"

She looks over as if waiting for me to answer.

When I don't respond, she continues. "God cast out his dissenters and assigned his supporters the best jobs. The lukewarm ones? He sent them to be thankless caretakers of the afterlife's waiting room, to serve humanity as a penance for their indecision. He called this third group the Morati, those who delayed."

Julian speaks up. "And that's why the Morati hate humans enough to trap them and use them to get back at God."

"And it is why we have to fight them at all costs," says Eli.

"So where do the rebels fit into all of this?" I ask, still not even remotely ready to let my guard down with them yet.

"The Morati used their collective materialization power to put the net architecture in place. And of course the power they siphon from humans in hives allows them to maintain the net. But some of the Morati were opposed to this abuse," Mira explains. "As time went on, the dissenters grew more vocal and a group finally splintered off, with the hope of returning Level Two to God's original purpose."

"And that's where I came in," says Eli. "I came up with a three-phase plan for defeating the Morati."

"Wait." I shake my head, not quite understanding. "Why you? Why didn't the rebels who are former Morati come up with the plans?"

Eli smiles serenely. "They did. Their plan was to find

humans who could help them. And that plan was extremely successful, wasn't it?"

Ugh. Eli's so full of himself.

"So, as I was saying, phase one was a simple system-wide breach program. When I had Julian upload it to the mainframe on a mission to the Morati's palace, it imprinted whatever memories were being viewed with scenes from the viewers' deaths. We thought it might push people to confront their bad memories too, get them on the path toward moving on."

That explains why my Neil memory on the church camping trip ended in glass shards and pain instead of the real way it ended. And why Beckah's animal shelter memory suddenly switched over to the one of her death. That jolt we all felt when we thought the system malfunctioned was part of the rebels' plan. A horrible thought occurs to me.

"But wait, those memories aren't permanently damaged, are they?"

"They better be. Whenever the viewer tries to access the imprinted memory, he should be confronted again with his death. It is the purpose of the program." Eli's answer is like an ice pick straight through my heart.

I shake my head in denial. I can't bear to think that one of my favorite Neil memories will be lost to me. Sure, it's still in my head now—that's how I even know it's ruined—but without my ability to retrieve it and relive it anytime I want to, sooner or later it will fade into oblivion. "How could you?" I punch the pillow Mira's holding in front of her, and she recoils in surprise.

"You all are the worst allies in the whole . . . universe."

Mira recovers and catches my fist as I lash out again. "I take it you were viewing an important memory when the program kicked in?"

"Yes. Very important." My throat feels raw, my spirit ripped to shreds. I sink down onto the sofa.

Mira caresses my cheek with the backs of her fingers. "There, there. All is not lost." She throws the pillow at Eli, and he deflects it in the air long before it can hit him. "It is time you try materialization out for yourself."

She glides off the sofa and extends her hand out to me, as if to help me up. When I refuse it, she simply chuckles, wiggles her nose, and makes the sofa disappear right out from under me. I crash to the floor, where the thick rug dulls my landing somewhat.

"It may seem like magic to you"—Mira winks—"but here in the afterlife you have the power to change the code of your surroundings with only your mind."

"Yeah, yeah . . . old news, Mira. But apparently I'm still too weak."

Mira gives me a tight, preachy smile. "I suggest you practice, then. You can start by trying to repair your memory." She forms an *O* with her lips, puts her hand under her chin, and blows. A cloud of gold dust sparkles and shimmers as it drifts slowly downward, forming a mirage of the sofa, which then solidifies. She sits down with a flourish. "If you want it badly enough . . ."

I give the three of them the most scathing look I can

muster, then enter my chamber to try to find a way to repair my precious Neil memory. I can't lose it permanently. It will feel too much like I'm losing a part of Neil, too—and an important part of myself. Even though I know my memories are a pale substitute for actually being with Neil, they fuel my dream of seeing him again. They give me the strength to go on. And strength is what I need if I'm ever going to be able to save Neil and my friends.

The hologram screen flickers when I pull up memory number 32105, taunting me. I concentrate on my desire to purge it of Eli's imprinting. As I am swept into the memory, heat rushes through me. I'm there in that forest that day, but I'm also somehow not. I experience the highs and lows of my roller-coaster meeting with Neil in a sort of split-screen reality. I feel the warmth of his skin, the nearness of his breath—but at the same time, it's as if I am also outside my body, observing the proceedings from another dimension. When I touch Neil's lips and close my eyes, I'm blasted with the squeal of tires and shards of glass. I surface in my chamber, gasping for breath, horrified to see that I'm covered in tiny cuts. It's the pain of one thousand cat scratches, and it's all I can do not to roll myself into the fetal position and surrender.

I wince as my sliced-up fingertips graze the control grooves, but I press on anyway. And I'm once again back in that glorious spring day, breathing the fresh air and anticipating Neil. As I relive the memory, I fight to keep myself as detached as possible from physical Felicia, though I long to feel the full weight of Neil's hand in mine. My success will depend on my absolute control of the situation. But when I see the naked look in his eyes, my resolve melts away and I fail for a second time.

It's like that a third, a fourth, a tenth time. Each time I emerge with more cuts, more pain.

As I go in for the eleventh time, I am exhausted. My concentration is shot, and self-doubt nips at me from all sides. The sights and sounds of my memory barely register anymore, as if I am no longer viewing the original but a copy many times removed. I feel myself floating above it all, a neutral observer of a scene where I have no stake in the outcome.

The moment of truth arrives. I observe how physical Felicia reaches up and touches Neil's lower lip lightly with her finger, and how she closes her eyes. I brace myself for the impact of sharp flying glass, but it doesn't come.

In an instant I'm snapped back into my body.

The heady fragrance of pine swirls around me, and my heart hammers in my chest. Neil removes my finger from his bottom lip. "Felicia . . . ," he says, his voice raw, and I stop him from asking my permission the only way I can, by kissing him first. And then the buzz of connection between Neil and me explodes into a fierce passion of exploring lips and hands.

An owl hoots, loudly enough that I startle. My eyes fly open, and for a second I'm disoriented by the heavy darkness. I'd be set adrift if it weren't for the anchor of Neil's hand on the small of my back and his arm around my neck. I am not afraid.

"Did you hear that?" Neil whispers into my ear. It tickles, and my shoulder bucks involuntarily, knocking against his chin.

"The owl?"

"No . . ." His body goes rigid, as if he's straining to hear something. "They're singing. They started the campfire songs without me," he says with genuine surprise. Of course. As the worship leader, Neil would be the one they would wait for to get started. We must have been away a long time for them to give up on him.

Sudden insecurity claws at my stomach. "Oh. Well. We better get back, then. It's your reputation on the line."

"Do you think that's the only thing I care about?" he asks, a sharp edge creeping into his voice. "Because it's not. I care about you. Even if you asked me to stay here all night long with you, I would do it."

As soon as he says it, I feel it in my bones that it's true. For some unfathomable reason, Neil believes I'm worth fighting for, worth giving up his high standing for. But still, I don't want it for him. I know I could be selfish, like I have been every day of my life up to this point, and stay here wrapped in his arms, forgetting everything but this buoyant feeling of finally finding a place where I belong.

"We have more than tonight," I say, reaching into his pocket for his flashlight. I slide the switch, and a beam of light comes between us. "I think we should go back."

When I look up, I can see the conflicting emotions flitting across his face. "It's okay," I assure him. "Really. I feel like singing, you know?"

He laughs and shakes his head. "You got it." He takes the flashlight from me and then laces his fingers through mine. We walk slowly, and not only because it's difficult to find our footing in the dark.

When we reach the edge of the forest, the roaring campfire jolts me back to reality. The youth group is arranged in a semicircle around it, in small groups of two and three, blankets thrown over their shoulders to ward off the chill. Pastor Joe is playing the guitar, and everyone's singing one of those happy, cheesy camp songs that make you laugh so much, you screw up the words.

We find an empty bench at the edge of the crowd and sit down, so close that our legs and shoulders touch. Neil drapes a blanket around our shoulders, and it's only then that I dare to look up and see the reactions of the others. Savannah flips me a thumbs-up when she notices me, and I duck my head to hide my smile.

Even though Andy looks a bit pissed off, no one stands up and demands that I return their golden boy to them. I shift to lay my head on Neil's shoulder and wrap my arms around his waist, feeling how his body trembles as he sings. The sound of it washes over me, and I close my eyes, content.

The singing stops abruptly. I'm back in my chamber. I roll onto my side and support my head on my arm as I think about what I've accomplished. I've managed to repair a memory with my mind. And that's when I realize that all my cuts are healed, and I feel . . . strong. Powerful, even.

I emerge from the chamber with a renewed sense of purpose and survey the hive. Eli's not at his bank of computers. He's not here at all. Mira and Julian are seated in front of a chessboard, already deep into a game, moving the pieces with their minds. I sit on the stair and watch them.

Julian makes a move, and Mira squeals. "Oh, no, no! You will not take my queen!"

Why are they sitting around playing games? I run my hands down my starchy white shift and suddenly wonder why I am still wearing it. I close my eyes and form a mental picture of one of my most comfortable outfits back on Earth. My favorite pair of boot cut jeans, an emerald-green silk blouse with a frilly collar, a gray cashmere V-neck sweater, and my worn-in brown leather boots. I also imagine my long hair pulled back in a smooth ponytail with a green velvet-covered hair band. It's exactly what I looked like on my first "date" with Neil.

When I feel the supple fabrics of my Earth clothes, I open my eyes and am overcome with the desire to see my reflection. My compact mirror appears in my hand. I peer at myself. Okay, a much paler version of myself. One with impossibly red lips and dark hair. One that looks like Snow White.

I set the compact down beside me and smile. It feels amazing to have these pieces of home, these pieces of myself I thought lost forever. I am overcome with the urge to dance, so powerful that I don't even care with whom. I sway to an imaginary beat in my head and spin around in circles across the hive until I fall into Julian's lap, laughing.

When I look up at his face, I stiffen. His lips are parted and his stare greedy. He runs his hand over my forehead, my scalp, and then smoothly yanks my hair band out, setting my hair free to fall around my shoulders.

I leap out of his lap. "Wanna dance?" I ask, pulling him to his feet.

Where our hands meet there is a low hum of electricity, nowhere near the levels of intoxication I felt for him before. Am I conquering my addiction to him at last?

By the confusion I see in his expression, I can tell he senses something has changed between us. My hate for him has diminished, but so has the desire. I give him a sad smile and squeeze his hands gently before letting them go. "Never mind. Don't want to interrupt your game."

"Are you forfeiting, Julian?" Mira asks with a nasty little smirk. "So unlike you."

As he sits back down, he glances at me. "No," he says forcefully, turning his focus back to the board. "I am in it to win it."

They continue to play, and I decide to do my nails. I could probably employ the Mira method and imagine them already done. But the painstaking process that goes into making your nails shine—the soaking, shaping, buffing, coloring, topcoat applying—I've always found it cathartic. And the result makes me feel finished, ready to face anything.

I drag the coffee table closer and move my hands in a

circular motion above it, willing all of my nail-care supplies to appear. When they do, I busy myself with the attainment of the perfect polish, scrunching up my nose at the strong chemical odor. It's strangely satisfying, though, to finally smell something, after what seems like centuries of thinking I'd lost that sense for good.

Oddly enough, when I finish and look up after admiring my pearly pink nails, the hive is empty. Was I that engrossed in my work that I didn't even hear Julian and Mira leave?

Excited to finally be alone, I decide to see this as a sign that now is the time to rescue Virginia. I owe it to her to at least try. And when I find Neil, I want him to be proud of the person I've become, a friend to rely on. Before I can change my mind, I knock out the code and slip out into the corridor.

All clear outside as well. Where could they be? I break out running, this time in the direction Julian pointed me in. Once I pick up Virginia, will I be able to find my way back here? Do I even want to? Or can I maybe make it on my own now?

My boots are too clunky to run in. I pause long enough to morph them into a pair of gray running shoes to match my sweater. Thinking I hear the low buzz of the scanner drones, I leap to the nearest alcove between hives and crash straight into Julian.

He laughs. "You should have seen the look on your face when I made that buzzing sound," he says. He mimics how freaked out I must have appeared.

"Ugh. Not funny, Julian." I punch him in the arm. "What are you doing out here?"

"I had a hunch you might make a break for it when you saw you were alone."

"Where'd Mira go?"

A shadow crosses over his face. "Eli got news that a hive collapsed in another quadrant, and they went to check it out."

"Did they cause it? Have they hurt more people?" I hate that Eli's tactics are so brutal.

"Hey, the hive collapsed on its own. We had nothing to do with it." He grabs my wrist. "I told you being out here alone isn't a good idea. Where are you going?"

I wriggle away from him and start walking. Though I'm not entirely convinced they had nothing to do with the hive collapse, it's not my main concern right now. "I'm going to get Virginia. I'll come back." The last part might be a lie. I'm not sure yet.

"You're nothing if not persistent." He falls into step beside me. "You'll need my help. Virginia will be weak. She's safer in her hive than running around out here with only you to protect her. Especially when you can't even protect yourself."

I hate that Julian is right again. I do need him. Despite being strong enough to materialize hair, clothes, and nail supplies, I doubt I'd be able to defend myself against a scanner drone—or something worse, because I don't know all the rules here. And of course I still hold out hope that he'll lead me to Neil eventually, so it pays to stay on his good side as long as I can stand to. "But won't you be going against Eli's wishes if you help me?"

He bristles. "Eli's not in charge of everything. And this is important to you."

It's great he finally understands that. "Fine. Come with."

Julian leads me through the maze of turns back to my old hive. There are no signs of imminent collapse in these sectors, though when I look closely, I detect hairline cracks in the infrastructure, cracks that etch out random patterns like glaze on a ceramic mug.

I practice homing in on Virginia's brain waves while at the same time protecting my explorations. In my attempt to do both, I effectively end up canceling my own weak signal. This is obviously going to take more training. Coming without Julian would have been a massive mistake.

At least my mental conditioning is vastly improved since Julian first broke me out, allowing us to make much better time than before. In fact, when Julian tells me we've arrived, without a single pit stop to plug in, at first I don't believe him. It's not until we step inside and I recognize the supine shapes of my fellow drones that I allow myself to get excited.

I bound up the stairs to Virginia's chamber and gaze at her. Even in her resting position her half smirk shines through. I glance down at Julian and see him inspecting the jagged edges of my former chamber.

"It took a real hit," he calls, his voice booming through the hive.

Virginia stirs, twitches her nose, like she senses something is amiss. She opens her eyes, and I put my finger to my lips. "Shhh . . . ," I say, trying to mimic the honey tones of Mira's most soothing voice. "It's me. I'm back."

She scoots away from me, her eyes bulging. "Who the hell are you?"

CHAPTER 13

I FEARED AS MUCH. The Morati's doping gas has made Virginia forget me, like it made her forget Beckah. "I'm your friend. Felicia." I enunciate every word and will her to remember our bond.

But my attempt only seems to annoy her. "How'd you get in here? Why do you have hair?"

"I'm here to rescue you."

As soon as the words are out of my mouth, I realize it's the wrong tactic to use with her. She stares me down. "Look, I don't know you. And I don't need to be rescued."

"Want to hear something random?" I lean over as if about to share a hot piece of gossip, and I know Virginia can't resist gossip.

She nods.

I lower my voice to a whisper. "There's a boy in the hive. He has hair too, and he's incredibly easy on the eyes."

"Seriously?" She shifts position so she can peek down, and her eyes lock with Julian's. She smiles in appreciation. "Wow, he *is* hot."

Virginia's complete one-eighty makes me giggle, and as she lifts herself out of her chamber, Julian laughs too. Virginia practically skips down the steps, and I follow her, hopeful I can convince her to come with us and preempt any plans Eli might have for overloading her brain. Even if she doesn't remember me, she's still my friend. And I don't want anything bad to happen to her.

She stops in front of Julian and reaches out to touch his face, as if to make sure he's real and not some figment of her imagination.

He flinches slightly when her hand makes contact with his skin. "I'm Julian," he says, encircling her wrist and giving her a dazzling smile. He pulls her hand away gently and then readjusts his grasp so he can shake it in greeting.

"Don't know what y'all are doing here, but it's fine by me. Certainly breaks up the monotony." She surveys the hive. "Where're you going to plug in?"

"We're not staying," Julian says. "This is a prison, and it's time you escaped. Let me show you something."

Julian leads Virginia over to the flat expanse of wall and taps in the code, triggering the door. "Take a look."

"Whoa!" Virginia peeks out cautiously and turns her

head right, then left. Shuddering, she backs up and presses herself against the nearest chamber. "I think I'd rather stay locked up."

I groan. Why does she have to be so difficult? I don't want to have to force her to come. "If you join us, we can show you how to get your hair back."

She shakes her head back and forth. "No way. I don't want my hair that badly."

Julian gives me a *What now* look as the door shuts seamlessly. I tap the side of my forehead in an *I'm thinking about it* gesture, and he nods.

"Why don't you sit with me, and I'll answer any questions you might have." He takes up his cross-legged, straight-backed yoga pose in the middle of the floor, and Virginia plops down in front of him eagerly. She really must be boy crazy.

"Can I check out your chamber for a minute?" I ask.

She startles at the sound of my voice, as if she forgot that I'm still here. "Go for it," she says, waving dismissively and turning her full attention back to Julian. He whispers something I can't quite hear, and she whispers back. At least Julian is good for distraction.

Once I'm positioned comfortably in Virginia's chamber, I scroll through her folders idly, trying to form some sort of plan. Since she never met me on Earth, she has no stored memories of me. But is there some way I can insert myself into her life? Like the way Eli imprinted all our memories with visions of our deaths? I scan her tags, praying for inspiration. And then

I see it. Ouija board. Of course. I click on the memory to live it first and see if there is anything I can use to my advantage.

It turns out to be a fairly standard teen Ouija board experience, at least if movies and books are to be believed, with Virginia in the basement trying to impress the girls on her cheerleading squad. Because they tease her, Virginia ends up getting out a Ouija board to show how grown-up she is. Someone uses the planchette to spell out a scary message, and they all freak out and then bond over the experience.

I wonder if I can stay remote enough in the memory to affect it instead of merely reliving it, like I did with my tainted memory of Neil at camp. I'll have to concentrate on manipulating the planchette to spell out what I want it to say. I go in.

Burrell, Virginia. Memory #26376
Tags: Ouija board, Rainbow style, Cheer squad, Sleepover
Number of Views: 12
Owner Rating: 2 stars
User Rating: 2 stars

Virginia's mother calls down the stairs that the pizza has arrived, and Virginia sighs with relief. Six pairs of eyes have been drilling into her all evening, obviously still upset that Virginia was chosen to replace their former teammate on the squad.

Virginia retrieves the pizza and sets it out for the girls. Amy makes a few snide comments, which have Virginia biting back her anger. But they eat in relative peace.

Soon Amy is taunting Virginia again, wondering aloud if the night's entertainment will consist of board games for babies. Virginia had planned to share a pedicure basket from her mother's salon with the girls, but doesn't feel like it anymore. She remembers the Ouija board her brother brought back from college and dares the girls to use it.

Amy says she's not scared. She declares Ouija boards to be fake and has no problem joining in.

They light candles and plunge the room into darkness to set the mood, huddle around the board, and place their hands on the planchette. Here's where I come in. The candles flicker, and I move the planchette to spell out:

W-H-E-N-Y-O-U-D-I-E

The girls freak out, pull their hands away from the board. Until one of the girls, Gail, insists they continue.

As if hypnotized, the girls comply. I cause the planchette to wobble wildly and spell out:

T-R-U-S-T-F-E-L-I-C-I-A

I swoop an arc from the *A* to the "good-bye." And with a *whoosh* the door to the basement slams, blowing out all the candles.

The girls' screams ricochet through the room. There's a pounding on the stairs. The door swings open, and the lights come back on. Virginia's mother checks to see if everything's all right.

The girls are shaken, but Virginia's mother comforts them by assuring them that Ouija boards are a load of bull. To make amends Virginia offers up her pedicure basket, and the girls react with enthusiasm. Because there are twenty colors to choose from, Virginia proposes to paint each nail a different color, rainbow style. The first layer of ice has been melted, and Virginia smiles for the first time that night.

I burst out of Virginia's memory. I never believed in Ouija boards before—never touched one, actually—but this one might be the key to getting Virginia to come with us. I mean, it's not like I actually talked to those girls. I only altered the memory so it seems like I did.

"Hey, Virginia," I call. Her seated posture is as perfect as Julian's, and her expression is spellbound as they stare at each other. "Don't you feel kind of woozy?"

Julian looks up at me sharply, and as he does, Virginia slumps over.

She picks herself up and climbs toward me, her movements sluggish. "Gotta plug in," she says.

I step aside so she can get into her chamber. Once she's positioned, I point out the Ouija board memory on her hologram screen. "I think you should view that one."

"Uh, sure."

When she's out, I watch her. She flinches every so often. Must be her reactions to Amy.

Julian joins me. "So what was your big plan?"

"I inserted myself into her memory so she'll know to trust me," I say, grinning. "They were playing with a Ouija board, and I was able to put pressure on the planchette to make it spell out what I wanted to say. Pretty cool, huh?"

"If it was so easy to alter her memory, how can you be certain someone hasn't messed with yours?"

Julian's comment renders me momentarily speechless and rips the grin right off my face. "But, why would they?"

"Maybe someone wanted you to trust them." He steps in very close and brushes strands of my hair over my shoulder. "Or they wanted you to react a certain way, so they pruned your life to form a new narrative."

My eyes narrow. "Wait—do you know something you're not telling me? Am I being *manipulated*?" I can't even begin to process the implications of Julian's suggestion.

Julian puts his hands up in a gesture of surrender. "How would I know? I'm asking you to think about it. Can you really trust your memories? Like, how can you be sure Neil even really exists? Or if he does, that he's the person you think he is?"

"Oh, now I get it." I materialize a rubber band and tie my hair back. "This is about your jealousy issues again." He's trying to unbalance me, get me to doubt my love for Neil. So he can what? Swoop in and pick up the pieces of my broken heart? Forget it. I *have* to trust my memories. They're the only link to my life that I have left.

He tilts his head back slightly, lifts one eyebrow, and peers down at me. "Think what you want. I'm just looking out for you."

"Ha! I might believe that if you were actually doing what you promised me you'd do." I cross my arms. "How hard can it be to take me to Neil? If you really know where he is?"

"It's complicated."

"I'm listening."

He turns sharply away from me. "I don't have to explain myself to you," he growls. Then he stomps down the stairs, returning to his position on the floor.

Arrogant jerk. I fume and wait for Virginia to surface, sneaking glances at Julian at regular intervals. Did he ever intend to lead me to Neil? I'm starting to seriously doubt it. Finally Virginia finishes her memory viewing.

"So?"

"I always forget what a bitch Amy could be sometimes," she says.

"That's all?"

"She was my best friend. I miss her."

"What about me?" I press.

"What about you?" Virginia says. Her disinterest stings and makes me feel thirteen again.

"I mean, what did the Ouija board say?"

"What's your name again?"

"Felicia."

"It said to trust Felicia."

"Bingo!" I say, excited that inserting myself into her memory seems to have stuck. "So trust me. Let's go."

She laughs. "Everyone knows Ouija boards are totally fake."

"Seriously?" Has all my effort been for nothing? "So, you think it's what—a coincidence?"

"It is a pretty strange coincidence, I'll give you that." She takes a hard look at me. "I mean, even if I did trust you, why would I want to go with you? I know what I have here, and I don't think it's that bad. I don't know what's out there."

I'm not sure what to tell her. If I explain Eli's experiments, it will only scare her more. Why would she want to go hang out with a guy who holds her life in so little regard? She wouldn't, and I can't blame her for that.

"Can we leave soon?" Julian calls up at us.

"Just a second," I tell her. I descend the stairs and lower my voice to a whisper. "We need a different tactic. The longer we wait, the higher the chance is that Eli hurts her. We can't let her overload."

"Do you owe her your loyalty even though she doesn't remember your friendship?"

"Of course!" And I need to do this, to atone for all my misdeeds on Earth, and prove to myself that I've changed for the better.

"If you insist." He seems to make some sort of decision. "Hey, Virginia! Do you smell smoke?"

Virginia flies down the stairs, missing the last one and

tumbling to the floor. "My chamber. It's *on fire*."

Julian winks at me as he scoops up Virginia. "Out!" he shouts. "Now!"

I rush ahead of them and pound out the code to open the door. Julian pushes me through just as an explosion rocks the hive, throwing us off balance. I twist in time to see Virginia's chamber destroyed before the door closes. And understanding dawns. That manipulative son of a— "You did this."

"What do you mean?" Julian lowers his eyes, the picture of coy innocence.

"My chamber. Virginia's chamber. Mind over matter indeed."

"Umm . . ." Virginia pulls at my arm. "What are those things?"

Scanner drones. "Flatten yourself against the wall. Quick." The three of us squeeze into an alcove. Virginia trembles beside me. A whole swarm, at least fifty, rumbles past us, low and steady, never breaking formation. But they aren't casting their yellow light. They're just flying.

"We're lucky," says Julian once the drones are gone. "If they had actually been scanning, they'd have picked us up for sure." He scratches his head. "You know, it looked like . . . like they were going to war or something. We'd better rendezvous with Eli and Mira as soon as possible."

Now's probably a good time to tell Julian I don't want to go back to the rebels. "I changed my mind about going back. I want you to help me find Neil. Right now." I'm tired of always having to put finding Neil on hold.

"No chance," Julian says. "Virginia's a liability now. Our hideout is a safe place for her to hang out while she weans herself off the drugs."

"I don't feel safe there." I take hold of Virginia's hand. "We can help Virginia detox on her own. On our way to get Neil."

"You know Eli's not going to let you go after all our efforts to recruit you." Julian wipes his wrist across his forehead, mussing up his bangs.

Julian's right once again. Eli's the type who will stop at nothing to get what he wants. But I don't care. "Then I guess I'll be on the run from the Morati *and* the rebels."

"Don't you *want* to help mankind escape from the Morati's bonds? What about all those kids? Won't you feel guilty hanging out drinking tea with Neil while little children are still strapped in?" He shakes his head slowly, sadly. "I never thought you were *that* selfish."

Am I selfish? I don't want to be. But I'm so confused. Don't I owe it to Neil to break him out? Don't I owe it to my friends to make sure they're okay? And if I help the rebels, does that mean I'll be responsible for putting other innocent people in danger?

"I'm sure you can do it without me," I tell him. My allegiance to Neil and my friends has to be my priority. And I don't want to hurt anyone. I couldn't stand it if my actions led to collateral damage.

"Why would we go to all the trouble to find you if we didn't need you?" Julian asks.

"I don't know!" I tug on Virginia and start walking. She hasn't said a word while Julian and I argue, and she looks nauseated. "But I don't really understand you all either. You're so secretive. And supercilious."

Virginia swoons, her knees buckling. The only reason she doesn't fall flat on her face is because I'm still holding on to her hand. Julian picks her up and carries her. "We can't stay here. The Morati might come personally to inspect the damage to Virginia's chamber. It's the second major anomaly in this hive."

He takes off running, Virginia's head lolling on his arm. I follow and try to keep up. Once we're twenty quadrants away, Julian stops. We enter a hive, and he sets her in a chamber to recharge. He does it so gently, I could almost believe he cares about her, too. My heart softens the tiniest bit more.

I push past him to pull up her account, and notice how low her credits have gotten. Not that she necessarily cares what she views at this point, and she doesn't need credits to relive parts of her own life. I pick out a memory from her favorites folder and then turn back to Julian.

"Why don't you ever plug in anymore?" I ask him.

"I meditate instead," he says. I wait for him to elaborate but he doesn't.

"But don't you miss reliving stuff from Earth? TV? Stargazing? Apple pie?" I can almost taste the tart sweetness of fruit and sugar-sprinkled crust in my mouth. Impulsively I grab Julian's hand and squeeze. His skin is warm.

This time Julian breaks off our contact. "Well, I'm not there now, am I?" he snarls.

It's such a strong reaction, I don't even know what to say.

"I prefer to live in the moment. You should try it sometime, instead of constantly pining for what you can't ever really have again." His words lash at me like a whip.

As I attempt to form a coherent response, the air in the hive shifts, and my whole being tenses. I turn slowly, and when I see Eli, I am overcome with a sensation akin to falling off a cliff.

"You look so surprised to see me," he says, his grim smile tinged with gloat. "I told you I could find you anywhere."

CHAPTER 14

"THE HIDEOUT IS OUR NEXT STOP," says Julian, interceding on my behalf. He steps between Eli and me, and suddenly I'm immensely grateful he stuck around.

Eli stares us down for a half minute and then emits a strange sort of sound, like a high-pitched grunt. I think it may have been a laugh.

"We need to stop playing games and wasting time," he says, turning on his heel as if he expects us to fall in line behind him like good little soldiers. "The Morati have been hunting for us with scanner drones, but our intel from other rebel cells suggests that at least some of the Morati have left the palace to conduct a search themselves."

It just got even more dangerous to be out on my own.

Will Eli punish me for coming to rescue Virginia?

Neither Julian nor I move. Eli pauses before reopening the door, and looks over his shoulder at us. He is not amused.

"I did not give you permission to leave." Eli clenches and unclenches his fists.

I'm going to have to come clean at some point, so I say it. "I rescued Virginia." I can't help letting a note of pride slip into my voice.

Eli's gaze darts around the half-full hive at the occupied chambers. He stomps over to the closest drone. "Where is she?"

Again, Julian moves to shield me from Eli. "I think Virginia can help us more by being with us. You said yourself she's a high potential." His voice is steady, his tone reasonable.

"She'll slow us down." Eli turns back to us, and crosses his arms over his broad chest.

I step forward so I'm standing next to Julian. His arguing my case has made me more confident. "Virginia's important to me. If you want me to happily contribute to the team effort, we have to take her with us. And it would also be nice if you'd tell me what's going on. You've told me about phase one. What was phase two?"

"Phase two was our attempt to force targeted subjects to relive the memory of their death over and over." He admits it without remorse or apology.

"And that's what you did to Beckah?" I caution myself

to remain calm, and step closer to him. Julian steps forward with me. "You made her think she was dying? Made her suffer?"

Eli raises his eyebrows slightly. "If she was one of our test subjects. I don't remember any names. We hoped it would force her to move on."

So there is hope that her disappearance from our hive means she moved on. "And did she?"

"So far all test subjects have overloaded. They couldn't handle the op. Swiss-cheesed their brains."

I dig my fingernails into my palms, but I barely feel a thing. "So that means she's in the isolation plains, like Mira said."

"Probably." He starts to pound the code into the wall to open the door, as if to indicate that our conversation is over.

"We have to go get her, too." I wedge myself between him and the wall so he can't open the door. I need him to know I'm serious about trying to help Beckah. Because she's my friend, and I promised her I wouldn't leave her.

Eli steps back, shakes his head, and waves me away like I'm a fly that won't leave him alone. "That subject is useless to us. Forget her."

I set my jaw. "I'll go get her myself."

"You'll be much too busy with phase three." He turns his head toward me and half smiles. A smile that doesn't reach his cold eyes.

"And what is phase three?" I ask, dreading the answer.

"Phase three is you."

"What do you mean I am phase three? What do you think I'm going to do for you?"

"Thanks to a certain someone"—Eli flicks his head in Julian's direction—"with an unhealthy interest in you, it was brought to our attention that you are special."

Julian chuckles at this, and puts his arm around me. I step to the side, away from him, annoyed that he's apparently been stalking me both in life and in the afterlife, for reasons I can't fathom. "How am *I* special?"

"I'm not entirely convinced you are," Eli says as if it pains him not to know. "But I did observe that you spent more time out of your chamber than others."

"Wait—you were *watching* me?" Now I am thoroughly creeped out. "Are there cameras in the hives?"

"Not that I'm aware of. I merely analyzed your pattern of net usage. Scientific observation." Eli shrugs his shoulders. "It was Julian's idea to pick you up."

And God knows what Julian's intentions are. Or if they have more to do with our history than they do with the rebellion. "Why didn't you tell me all this before?"

"We didn't want to overwhelm you. There's only so much a drone can handle when it first leaves the hive," Eli says.

"Hey. Good morning." Virginia rubs her eyes drowsily, stumbling out of the chamber Julian put her in earlier. As much as I love her, I'm a little annoyed at her timing—coming out of a memory right as I'm getting some real answers.

Eli scans her from head to toe in a quick, clinical

procedure and flicks his gaze away. "This is the girl you risked everything for?" His disdain is palpable.

Startled, Virginia cowers in Eli's shadow and scuttles over to Julian.

His bullying makes something inside me snap. I stand up as straight as possible and face Eli full-on. "Okay, Eli. Here's the deal. We go pick up Beckah and find my boyfriend, Neil. And then maybe you can find out for sure if I'm special enough for phase three."

Eli's lips twitch, but his eyes don't as much as blink. His arm shoots out, grabbing and twisting me until my face squishes up against the wall. I feel cold metal on my wrists, hear the tinny ring of handcuffs clanking shut. He yanks the chain between the cuffs, and I sway, no longer steady on my feet. He cinches my upper arms with his steely fingers and pivots so I can see Julian and Virginia's shocked expressions.

He leans into me. "No deal."

"Let her go, Eli," Julian says sharply, but he doesn't make a move to free me.

"I don't want this to get out of hand." Eli's voice is low, perfectly modulated. "We're all going to quietly head back to meet Mira and proceed with phase three. Because if there's any trouble, I can't guarantee our new friend Virginia's safety."

A wave of psychological nausea pounds me into submission. I can't let him hurt Virginia. I nod weakly to signal my acquiescence to Julian, and he dips his chin in return.

"I think we're ready, then." Julian pulls a shell-shocked

Virginia with him and pounds out the code. The door opens, and they hesitate before slowly exiting the hive.

"Move out!" Eli orders. He escorts me firmly down the corridor behind Julian and Virginia, and we all four make our way back to the rebels' latest hideout.

During the forced march I seethe with resentment for Eli. But for Virginia's sake I don't struggle. Don't make a scene. His whole demeanor is laced with swagger. He enjoys my knowing he has the upper hand.

Once we're back at the hideout, Eli presses a key into Julian's hand, even though he could have dematerialized the cuffs himself. As Eli stalks over to his work space, Julian frees me so I can help Virginia into a chamber. Our journey has taken a lot out of her, but it's amazing, despite the soreness in my arms, how fit I feel in comparison. Was I as haggard and worn when I first got out as she is now?

I sit down on the sofa, noting that Mira sits on a chair with her sights fixed on me. I won't get away easily again.

As I wait for Eli to spring phase three on me, I pick at my sweater and pinch the lightly stretchy material of my jeans. Something's missing from my outfit. My charm bracelet. As soon as I think about it, it appears around my wrist, the weight of it uncomfortable against my skin. I look at the now single dolphin and have to think of Autumn. And I know that if I am to be truly strong, if I am ever to pave my own path away from the rebels and eventually move on, I am going to have to confront my betrayal of her, the reason the second dolphin is now missing from my bracelet.

I stand up, and Mira springs up, as quick as a cat. "Where are you going?"

"To plug in," I say sharply. "Is that still allowed?"

"Of course." But she waits, arms folded, until I'm halfway up the stairs before she sits back down.

I climb into the chamber above Virginia, pull the cables out, and lie down. When the hologram screen lights up, I begin to have second thoughts. I don't really need to do this, do I? Surely there are other ways to build strength? But my gut tells me I have to go in and face the weakness that ruined my friendship with Autumn. I steel myself for impact, like taking a deep breath at the edge of an icy lake, and I dive in.

Ward, Felicia. Memory #31434
Tags: Germany, Autumn, Julian, Halloween
Number of Views: 1
Owner Rating: Not rated
User Rating: Not shared

The field house is dimly lit and draped in snaking black streamers and thick vines of fake cobwebs. As I grope my way through the room, strobe lights illuminate the few people here this early in jarring bursts. I sit down at the bar, where I am supposed to meet Autumn. In Germany the legal drinking age is sixteen, so anywhere off our housing compound I could order a mojito. And I would. But because this area is considered U.S. property, U.S. rules govern here. I have no chance in hell of the bartender serving me a mojito, even if I am dressed up as a devil.

Since their espresso machine sports a visible OUT OF SERVICE sign, I order a Diet Dr Pepper. The bartender serves it to me in a glass with a twisty straw, like I am eleven. I resist the urge to throw the straw back in his face and instead swirl it around in the dark, murky liquid, faster and faster until a tiny whirlpool forms.

"Felicia!" Autumn crashes into me, laughing. Dressed as an angel, in a long flowing white dress cinched with a gold belt, an ivory chiffon wrap, and a gold halo headband, she's loose and languid. Her breath reeks of vodka and peppermint. She takes my cola and gulps straight from the glass. "Ugh! What is this?" She smacks her lips and then sticks her finger into her mouth and pretends to gag, giggling. "It's vomitous!"

"You're in a good mood."

"Hell yeah, I am!" She slams my drink onto the counter so that it sloshes over the side, and then she pulls out a mirror and a tube of lipstick from her tiny gold clutch. Dabbing a shimmery pink on her lips, she leans in close to my ear and shouts, "He finally kissed me last night! And he's meeting me here in a few hours."

My heart thuds in my chest and my body goes numb. The blood rushing to my head drowns out the sound of the party music. I stare at her, uncomprehending.

She's grinning ear to ear, looking up dreamily, her big hazel eyes in soft focus. She hasn't noticed how still I've gone.

She'll expect me to be happy for her, but my insides twist with jealousy. What game is Julian playing?

"Uh . . . that's great. Finally." I shape my mouth into an approximation of a smile.

"I need a drink!" Autumn declares. "And not that swill you're drinking. Mojitos!"

"Haven't you had enough?" I ask, squeezing her arm. "Your breath could power a small city."

She throws back her head and laughs, pulling me off my stool and onto the edge of the dance floor but no farther. She knows I like having an escape route when places get crowded. "I love this song!" She shimmies her hips back and forth in a sexy merengue, a souvenir of her family's most recent posting in the Dominican Republic. I have to smile as I watch her. With Autumn it doesn't matter what type of song is playing, it could be The Beatles or a Gregorian chant, she always pulls out her merengue in the end.

Unlike for most parties I've been to at the field house, the DJ is spinning a good mix of dance songs. The more I dance, the less I fume—until the combination of Autumn's sparkling eyes and the pulsating beat of the music wins me over completely. Despite her flaws, Autumn is my best friend. She has stood beside me, metaphorically speaking, anyway, for more than half my life. A meaningless fling with a jerk like Julian, as irresistible as he is, is not worth losing her over.

After an hour of dancing I'm in need of some fresh air. I mouth to Autumn that I'm going outside, and head for the back patio. Autumn latches on to my hand and lets me lead her around the mass of costumed revelers. We burst through the door, giggling. The brisk October air makes me shiver, despite my long-sleeved black turtleneck, black wool tights, and red form-fitting sweater and skirt. But Autumn doesn't seem to feel the chill.

She pulls a flask from her clutch and drinks deeply. "Want some?" she says, wiping her mouth with the back of her hand.

I accept it from her, take a sip, and grimace. It's straight vodka—and it burns going down, making me long for my orphaned glass of Dr Pepper. "How can you drink this stuff?"

She snatches the flask and pouts. "I like it." She drains the rest of the flask and then pops a red-and-white-striped peppermint into her mouth.

She narrows her eyes at me. "Hey, did you read the chapters from our book I gave you last week yet?"

"Yeah," I say, my teeth starting to chatter.

"So what did you think?" Her cheeks flush as she waits for my response.

"Wasn't it a bit . . ." I search for the right word. ". . . over-dramatic to have Chelsy smash a vase over Tyler's head?" I cross my arms over my chest for warmth.

"I told you. They call Chelsy 'Winter.'" She cocks her head. "Tyler cheated on her with Summer. She was upset." She looks at me as if this should explain everything.

I don't feel like fighting with her. I want to go back inside. "Okay. If that's what you want."

She nods her head, surprised but pleased that I've acquiesced so easily.

We return to the dance floor. Autumn's movements become increasingly uncoordinated, until I start to worry I'm going to have to drag her limp body home.

I'm keeping such a close eye on her, I don't even notice Julian standing there until Autumn lurches forward and plants a sloppy kiss on him. "You came!" she slurs, holding on to his bare arms for support. "But you didn't wear a costume. You naughty, naughty boy!" She dissolves into giggles and clumsily rips off her halo headband. "Take this . . ." She bites her lip in exaggerated concentration as she tries to put it on him.

He plucks the halo from her hand and sticks it back on her head, smoothing out her hair so it frames her face. He says something into her ear, and she laughs. He lifts her arms and places them on his shoulders, and they start swaying to the music.

I should have left before Julian showed up. His arrogant charm irritates me. I look for a place to sit down, but Autumn stumbles over. "Let's go!" she roars into my ear, pushing me toward the exit. We spill out onto the sidewalk, and Julian joins us, brandishing his coat.

"What's up?" I say, raising an eyebrow.

"Julian got a text from Nicole that they're all over at the Irish pub," Autumn says, grabbing on to Julian's hand. "She wants us to come too!"

My stomach clenches when I see Julian give her an

adoring smile. "I'm not so sure that's a good idea . . . ," I say.

"Please, please, please!" Autumn stomps her foot like a toddler denied a cookie. "You know I want to go to Nicole's birthday party. If we go tonight, she'll invite us. I know it."

I kind of doubt Nicole will be impressed by the state Autumn is in at the moment, but maybe she'll sober up in the cab ride over. I throw up my arms in surrender, and we hustle over to the main street to hail a taxi.

Autumn slides in first, followed by Julian and then me. I give the driver instructions, sit back, and look out the window to avoid the happy couple.

Julian's lips brush my neck. "Alone at last," he murmurs.

I push him away roughly and peek over at Autumn. She's slumped over in her seat, snoring. After all the vodka she's drunk, probably not even a car crash could wake her.

"What's going on, Julian?" I hiss, my jealousy bubbling to the surface. "You kissed her even though you told me you didn't like her like that."

Julian looks petulant. "Hey, it was you who wanted to keep the charade going. She was getting suspicious. I did it for you. It's what you wanted."

I snort. "And you didn't enjoy it the least bit either. Am I right?"

"Of course not." He grazes his knuckles softly down my cheek. "I am all yours."

He leans in close and smashes his lips against mine. And with that, my resolve to stay away from him is overpowered by my desire. I press against him, forgetting

Autumn, forgetting myself. Nothing else on Earth matters more than this.

As he kisses me, Julian's hands are everywhere at once. In my hair, caressing my neck, pushing my skirt up higher on my leg, pulling at my sweater. "You have too many clothes on," he says as he softly bites my earlobe, his voice a low growl. I slide my hand under his shirt, over his heart. It's beating as wildly as mine.

The taxi squeals to a stop, the driver blaring on his horn and shouting obscenities at someone who has cut him off. Startled, I break away from Julian's kiss to see Autumn staring straight at me. Her eyes grow huge. I gulp, tugging my skirt down and readjusting my devil's horns headband. "It's not what it looks like!" I say desperately.

The driver announces our arrival at the Irish pub, and Autumn is out of the car in two seconds flat. I've never seen her move so fast. Certainly never with a flask of vodka in her. "Pay him!" I yell at Julian and rush out after Autumn. I catch up to her before she can enter the pub, and grab her hand.

She spins around, shaking me off. "Don't. Touch. Me." Her tone is scalding, her eyes filled with pure hatred.

"I'm so sorry. I . . ." I wring my hands, and something on my wrist catches her attention. My charm bracelet has come loose from under the cuff of my turtleneck.

She snatches at it, lifting my arm violently in the process. Then she rips off one of the dolphins. "You don't need this anymore. My friendship means nothing to you. And now . . . you mean nothing to me."

Autumn yanks open the door to the pub and lets it slam shut behind her. Dazed, I turn to look for Julian, but he's not on the curb, where I expect him to be. He has moved to the front seat of the cab, and he's gesturing to the driver. Some problem with the fare? I stalk over to the taxi, ready to give him hell for his part in pissing off Autumn, but when I try to open the back door, it's jammed. Or locked.

I jiggle it. "Hey! Unlock this!" I shout.

Julian turns in his seat and peers out the window at me. He has the saddest eyes I've ever seen. He presses his palm against the window, and as if hypnotized, I press my hand on the other side of the glass. And the cab drives off. I'm stunned. What the hell is he doing?

I pull out my phone and call him, but a recording informs me the number has been disconnected. In frustration I kick the curb with my shiny red heels. I end up only scuffing the toe and banging my foot. I hobble over to the outside wall of the pub. I sink to the ground against the rough concrete and bury my pounding head in my hands, not able to believe what just happened.

When I surface in my chamber, I blink back tears. Autumn's last look at me is burned into my consciousness, like the glare you still see on the back of your eyelids after staring at the sun. It will follow me for all of eternity. I crawl out of the chamber and freeze.

All three of my prison guards are standing on the stairs in front of me, wearing grim expressions.

"What's wrong?" I ask. "Phase three misfire?"

"Some of our quadrant leaders from other cells are reporting strange occurrences," says Eli. "First there was an isolated hive cave-in, but now an increasing number of hives have crumbled to the point where they are unusable."

"But isn't that what you wanted? Fewer batteries to power their evil plan?"

"Not like this," he says. "Not with what they are doing with those displaced."

I shudder, expecting bad news. "Which is what?"

"Unconfirmed. But we do know the Morati are rounding them up. And it looks like they plan to turn them into an army."

CHAPTER 15

"I . . . I THINK I NEED TO SIT DOWN." My head spins. I stagger down the stairs, over to the closest chair, and fall into it. Eli, Mira, and Julian sit as well. They look shell-shocked and, for the first time, actually scared. Seeing them like this hits me hard. The Morati threat is tangible now in a way it wasn't before.

Mira, usually so talkative, does nothing except pull at the ends of the hair at the base of her neck. Eli stares off into space. Julian—I don't even want to look at Julian.

"Okay. So what makes you think they are building an army? And how is that even possible?"

"The Morati are ruthless, and the Lethe drug is not the only tool at their disposal," Eli says, more composed than the rest of us but still shaken. "Reports from my scouts say there is also an experimental drug derived from the underworld river Phlegethon."

That day in Mrs. Keats's Mythology class pops into my head, fresh in mind thanks to my recent viewing. Alyssa's smug expression as she answered every question right, including the one about the River Phlegethon. "It's where dead souls boil with anger," I say.

"Exactly. If the Morati have found a way to stabilize it, they could use it to marshal any displaced subjects against us."

It's bad enough the Morati have so little regard for humans that they use us as batteries. But at least, despite being imprisoned, we still have had free will about what we choose to access and do with our time. If this drug can turn us into some kind of automated supersoldiers for their cause . . . It's unfathomable. What if it happens to Neil? My father? To me? "But they can't do that," I protest. "What will happen to the people? Won't it torture them to burn with rage?"

"The people?" Eli looks slightly confused, as if he hasn't contemplated this aspect of the Morati's plan. As if he doesn't care. "Well, they'll be like mindless zombies, so consumed by pain that they'll attack anyone in sight."

Julian clears his throat. "We can't let it happen." He gets up, his jaw set with steely resolve, and scoots his chair so it's facing mine directly, and sits back down. We're so close, our knees knock together.

"You have to make a decision, Felicia. Are you ready to join this fight for real?" Julian glances at Eli and scowls slightly. "As a volunteer, not a conscript?"

Am I? Until a few minutes ago I would have said no, mostly out of resentment for Eli's recent behavior. But this is bigger than me now. There's more at stake than my pride.

If I do join the rebels, I need to be prepared to make sacrifices. Will Eli's phase three require me to give up my chance to help Beckah and reunite with Neil? Can I put the rebels' plans above my personal goals? I'm not sure.

But if I don't join the rebels, am I condemning people to a fate worse than death? Could I live with myself if I stand by and let the Morati infect people with the Phlegethon? Even if I don't trust the rebels completely, even if I'm not sure I can really make a difference, I know we can't let the Morati win.

"Okay." I grip the arms of my chair. "I'm in."

Mira leaps up. "We need to train you to fight," she says excitedly. "Remember how Eli threw you across the room? You could learn to do that too."

"It will be another tool in your arsenal," says Julian. He leans forward and clasps his hands in front of him as if he anticipates some sort of resistance from me. "You're nearly weaned off the drugs. You can materialize objects. You're even learning to find people and communicate with your mind."

But I don't need them to convince me about learning to fight. I want to be able to protect myself. What I need is conviction that I'm making the right choice. I push back in my chair, scraping it across the carpet so I can get up. "I'm ready."

With something to focus on, Mira's face loses the hollowness from before. She lifts both of her arms behind her head and pitches them forward, as if throwing something large and heavy. Sparks fly through the air, and a dartboard materializes on the right side of the hive, in front of all the ripped-out chambers.

"I like to go through the physical motions of an action," she explains to me. "I like the drama of it. But to each his own. It works without the theatrics too."

"Watch and learn," says Julian, gyrating his arms in large circles a few times to warm up.

Eli doesn't get up but watches Julian and Mira materialize darts and throw them at the board, in his usual detached manner. He's not the slightest bit moved by Mira's enthusiastic showmanship, her fancy techniques with the darts—though, he does nod when they hit their marks with deadly accuracy, like an inspector checking off a list.

"You give it a try." Mira smiles encouragingly.

I furrow my brow in concentration, but at first I can't get any darts to appear in my hand, let alone hit the board.

"Relax," advises Mira. "Feel your energy flow through you, and then let it loose."

I take a deep breath and tap into the power at my core. A dart appears in my hand, and I let it fly. My aim is wide, and the dart clatters to the ground.

It takes me several attempts, but finally I hit the edge of the board. Encouraged, I risk making a fool of myself and imagine five darts at once. I throw my head forward abruptly, and then take a peek at the board. All five darts are arranged in a tight circle around the bull's-eye.

Mira glides over and gives me a high five. "Classy move! Impressive, especially for a beginner."

Julian nods his head in appreciation of my work. "Now let's see how good you are at deflecting darts."

I grit my teeth and let them put me through my paces. It reminds me of seventh-grade gym class, where I had an ambitious teacher who wanted to make sure every single kid could climb a Peg-Board and perform at least ten pull-ups before the end of term. It was excruciating then, and it's no different now. Even when I beg for a rest break, they keep coming at me. To "toughen up" my mind. The only thing that keeps me going is the thought of slamming Eli against a wall at the end of all this.

We run through more materialization drills and keep working on my deflection skills. During my training, Virginia comes and goes from her chamber. I feel like I've been at it for days, and when my body starts to convulse from the strain, Mira forces me to continue, to push through. "Mind over matter!" she always yells as a reminder, like some sort of sadistic fitness trainer.

In the middle of a stick fight, Eli whistles loudly to get our attention. The sticks thump onto the rug.

"Fun's over. We need to discuss the latest reports," he says, putting his typical humorless spin on it.

While Eli occupies the other two, I sneak off for some R&R in a chamber. I'm exhausted, but also excited about how much I've learned. Since I'm still dressed in my "date" outfit, it only makes sense that I access my first date with Neil.

Ward, Felicia. Memory #32236
Tags: Ohio, Neil, First date, Playground
Number of Views: 536
Owner Rating: 5 stars
User Rating: 4 stars

I spin my locker combination and pull open the door. Throwing my books on the top shelf, I catch my reflection in the small mirror, and I pause to examine it more closely. Could it be? Is my skin glowing? I have to admit, I look healthier than I have in months, and it's not only the makeup I put on today. The green silk blouse I'm wearing brings out the amber flecks in my brown eyes. Instead of their usual muddy tint, they sparkle like topaz.

Hands reach around my face and cover my eyes. "Guess who."

"Is that you again, Principal Joplin?" I tease.

"Straight A's for you, young lady," says Neil, imitating the booming bass of our school's headmaster. Neil removes his hands from my eyes and puts them on my shoulders, turning me to face him. The look in his eyes makes me light-headed.

Being this close to him in the crowded senior hallway unbalances me. I back away, crashing into my locker. "Are you ready to go?" I ask, trying to cover up my embarrassment over being a total klutz.

He nods, his expression inscrutable, and we walk out to his car. Nervous energy crackles between us. I'm not sure what to say, and I guess he's not either, because we don't talk. His movements—as he opens my door for me, buckles his seat belt, and turns the steering wheel to leave the parking lot—seem shaky.

He puts on the radio, and I'm thankful it fills the silence. I tap out the beat with my palm, and sing along under my breath to the songs I know. I sneak looks at him as he keeps his full attention on the road. He's a conscientious driver.

We pull into his driveway. When he reaches for the gearshift to put the car in park, I tap his hand lightly. "Can we go to that playground we passed? The one just around the corner?"

Somehow the thought of going into his house right now, and sitting together awkwardly on the sofa, freaks me out. The playground will be a neutral place.

"Yeah, sure," says Neil, visibly relieved. "I haven't been there in years. About time I check in on it." He smiles so warmly, his dimples show, confirming I've made the right call.

Neil walks beside me to the playground. Close, but not touching. His hands are jammed into the front pockets of his lightweight Windbreaker, and whenever we come across an errant stone on the pavement, he kicks it.

I rack my brain for some small tidbit or factoid I can share to break the silence, but can't come up with anything. I could dance around my feelings all day, or I could commit to them, despite the risk. It's possible Neil realizes our kiss in the woods was a big mistake. Now that he's had time to think it over, maybe he's looking for a way to let me down gently. I take a deep breath. "So . . . I'm really glad you talked me into going to the church camp. I had a great time." Understatement of the year.

"You did?" Neil gulps, drawing my attention to his neck, and the way his polo shirt is buttoned up tight against his collarbone. "I mean, I'm glad. I mean, I did too."

I zone in on the top button of his shirt, and before I can stop myself, I reach up and undo it.

"Race you to the swings!" I take off running, to hide my blush.

Neil thunders behind me and makes up my head start easily. We lunge into the swings, leaving wood chips in our wake. Laughing, we pump our legs until we're touching nothing but sky.

Finally I put my feet down and let them scrape against the dirt underneath the swing set to slow myself down. Neil does the same.

"Twists?" I ask. It's something I remember doing as a kid, the last time our family was in D.C., before my experience in Nairobi made me grow up way too fast. And the chains on these swings are long enough for it to work.

"You're on!"

I twist myself as high as my legs allow. Because he has longer legs, Neil gets two more twists in. We let loose at the same time, and our swings spin and pitch violently, the chains clanking as we unwind.

Once our swings come to a halt, Neil reaches for my hand. It feels like the most natural thing in the world, and I wonder how I could have ever doubted his affection for me.

"Now that we got that out of our system . . . let's talk hobbies." The teasing note in his voice is back, the color on his cheeks high. We continue to sway together, each anchored by one foot on the ground.

"Well," I begin, "we all know you enjoy singing and acting and Boy Scouts. . . . Anything else you'd like to share with the audience today?" I make a fist and thrust it into his face, an imaginary microphone.

He clears his throat and puts on a mock serious expression, one eyebrow cocked, his nostrils slightly flared. "I also enjoy kayaking, camping, writing bad poetry . . . and making out with my girlfriend."

At the word "girlfriend" my heart skips a beat. Does he mean me? Or does he have some other girlfriend I don't know about? I chuckle weakly and drop my fist. "A well-rounded array of hobbies indeed."

"And what about you?" He copies my interview approach. "We all know you enjoy . . ." And here he stumbles. He bites his lip, probably wondering if he should mention the piano or not. But he recovers quickly. "Um . . . listening to music and . . . camping." He's grasping at straws, trying not to offend me or plunge me into a bad mood. "Anything else you would like to share?"

I smile sweetly. I decide to skip mentioning my dormant piano playing as well. It's a wound I don't want to rub salt into at the moment. "I also enjoy picking apart movies for continuity flaws, swimming, and making out with my boyfriend."

We stare at each other then, and all the blood in my body seems to rush to my head.

"He's a lucky guy, your boyfriend," Neil says. He gets off his swing and bends down toward me, in such a way that I'm sure he'll kiss me. My insides flip-flop in anticipation. But instead of his lips heading toward mine, they move in the direction of my ear. "Are you up for the challenge of the merry-go-round?" he breathes dramatically.

He pulls me to my feet, and we dash over to the merry-go-round. The rut that circles it is etched into the dirt like a moat protecting a castle. I hop onto the pebbly metal platform, careful not to trip, and grab on to the center bars.

"Hold on tight!" Neil says as he pushes against the bar and begins to run, digging his heels into the Earth. After about ten rotations, the centrifugal force threatens to overwhelm me, but I stick out my hand for Neil to grab anyway. He locks his hand around my wrist and jumps on. We jostle against each other until we're lying perfectly still, our fingers entwined.

Our heads bump lightly together as we spin, and the sun's rays warm our exposed skin. When the merry-go-round slows, and then grinds to a halt, I turn my head to face Neil. We grin at each other with big cheesy smiles. He shifts his body so he's propped up on his side, and he reaches out his hand to brush the tendrils that have escaped from my ponytail away from my face. My scalp tingles, and the tiny pulses of pleasure radiate down my body. My muscles relax, and I close my eyes. His kiss is tender, his lips impossibly soft, and I marvel at how perfectly we fit together, like he's a piece of me I didn't know was missing before.

And of course I have to go and ruin it by crying. I'm not loud about it, but by the time the first tear trickle reaches my ear, he knows. A shadow passes over the sun, and I shiver.

He hugs me tightly, pressing me against his body in a way that makes me want to wrap my legs around him. I redden at the thought. I break away from him and sit up, hugging my arms to my chest.

"You're cold," Neil says, concerned. "Let's go inside. I'll make you coffee."

"Do you have tea?" I blurt. Having this chance to be with Neil feels like a fresh start, and coffee is a vice I'd rather leave in my past.

"More than what lies at the bottom of Boston Harbor." As we walk to his house, Neil gives me a rundown of all the different types of tea that inhabit his parents' well-stocked cupboards.

"Chamomile is good," I tell him as he unlocks the door and ushers me inside.

Neil's living room is light and airy, and impeccably neat. A sofa and armchairs are arranged in front of a fireplace, and the walls are lined with bookshelves.

"Have a seat," Neil says. "I'll get our tea."

I sit on the sofa—right in the middle—and pull a throw pillow from the nook of the armrest to stow behind my back. My eyes flicker around the room, taking in the various family photos on the wall, always of the same three people—Neil and his parents. But then I see one smack in the middle of the mantel that makes me pause because there are four people in it. I cock my ear, listening for the telltale signs of tea-making in the kitchen, and approach the photo, skimming around the coffee table carefully.

In it Neil looks about thirteen, and there's another boy standing next to Neil's father, blond but with the same wild curls, who must be a couple years older. Does Neil have a long-lost brother? There has never been mention of him, so I have to assume it's a sensitive subject. What happened to him? Did he die?

My heart pounding in my throat, I sit back down. Just in time too, because Neil comes in with two steaming mugs. "We'll let these steep a couple minutes, and in the meantime I can play you a song." He ducks his head and shrugs as he places our tea on doilies on the coffee table in front of me. "If you want."

"A private concert? Of course I want!" I smile at him brightly and swallow my questions about the mystery boy.

He returns to the entryway and pulls his guitar out of the closet, and then sits on the footstool in front of me. He strums a few chords, then scratches the side of his neck with the bright orange guitar pick. "I haven't played this song for anyone before. But I play a lot when I'm home alone."

Leaning forward, I press my palms together and squeeze them between my knees. As he starts to sing, I'm struck again, as I am every time, by the emotion he's able to convey. He sings of loss, of forgiveness, of learning to live—and love again. It's an arrow through my heart, because it's everything

I both feel and long for. It's like he's reading my mind.

When it ends, I'm paralyzed.

He places his guitar on the chair and scoots the footrest closer to me. He takes my hands in his, looks deep into my eyes. "I . . . I thought it might help you to see I understand what you're going through. I mean, not exactly, of course, since you haven't told me what happened, but . . . Remember when you asked me if I'd drink from that river, the Lethe? At one time I would've—without question. I'd have thrown myself into that river. Anything to take the pain away. But you can get through it. I did. And I want you to know that whatever it is, I'm here for you. Whenever you're ready to talk." He's so earnest, if he told me he'd jump in front of a lion for me, I think I'd believe him. But that doesn't make it any easier for me to bare my dark secrets to him.

I lower my eyes to escape his gaze, which has grown so intense, I fear it can see straight into my soul. "I better get home," I say, getting up and heading toward the door. "Grammy's going to wonder where I am."

"Wait—I'll drive you." He jumps up and brushes by me, opening the door.

"It's only a half mile," I say, ready to refuse him, until I see his eager expression. "Will you walk with me instead? I feel like walking."

"Yeah . . . yeah, sure." And when we step out the door, hand in hand, I glance back, realizing we never touched our tea.

We walk past the playground, past cul-de-sacs, past an array of pastel-colored houses. Neil and I talk about our friends at church and our classes at school. It feels so normal and nice.

At my door I pull out my key, insert it into the lock.

"Wait," says Neil. "Before you go . . ." He leans in and cups my face with his hands. He kisses me softly, his warm touch melting away all my remaining uncertainty. It's a feeling I could get lost in. I pull him closer, kiss him back harder.

The door opens, creaking on its hinges, and Neil and I break apart, startled.

"Good evening, Neil," says Grammy. Her smile is polite, her eyebrows slightly raised.

"Hello, Mrs. Ward," he says, backing away. "So, see you tomorrow, Felicia?" He looks like he's trying to keep a straight, serious face, but a smile—and those dimples—breaks through.

"Yes, tomorrow," I promise as Grammy guides me into the house, even though I don't know how I'll survive the hours until I can see him again. Grammy retrieves my key and shuts the door, but I rush to the front window and pull back the curtains to watch him. And I stay there until he rounds the corner, out of sight.

CHAPTER 16

SUDDENLY I FEEL LIKE I'm being ripped apart. It is pitch black, and dust and small stones are raining down on me, bouncing and pinging against the sides of the chamber like hail. I'm disoriented by the lack of hologram screen glow, and have to squint to keep the dust out of my eyes. With rising panic I try to turn the screen back on, but the system is completely fried.

I shift my body toward the open side of the chamber and bang my arm on something hard. It's blocked. After closing my eyes to find my calm center, I shuffle toward the stair exit, bumping my head in the process. I kick with my feet. Air. A burst of relief. I shuffle farther and kick again. Rocks? A sinking feeling in my stomach.

"Help me dig!" I hear Julian's voice, but it's muffled, like I have earplugs in. I'm trapped in my chamber.

Frantically I pat at the ceiling above me, feeling for cracks. There are a few thin ones, like hairline fractures. And a larger one, over my right ear, that continues to spill an alarming amount of sandlike sediment. At this rate I'll soon be completely buried, like a cursed princess trapped in the bottom of an hourglass.

There's just enough room for me to twist myself around so my head is nearest the stair. I crawl on my belly and claw at the large chunks of stone that block my exit from the chamber. The jagged edges slice my fingertips and scrape my knuckles. I catch a fingernail, and as I pull my hand away, the nail peels off. I yowl in pain and jab my finger into my mouth, biting my injured finger between my lips, cursing the fact that the stronger my mind gets, the more I seem to inhabit my body and the more I feel pain. Shouldn't I be able to will the pain away?

Whimpering, I try to calm myself. Physically there's no chance of me getting out of here. But mentally? Am I powerful enough to move these heavy boulders that block my exit?

I tense and stretch my entire body, and then relax. I open my mind to let the energy flow around me, and I feel a tickle at the edge of my consciousness. It doesn't seem threatening so I let it in. It's Julian. He's telling me to push with all my might against the barrier while they pull with theirs. "I'll try," I mutter.

Tentatively touching the barrier, my arms stretched out

like Superman, I imagine all my energy focusing on that one spot. I harness this power and let it loose. There's a loud boom, and then light streams into the chamber. We've managed to punch a hole—small, but wide enough for me to crawl through. Fortunately for my banged-up hands, the inside surface of the hole is as smooth as polished marble.

Julian helps me out, and once my feet hit the floor, I brush away the dust on my clothes.

Mira and Eli stand with Virginia by the open doorway. I'm relieved to see that Virginia is unharmed, and a little disappointed to see that Eli is fine too. Mira's eyes dart back and forth, scanning for outside threats, while Eli gives me a once-over, as if confirming to himself that I am all in one piece. "Based on your little display, I would say phase three is all systems go." He climbs over some rubble, motioning for us to follow. Eli's mention of phase three makes me squirm.

As Julian and I move toward the exit, I place my hand on his shoulder. The buzz between us is entirely gone, and I'm glad. "Thanks for telling me to push back there while you were pulling. It really helped me to focus." I grimace. "Though I'm sure our success had more to do with your effort than mine."

"Our effort?" Julian scrunches his eyebrows together. "No, Felicia. That was all you."

"You mean . . . you had nothing to do with getting me out?" I shake my head in disbelief.

"No." He puts his index finger to his lips, indicating we should be quiet, and then whispers, "And frankly I'm surprised you aren't a quivering mass of jelly after a stunt like that."

He's right. I should be out cold. But aside from some minor aches and pains, I feel fine. Good, even. I keep my voice low. "Where are we going? Another hideout?" I catch sight of my nine remaining nails. The polish is scraped off, uneven. I imagine a full set of smooth, perfectly oval nails, and they're mine. I could get used to this.

Julian nods. "The plan is to meet up with the others at the main rebel base. Assess our strength."

"Did the Morati cause the hive to collapse?" I ask.

"The Morati receive no benefit from destroying hives."

"Then who did it?" I assume it wasn't the rebels, since the cave-in could've hurt me or them.

Julian shrugs his shoulders. "That's a good question." It is. Perhaps a higher power is finally interfering? If so, it's about time.

In front of us Mira and Virginia tiptoe along the corridor while Eli trudges beside them like a tank. As we follow, I survey the damage around us. The great majority of the hives are intact—pristine, even. Maybe only one in twenty has been affected, some worse than others. I peek back at our former hideout. Though the walls still stand, most of the roof has collapsed. It's no wonder I was buried.

We walk for a long time, pausing only for brief periods to give Virginia short bursts of chamber time. Sometimes Eli carries her to avoid having to stop. The silence Julian and I share is companionable for once. We touch each other casually to point out cracks and crumbling hives we come across, and Julian laughs when I imitate Eli's heavy gait. These welcome distractions help me to stay focused on putting one foot in front of the other. I don't want to think about what phase three might cost me. And I fear if I dwell on the Morati threat, on which people they might be infecting at this moment with the Phlegethon and turning into attack zombies, I might wish for a swift end and throw myself under the next cave-in.

At first I think the diminishing amount of light as we continue our trek through the hives is a trick of my tiring mind, but when I turn and look behind me, I notice a stark difference between the way we've come and the gloomy horizon ahead. The shadows grow fuller, the atmosphere more oppressive.

My pace slows, almost as if my body dreads going any closer. Julian leans toward me, his elbow knocking against mine. "Fog rolling in," he whispers. "We should take shelter." I stay close on his heels, and we duck into a hive, one that now resembles an abandoned hovel. The others are already inside, and Mira and Eli put their materialization skills to good use to make the place more comfortable. In fact, Mira re-creates the entire furniture set from our ruined hideout, right down to the throw pillows.

"Is this where we'll meet the rest of the rebels?" I ask.

"Oh, no." Mira laughs. "It's a rest stop on our journey. Luckily for you and Virginia, a couple of the chambers here still function."

"Actually, I don't think I need to go in anymore," I say as I set Virginia's profile for her. She gets in gratefully. "I'm totally cured."

"Yes, you are over your addiction," Mira says, glancing quickly at Julian as if to gauge his reaction to her words. He keeps his face blank. "The point of going in the chamber now is to build up your mental toughness by reliving some of your less pleasant memories. But then, I think you already know that."

Mira's right. Reliving my betrayal of Autumn hurt, but it also made me stronger. One of these times I might even be ready to face the memory of my death—though, it would certainly undermine the rebels' plan for me if I were able to move on. "Yeah, okay. But where are we? Why all the fog?"

"We're on the edge of the isolation plains. We must cross it to meet up with the others at our headquarters," explains Eli.

At his mention of the isolation plains, my ears perk up. That's where Beckah might be. I can look for her. Save her. "Great." I fake a yawn. "I guess I'll go ahead and plug in, then. Build up some mental toughness."

I inspect a couple of the chambers until I find one that works, and I scoot in. It takes less than a minute to pull up my profile and decide what unpleasant memory I should access.

Ward, Felicia. Memory #31551
Tags: Germany, Mother, Nervous breakdown
Number of Views: 1
Owner Rating: Not rated
User Rating: Not shared

I slam my cell phone twice against my desk. "Dammit! Why won't you pick up?" It's been a week since Autumn's meltdown and Julian's mysterious disappearance. I've seen Autumn at school, and the looks she's been giving me, when she acknowledges my presence at all, are as sharp as icicles. I don't need to call her to know she won't answer. But Julian? Did he flat-out bail on me because the drama got too hot?

I heave my book bag onto my bed and then upend it to pour out its contents. Balled-up papers bounce off my bedspread and roll onto the carpet, joining the sea of candy wrappers, empty cola cans, and discarded dirty clothes. I have a makeup exam in physics tomorrow and need to study if I am going to improve upon my D+, the lowest grade I've ever gotten in my life. I owe my second chance to my excellent track record, and Mr. Hall's squeamishness about "women's issues."

I shuffle through my books and break out in a cold sweat. I've managed to bring every book home except the one I need. I rub my temples and blow out my breath in short bursts. Don't panic. Don't panic. Don't panic.

My stomach sinking, I go through my options, each more pathetic and desperate than the last. I could fake sick tomorrow and hope Mr. Hall takes pity on me again. I could go to Autumn's and beg to borrow her book. Or I could borrow Mother's car keys once she falls asleep and break into the school to get my study materials from my locker.

That last option has me giggling hysterically. When I sober, I absentmindedly dial Julian again. Still the message that his number's been disconnected.

Lost in thought, I don't even hear my mother come into the apartment until she's right outside my bedroom door. "Felicia?" she calls. "You home?"

I bolt across the room and wedge myself through the door, blocking her view into my room. Last thing I need right now is her nosing around. "Hi, Mother. You're home early."

"I thought we could cook dinner together tonight," she says, moving to turn on the hallway light. When she flips the switch, she gasps. "You look terrible! Are you sick?" I'm dimly aware I don't look my best. Because I haven't done laundry in weeks, I've resorted to the dregs of my closet—a pair of saggy jeans with grass-stained knees and a Frankfurt consulate T-shirt from an open house last year. I didn't bother to put on any makeup today, my hair is stringy, and the skin around my eyes is tender and puffy.

Mother approaches me and places the back of her hand against my forehead. "You're clammy. Why don't you tell me what's wrong." She pushes against my door.

"No!" I shout wildly, pulling on the doorknob so she can't enter my room.

"What's gotten into you? Open this door right now!" She says it with authority, in her best *Don't mess with me or else* voice.

"It's my room," I say. "And you're not allowed to come in."

Mother crosses her arms. She is not amused. "I'll give you three seconds. Three . . . two . . . one . . ."

When I don't budge after her countdown, Mother's eyes go wide. "Are you disobeying me?" she screeches. "What are you hiding from me?"

"Nothing."

She backs away, as if giving up, and then lunges at the door, forcing it open. Triumphant, she marches into my room. She doesn't make it far before she spins and stares at me disbelievingly. "What is this mess?"

As furious as I am with her trespassing, I know if she has taken it this far, I need to tread carefully. I bend down and start picking up clothes to put into the hamper. "I've been so busy . . . studying . . . I've let a few things fall by the wayside."

"Yes. You have." Her lips are pursed as she scans my room, and her eyes zoom in on the books and papers strewn across my bed. She plucks one of the balled-up papers from the floor and smoothes it out. It's a pop quiz from my German class this morning. She shakes her head, grabbing at the rest of my school papers and uncovering my red badges of shame.

"You can't have been studying very hard if you've been getting these grades. C, C minus, C, B minus, C plus . . . I've been much too lenient with you." She sees my cell phone, still in my hand, and her eyes narrow. "I'll take that," she says as she snatches it from me. "Until you get your grades back up, no phone, no friends, no TV."

"How are you going to enforce that?" I scoff. "You're never here."

She reaches over and grabs the skin above my elbow, twisting it in a painful pinch. "Do I need to get you a baby-sitter, young lady?"

I glare at her, but I say nothing. Finally she stalks out of my room, taking my papers with her. I slam the door behind her, then slide down it and grunt in frustration. "I hate you, I hate you, I hate you." I chant the words under my breath, wishing I were ballsy enough to spit them in Mother's face. Then I jump up and tear back my bedspread, causing all my books to scatter onto the floor. I dive face-first into my pillow and beat my fists against my mattress.

I no longer care about my stupid test tomorrow, or Autumn, or Julian or my mother or any of this crap. I just want things to be normal again, to sleep without slipping into the same terrifying nightmare. The one where I'm trapped. Where my heart palpitates so fast, it might burst. Where a sinister presence shines with otherworldly light. I am so tired. So, so, so tired . . .

I open my eyes with a start, and for several terrifying seconds I think I've awakened in my nightmare. But then I hear the low voices of Mira and Eli, and I remember where I am. I lie still, straining to hear what they're saying. I catch only bits and pieces, but it seems like Mira is stressing my importance to the mission and how dearly the Morati would like to capture me. Could phase three entail using me as bait or as a trade? I wouldn't put that past Eli or Mira. But then why would they go to the trouble of training me? I must have some other purpose—and I wish I had enough power to force them to be honest with me. Probably God himself couldn't manage to get the whole truth out of these three.

Careful not to trip on the debris outside my borrowed chamber, I clamber out.

Mira looks up from her conversation with Eli, bemused. "Feeling stronger?" she asks, wrinkling her nose. "Can we finally ditch these digs?"

I tap Virginia on her arm, and she disengages from her session. She pets the sleeve of my sweater and looks up at me. "Say, how do I go about getting something besides this plain, itchy shift?" I'm relieved she's back to her old self.

"I don't think you're strong enough yet, but once you are, I'll show you how you can wear anything you want."

"Cool," she says.

"We're ready when you are," I confirm to Mira. "Where's Julian?"

"He's outside on lookout duty," she says. She springs off the sofa and dematerializes the furniture.

We walk through the door together, and are immediately swallowed by the fog. It furls around me, probing, skimming the surface of my skin. It whistles a somber tune, so heart-rendingly sad, it makes me want to curl into a ball and rock myself into oblivion. "Stay close," says Julian in my ear as he links his arm through mine. "And think happy thoughts."

With Julian as a buoy, I glide safely though the fog. "Depression gas," says Julian. "Derived from the Kokytos, the underworld river of lamentation. The Morati use it as a border around the isolation plains."

Mira frowns deeply. She and Eli are supporting a totally wrecked-looking Virginia between them. "More potent than ever before too." Not potent enough to affect any of them, though, I guess. Maybe because they've been out and active longer than we have?

The plains are wide open, a vast expanse of white. When I squint, I can see they're dotted with slabs of gray, like a graveyard right after a heavy snow. Mira explains that these structures are where the isolated people are housed.

As we get deeper into the plains, I realize the whiteness comes not only from the smooth polished surface of the ground, but also from a strange moss that gets deeper and thicker as we walk, until it feels like we're wading shin-deep in cotton candy. Plodding through, I reach out to search for Beckah, concentrating on picturing her shy smile. I feel the presence of many souls, and I sense their suffering. This is a terrible place to end up—cut off from the net, cut off from all contact with others. I steady my thoughts and keep throwing out my line, hoping to reel Beckah in.

With each step, with each failed scan, my mind grows wearier. I've nearly given up on finding Beckah, when I sense a brain wave I recognize. It's her. I've found her! I home in on her signal and break out in a sprint, the others hot on my heels.

When I reach her, I pry open the tiny, hivelike sepulcher that encases her. Julian helps me lift the heavy lid, and I gasp when I see Beckah lying supine, her hands crossed at the neck, eyes open, blank and sightless.

Without the net architecture, I have to try to enter Beckah's mind directly. But when I bear down, ready to grasp the first thought I find, I recoil in shock. Beckah's mind is nothing but static.

CHAPTER 17

"SHE IS GONE," Eli says dispassionately. "And we have to keep moving."

I run my hands over Beckah's face, refusing to believe there's no chance for her, that this body is just an empty shell. "No! There has to be a way!" I chew my lip, racking my brain for some strategy, some inspiration—anything that would bring Beckah back. "Tell me there's a way, Julian. Please!"

Julian shakes his head sadly and tugs on my sleeve. "Eli's right. We have to go. There is nothing more we can do."

I rip out of his grasp and shake Beckah's shoulders—first gently, but increasingly violently. "Wake up! C'mon, Beckah. Wake up!" Her head lolls back and forth, and her arms flail like a rag doll's. White moss flutters around us, and I almost wish it would swallow me whole.

"Scanner drones!" hisses Mira. "Julian, take Felicia to safety, now!"

As quick as a flash, Julian throws me over his shoulder feet-first like I'm nothing more than a goose-down pillow. "No!" I cry out as I thrash against him. "We can't leave her here!"

As Julian runs back the way we came, he clamps his hand over my mouth. I see Eli and Mira waving their arms at the scanner drones, Virginia terrified between them. The scanner drones veer toward them, hovering low, making figure eights as they go. Once they're close enough, their amber light spills over Virginia, rooting her to the spot. I scream, but it comes out as a gurgle against Julian's hand. Eli and Mira push back against the beams that try to trap them.

I don't know what happens next because we arrive at the fog. Julian barrels me through, insisting everything will be fine, in an attempt to counteract the wailing wraiths of mist. The mist tells me I'm a failure for not being able to save Beckah, that I'm a bad friend for abandoning Virginia. I know it's right. I had my chance for redemption and I failed.

We arrive at the hive we just left, and Julian curses. As I attempt to swallow down my despair, I notice that all the chambers inside have collapsed. I won't be plugging in here.

Julian sets me back on my feet and drags me into the corridor, toward the other hives and away from the isolation plains.

"Why are we backtracking?" I struggle against his firm grip. "We need to meet up with the others. . . ." I have to know that at least Virginia is okay, even as I admit to myself that Beckah is a lost cause.

Julian doesn't stop but ducks into another hive, surveying the damage. "What we need to do is lie low. Get you into a chamber and calmed down."

I go limp, stop fighting him. It doesn't matter anymore. Julian always seems to get his way. "I'm calm. You can let go now."

He regards me with skepticism but complies.

I massage the skin of my forearm and then yank the cuff of my sweater back over my wrist. "Thanks."

Detecting movement on the horizon in the direction of the hives, I squint to get a better look. It's a pair of humans, like us. I materialize binocular glasses and then gasp, covering my mouth with my hand. Julian knocks me into a recess between hives. "What did you see?" he demands.

"They're humans . . . but . . . I think they're infected with that rage river virus Eli was taking about." I shiver. "They're shuffling around and sniffing at the air."

Then we hear it, a bone-shattering roar of rage.

Julian curses under his breath. "They saw us!"

I peek out from my hiding place and see the infected drones racing at us, their eyes popping out with rage, their mouths foaming and spitting. At their pace they'll be upon us within seconds.

"Get a weapon!" Julian commands, materializing a bow and a quiver of arrows. He strings the first arrow and aims at the head of the larger drone. The arrow pierces his eye, causing him to stumble. But not fall.

As Julian strings his second arrow, I look at him in a daze. I can't think.

"Felicia! Do you want them to infect you, too?" His second arrow hits the man's other eye, but even blinded he keeps coming.

I steady myself and will giant-size darts into my hands. The man is innocent, and I don't want to hurt him, but I don't know how else to keep him from attacking us. I call up a burst of energy and heave it forward to slam the smaller man to the ground. Then I send the five darts flying, pinning him down to incapacitate him. My aim is true. The man roars and spits, his limbs popping and jerking so wildly, I have to think of a slab of bacon frying in a skillet.

Julian has shot the blinded man a third time—through the forehead—but it hasn't even slowed him down. He's close, leaping and tearing at the air, poised to strike at Julian. Julian drops his bow and materializes a sword. When the man claws toward Julian's face, Julian lops off his head in a clean slice.

I cautiously approach the man I peppered with darts. Despite all his gurgling, moaning, and hissing—and the prominent veins straining against his skin like cords ready to burst—I can recognize him as a man in his late twenties. Someone's son. Someone's boyfriend or husband. Maybe even someone's father. He's a chilling testimony to how far the Morati are willing to go.

"Chop off his head, and he'll disappear," says Julian,

coming over and putting a reassuring hand on my shoulder. "See, the other guy is dissolving into nothingness as we speak." He offers me his sword.

"To cycle back through again, right?"

"Probably. But with everything that's been changing around here, I honestly don't know what the rules are anymore."

My eyes flit back and forth between the man's eerie, possessed eyes and the sword. Is it better to leave him here or put him out of his misery? I take Julian's sword and raise it above the man's head, but I can't do it. My conscience won't let me. Instead I let the sword clatter to the ground.

"He's a goner either way. Even if you don't strike the killing blow . . . you contributed."

"Let's just go," I say, unable to look at the man again.

Julian sighs. He picks up the sword, and the man's godawful cries cease. I can't believe Julian can be so calm about killing two people, especially when my nerves are run ragged. I mean sure, technically they're already dead, but he was so casual about it, so steady, it makes me wonder if he's killed before.

"I don't like this at all," he says. His whole body is on alert as he scans our surroundings. "Scanner drones should have picked up their activity and headed this way. . . . Something's up."

"Maybe the scanner drones are otherwise occupied," I suggest. "Taking Virginia back to their lair."

"Don't worry so much. I told you she'll be fine!" He nudges me toward a still intact hive, and we enter.

Julian materializes the same eggplant-colored sofa I've come to know so well. I sink into it, and Julian sits beside me, propping up my chin with his knuckles. He tries to catch my eye, but I refuse to look at him. "You're safe," he says.

"For now. But for how long?" Everything is falling apart, and I can barely hold myself together anymore.

Julian pulls me into an embrace, rocks me slowly, kisses the top of my head. "Shhh . . . We'll lie low here for a while and then join everyone at base. They're fine. You'll see."

"Beckah definitely won't be fine."

"No," he agrees. "Beckah's gone. A victim of the war. She was your friend and you honor her with your courage, but you have to let her go now."

"You have no right to comfort me," I say, lashing out at him. "You helped do this to her."

Julian sighs. "I told you, I didn't know about that." He crosses his heart and then hovers his finger above my heart, making the same motions. "If it had been up to me, I would have done things differently."

"Oh, yeah?" I scoff, disbelieving. "Like what?"

He shifts his weight and settles in next to me. "Well, first of all, I would have come for you a lot sooner."

I finally ask the question that has gnawed at me forever. "Why did you leave that night at the Irish pub? You didn't even say good-bye."

"Do you have regrets?" he asks, his voice raw. "If you could go back and do one thing differently, what would you change?"

Just one thing? Hard to say with all the mistakes I've made. But I know the most likely answer is one Julian won't want to hear. "Autumn and I should've never gone to the sushi restaurant that day," I say carefully, not looking over at him. "I should have never met you."

I steel myself for an angry outburst, but Julian merely chuckles. "Not that I really want to bring up my competition, but you do know that if you'd never met me, you might have never met Neil. You see, I am a part of you . . . like it or not."

I nod, conceding his point, but hating that he knows so much about me. "So what would you do differently?" I ask.

He leans in closer. "I wouldn't have left you that night," he says so softly, I have to strain to hear him. "At the time, I thought I had to go, that it would be better to make a clean break."

"That's your big regret?" I ask, incredulous. "I can't imagine I was ever that important to you."

He reaches over and touches my cheek, turning my head toward his. "Do you even realize the effect you have on me?" His voice cracks with emotion. "I tried to forget about you. To go on living my life. But I never could."

Julian's confession shocks me, but it doesn't change anything. I lift my hand to his on my cheek and pull it away gently. "Don't do this, Julian. You know I love Neil."

"Wait. So tell me this . . ." He regards me with a calculating expression. "Do you really think, if you hadn't died, you'd still be with Neil? I mean, you didn't know him long enough to say definitively that you'd be together forever. You were only seventeen. You don't go making lifelong commitments at that age."

Ahh . . . another of his ploys to push me off balance. But I never have allowed myself to question my love for Neil. I won't start now. It's the kind of thing that can drive you crazy if you've had enough time to think about it. And I have. Centuries, at least, by the feel of it.

Instead of answering Julian, I place his hand in his lap and get up, turning away from him because I don't want to see his reaction. I have an overwhelming urge to visit Neil, to find comfort in my memories of him. I slip into a chamber and pull up a memory.

Ward, Felicia. Memory #32689
Tags: Ohio, Neil, True love waits
Number of Views: 67
Owner Rating: 3 stars
User Rating: 2 stars

"You think I should go up in front of the whole church and sign the card, don't you?" I huff, turning down the volume on the radio.

Neil flips the turn signal and smoothly changes lanes. "I don't think that. Some 'concerned congregation members' think that. Maybe Pastor Joe thinks that." He reaches over and rubs my knee. "I think you should do what you're comfortable with."

I stare at the road ahead in silence. Our meeting with Pastor Joe has upset me greatly. Why do people have to get into our private business? Why do they need me to make some public pledge to save my virginity for marriage? We've been together fewer than six weeks, and already they suspect me of corrupting Neil? Sure we've "slept together," if you count our increasingly frequent afternoon naps in Neil's bed, but it has never been anything more than innocent cuddling and kissing. I've yet to even see him without his shirt, for God's sake.

I pull the book Pastor Joe gave me from my bag. "*Passion and Purity*," I read the title aloud and then thumb through it in disgust. I remember the title from one of my discussions with Savannah. She swears by it. She even told me, without a trace of irony, that "Thou shalt remain a virgin until marriage" is the lost eleventh commandment. I shove the book back into my bag. Neil doesn't comment.

"And how do they know if I even am a virgin anymore? I can't pledge something I don't have," I say, kicking at the floorboard under my feet.

But when I glance over at Neil and see how still he has gone, I rush to reassure him. "I mean, I am. But it's not because I signed some silly piece of paper." I snort. "It's because my mother always told me if I had sex, I'd get pregnant and my future would be ruined." I raise my voice. "But you know what, Mother? Looks like my future is already ruined, so I might as well do the deed, right?"

Neil emits a strangled noise from his throat and starts to cough furiously.

"Are you okay?" I ask.

"Uh . . . fine." He brakes at the stop sign and then turns right. "But you know your future isn't ruined. We've discussed this. Like a zillion times."

Despite the fact that I still haven't confided my checkered past to him, Neil keeps insisting I have a bright future. And I guess if everything were up to him, maybe I would. But that's not how the world works.

"Yeah, well. I'm still not convinced," I say, twisting the strap of my bag. "And what about your future? Have you considered that, because of me, you could lose your position as worship leader? And everything you've worked for?"

Neil taps his index finger on the steering wheel, thinking. Finally he asks, "Is there any way you would consider making the pledge? I mean, not for them. For you."

I'm not sure of the protocol here. It's like church is some foreign country and I missed out on the cultural briefing. I started going because Grammy needed me to drive her. I started to enjoy going because Neil was there. But that doesn't mean I've bought into the idea that God cares if I stay pure or not.

"It's nothing I was ever confronted with before," I say honestly. "I always figured someday I'd fall in love, and sex would happen naturally. I never thought I'd need to be married necessarily. And now everyone's pushing the issue. I . . . don't think I'm ready to make such a commitment."

Neil pulls into his driveway, puts the car in park, and kills the engine. "But you know I've made the pledge. . . ." He looks at me for confirmation.

I squirm in my seat. "Yeah . . ."

"And I do take it seriously."

My heart sinks. "Does that mean . . . you want to break up with me?" I ask in a small voice.

"No—of course not!" Neil's denial is forceful. He unlatches his seat belt, leans over to brush wayward strands of hair behind my ear, and lets his hand rest on my neck. "Every relationship has its hurdles . . . and the big test is if you still want to be with someone despite those hurdles. And I do. I want to be with you."

I nod. "So if you aren't breaking up with me, and I'm not signing the pledge, then . . ."

Neil sighs. "Well, my parents won't be happy about it, but if the congregation insists, then I'll give up the worship leader position." My heart swells, but I'm scared, too.

"And everyone will think you're getting it on with a slut," I say sarcastically, instantly regretting my words when Neil reacts as if he's been slapped.

"I hate that word." Neil draws back and unlocks his car door. "And I told you—I don't care what everyone thinks." He gets out, walks around the car, and opens my door for me. He's not smiling.

I put my bag on my shoulder and get out. "What about what Andy thinks? Didn't he warn you to stay away from me?" Andy also told me that Neil has a weakness for damaged girls, that I'm another in a long line of his mission projects. He accused me of taking advantage of Neil's kind-heartedness, and told me it was his job as Neil's best friend to look out for him.

"Right, like Andy's anyone who can afford to be judgmental."

Face-to-face, we regard each other a long moment. I

sigh and run my hand down his cheek. "I appreciate what you're willing to sacrifice for me . . . but you shouldn't have to. I can't ask that of you. I can't." I lower my hand and hang my head, biting my lip.

Neil draws me into a fierce hug. "Look, we'll figure it out, okay?" He kisses my forehead. I want so much to believe him.

As we walk into his house, Sugar runs to the door and rubs her face against Neil's shin, meowing. I'm struck by a sudden, irrational jealousy when I see her. Maybe because her relationship with Neil is well defined, without any of these squishy gray areas and emotional land mines.

"Tea?" Neil asks, laughing as he picks up Sugar to carry her into the kitchen.

I laugh too. The tea question has become our inside joke, since every time Neil brews it, we forget to drink it. I've made Neil waste a lot of tea. I just hope I don't make him waste his life, too.

I'm cozy and thinking of warm tea when the harsh glow of my hologram screen breaks into my consciousness. I twitch. Someone's touching me, running fingers through my hair.

"Felicia?"

I groan, not wanting to open my eyes. "What, Julian?"

"I have been sitting here this whole time, thinking about you and me. About us."

I sit up and look at him full on. Is he delusional? "There is no us."

He acts like he doesn't hear me. "We can break away

from the rebels. Let them fight the Morati and see where the chips fall. If we stay out of it, we have a chance to live."

I've avoided thinking too much about the personal consequences of waging this war, but it makes sense that there's a good chance I won't make it out "alive." Would he really be willing to help me escape the Morati and the rebels? Would I be willing to leave Virginia with them if it meant a new chance for finding Neil?

"Maybe you're right." I throw my legs over the side of the chamber and push myself out. "We could run off, find Neil, and all live happily ever after. Assuming the rebels manage to defeat the Morati without us, that is." Saying it out loud, it all seems so absurd.

"You're still going on about Neil?" he asks, a nasty edge creeping into his voice. "You sound like a broken record."

"Of course I am," I say, annoyed. "You told me you'd help me find him, but you haven't kept that promise. But you know what? I don't need you anymore. I can find people on my own now." Okay, so I haven't found anyone but Beckah, but I won't give up easily.

Julian crosses his arms and smirks. "You won't find Neil."

"Sure I will," I say, jutting out my chin.

"You won't," Julian repeats. "Because Neil is still on Earth."

CHAPTER 18

"BUT HOW CAN THAT BE?" My eyes cloud over, and I feel like I'm going to faint. "I've been dead for so long, Neil would've died by now too."

Julian starts pacing, reminding me of a high school teacher about to impart an important lesson. "Time exists differently here. It's been only two Earth years since you died."

"Two years?" I lean on the wall next to the chamber for support. "Why didn't you tell me? Why did you lie?"

Julian clenches his jaw. "I didn't lie. I said I know where Neil is. And I do. He's on Earth."

"Seriously?" I'm so frustrated with Julian, I could scream. "You think you can get off on a technicality? You let me believe I could find Neil. Here. In Level Two."

"You can find him," Julian says nonchalantly. "There's a window to Earth here."

I perk up. "Really? Where?"

Julian materializes three bowling pins and starts juggling, as if he's totally over our conversation.

"Where's this window, Julian?" I ask again, my anger mounting to the point where I push one of his pins with my mind.

The pin drops to the ground, and Julian bends to pick it up with a huff. "The window is in the Morati's palace. Ask them to give you a glimpse of what your boyfriend is up to these days. I'm sure they'd oblige." He covers his mouth but not soon enough to disguise a smirk.

"Are you serious? Or are you lying again?" I don't know what to believe anymore.

"I wasn't lying before," Julian insists. "I'm not lying now. I even saw it for myself once."

So that's it, then. Unless Neil dies soon, which I hope he doesn't, he won't come here for a very, very long time. And who's to say that by then he'll still care at all about me? He'll probably live a long life, get the worship leader position back, marry someone worthy of his goodness, be happy. There's no room for me in such a scenario.

And if I could get past the Morati and summon his image up using this portal? It'd be bittersweet at best, heart-wrenching at worst. All I have of him are my memories, and they are not nearly enough. And if the rebels somehow do defeat the Morati, will I be able to let go of Neil and move on to whatever comes next, or will Neil be a stone that keeps me tied to this dimension indefinitely, waiting for some measure of closure? The energy I have built up inside me since Julian broke me out of my hive ebbs away, like an ocean at low tide.

Julian must notice my change in mood, because he brushes my hair back over my ear with his fingers in a gesture that's probably meant to be comforting. "The truth hurts, doesn't it? I didn't want to tell you . . . but you forced my hand."

"You should have told me back at my hive," I say.

"No, I couldn't. You wouldn't have come with me. We needed you. *I* needed you." He takes my hand and rubs semicircles in my palm. "I still do."

I don't even have enough will left to tear my hand away. "Oh, don't start that again." A weak protest, but he retreats.

We stand there in silence. For the first time in forever, I have no idea what I want to do. Would I be better off fleeing with Julian and then ditching him the first chance I get? Going back to the rebels so I can at least make sure Virginia is safe? If I stay in a hive, chances are I'll be picked up by the Morati and infected with the rage virus. I may be emptied out, but I couldn't stand to be filled with that.

"If we do go on the run," I say, musing aloud, "won't Eli be able to find me again, because he's touched me? We wouldn't get very far."

Julian snorts. "Well, first of all, a far more important

basis for finding people is a deep connection and mutual affection. Like a long-standing friendship, familial bonds, or a committed romance. Eli touched you, yes. But you barely know each other. His power to find you will fade over time."

"But what if it doesn't fade fast enough? Eli could be looking for me right now, and he's found me before."

"They all likely headed to rebel headquarters, which is across the isolation plains. We're still on the other side, so Eli can't reach you because of the fog interference." Julian moves toward the door. "But whatever we do, we shouldn't stay here. It'll help to get some distance between us and them, at least while we figure out a new plan."

"Yeah, okay," I tell him, materializing a hair band and pulling my hair back into a ponytail. I follow him, ready to run.

Julian peeks out the door, and then jumps back, knocking into me. "Change of plans," he says as he whirls around to face me, his eyes huge. "We are going to have to go through the isolation plains."

"What do you mean?" I thought he just said we shouldn't go that way if we want to avoid the rebels.

"An army of the infected is out there, and that means some of the Morati are probably with them." He grabs my shoulders. "Stay close to me. Don't look behind you."

Julian slips out of the hive and flattens himself against its cracking wall. I do the same. We advance quickly toward the fog, picking our way through debris as we try to stay out of sight. I think I hear hissing behind me, but I keep my sights ahead, pushing down my panic.

At the border to the isolation plains, Julian takes my hand. The fog is denser than before. I can see nothing, and if it weren't for Julian's fingers curled around mine, I might think I have ceased to exist. The fog howls my name over and over until I want to claw all consciousness from my head and forget who I am. But Julian pulls me steadily, and guides me to the other side.

The fog has invaded my throat, and I choke it out with a cough. As we run through the isolation plains, Julian holds on to me tightly. He probably thinks I'll try to save Beckah again, but I know now she's a lost cause. I say a little prayer for her when we pass by her mini-hive, and I silently beg for her forgiveness for not being able to help.

Gradually the white moss grows deeper and thicker, shin deep, knee deep, until it's like a morass around my thighs. I imagine sinking into it, suffocating.

"Don't worry—this is the deepest point," assures Julian. "We've almost made it."

We reach a steep incline and climb up, and when I look back to survey the plains behind us, I stub my toe. Have I accidentally walked into one of the tomblike hives?

No, it's not a hive but a low wall surrounding a fountain. The clearest, most inviting blue water I've ever seen gurgles out of it, and my heart fills with the desire to submerge myself in its depths. As if in a trance, I pull out of Julian's grasp, but he catches me before I can dive in.

"No! That's the Lethe fountain." He twists me around to face him and shakes my shoulders. "If you drink of it, you will forget yourself forever."

Maybe that's what I want. Finally I am getting a chance to let everything go and to swim in eternal bliss. Before Neil, I would've done it in a heartbeat. And now? I wrestle with myself. There's the part of me that begs for release. Beckah's all but gone. Virginia's probably captured. Neil is lost to me. Who's left but Julian? And he's merely someone who thinks obsession equals love. Then there's also the part that assures me I'm strong, that giving up is not an option.

"Let me make my own choice, Julian."

He looks at me, his eyes pleading, but he lets me go.

I kneel beside the wall and reach out the fingers of my right hand to the water, skimming over its turquoise surface, and breathe in the fine mist. It's heavenly, so much so that my thoughts begin to float away like soap bubbles on a breeze. I lean in, closer and closer, until the tip of my nose is submerged in the warm pool, until my lips touch liquid, parting to let my tongue taste sweet release from all my pain.

But before I can take a sip, I picture Neil and think of his unwavering belief that our trials shape who we are and make us stronger. Yes, I've lost him. But I don't have to lose myself.

Gasping, I pull back and collapse at Julian's feet.

"You passed the test," he says simply as he helps me up and pulls me into a hug. There's not a trace of passion in it, just relief, and I burrow my head into his chest.

I almost threw myself away. But I didn't, and now I know I never could.

After the fountain we cross through the northern border of the fog, and this time its cries barely register. Then we're back among the hives. This quadrant has more damage, more crumbled hives, and more debris to climb over and avoid.

"I know you probably don't want to hear this, but I think our only chance for survival at this point is to go to rebel headquarters like we originally planned," says Julian as we run. "I've seen the army—and if we stay on our own, we're going to be swept away."

As much as I dread seeing Eli—being used by Eli—it's still the best option to join the rebels against the Morati. The two rage-infected drones were threatening enough; I can't imagine facing a whole army by ourselves. "I agree."

Julian trots over to a nearby hive, still completely intact, and signals for me to follow. He taps the code, and we're in. "Let's take a tactical break. You toughen yourself up with the most horrible memory you can think of, and I'll work on contacting Mira and Eli to see what they know."

Fortunately, this hive is only about three-fourths full, giving me plenty of berths to choose from.

I need to be as strong as possible for our reunion with the rebels. It's time to face the memory I most dread, the one that scares me even more than reliving my own death. I take comfort in telling myself that I don't have to go all in.

I can fight to float above, like I did when I fixed my damaged campfire memory with Neil and inserted myself into Virginia's Ouija board memory. I place my fingers in the grooves, lighting up the screen, and then go in.

Ward, Felicia. Memory #31666
Tags: Germany, Autumn, Nightmare, Myanmar
Number of Views: 1
Owner Rating: Not rated
User Rating: Not shared

I'm Felicia, but I'm not. I'm her shadow twin, inexorably connected to her but physically detached. As much as I yearn to, I can't change the ending of this story. I can't whisper into her ear and tell her to make different choices—and even if I could somehow manipulate the memory, it wouldn't change what really happened. For I am a mere observer, and what she is about to experience for the first time is set in stone.

She's upset, or, better said, livid. Events of the past few weeks have had her simmering, and her latest setback—a meeting with Mr. Bennett where he kicked her out of his advanced writing seminar and asked Autumn to join instead—has finally caused her to boil over. It's lunchtime. She has classes yet to attend. Tests yet to take. But she can't breathe in the air of this school for one more second. She needs to escape.

We're on the bus now. Felicia is officially skipping for

the first time in her life. Her nostrils flare as she jabs her pen into the hideous fabric seat cover she's sitting on. Defacing public property. Add it to her growing list of crimes.

The consulate housing complex seems different this time of day. Most everyone she knows is at work, or school. The playground is booming. Shouts and squeals of happy toddlers worm their way into her consciousness, but she pushes them back. Shuts them out. Misery wants company, not a painful reminder that other people's lives are happy and uncomplicated.

Slamming her way into the apartment, Felicia wants nothing more than to strip off her clothes and stand for hours under scalding hot water. But that is not to be. Because when she enters her bedroom, she's greeted by the most gruesome sight she can imagine, and at first she thinks it must be some sort of sick joke Autumn is playing to get back at her.

But the stench. That's what finally convinces her that what she's seeing is real. Autumn is dead, lying spread-eagle on Felicia's bed, her mouth open, her eyes empty. She's crisscrossed with deep slashes that have bled crimson onto her once white tank and shorts, and Felicia's once white bedspread. Autumn is not going to get up ever again. Not to yell at her. Certainly not to forgive her.

Felicia's eyes grow huge with that realization, and time seems to slow, to shift. She has the sensation of weightlessness, the feeling that the atoms that make up her body could separate and scatter at any moment. She recognizes this state of mind. It's what she felt in Nairobi that day when the muggers attacked her. And her nightmare begins, the same nightmare she had in Nairobi and ever since then.

Light surrounds her, crushes her as it invades her pores, blinding her with its brightness. It's ice. It's terror. It's pain. And then he appears. She can't yet see his face, just the soft curve of his cheek, shaggy blond hair, broad back, slim hips, strong legs. She gasps. Because she didn't know who he was back then, when she was at the cusp of thirteen. But she realizes she knows him quite well now. She has tangled her fingers in that hair, dug her fingernails into that back.

He turns then, his dark blue eyes flashing, his generous lips curving into a hard smile. "Time to go," he says.

She screams. She's huddled on the floor of her bedroom, heart pounding wildly. Why is Julian in her nightmare?

She can make even less sense of Autumn's death. She risks a closer look, sees the bloodied blades that made these cuts scattered across the bed. On the floor. Did Autumn do this to herself? Is it all Felicia's fault? Or was Autumn murdered? But why? She has no answers.

Felicia backs away from the bed, her mind a tangle of half-coherent thoughts. Her home is no longer safe. There could be a murderer on the loose, one who is not done killing. Or will the police think that Felicia murdered Autumn? Nicole can testify about the whole nasty incident that happened on Halloween night. The horrible things Felicia and Autumn shouted at each other afterward in the hallways at school. They'll say Felicia had motive. No one will believe her side of the story. She can't stick around and blindly hope they'll understand. She needs to go to her dad. Where is he? Myanmar? Yes, that's it. She needs to go to him. Right now. Before they come, before they look at her with accusing eyes and put her name on a list that prevents her from crossing borders. She's savvy about these things. She knows how they work.

Like a robot Felicia pulls a rolling suitcase out of her closet and throws some random clothes into it. Her passport. Some tiny shampoo bottles branded with the name of a hotel chain. She can't wash Autumn's blood out of her mind, but at least she'll have clean hair.

She grabs her laptop and the suitcase and stumbles through the living room and into the kitchen in a haze. She pulls the note off the fridge with Dad's contact details in Myanmar. She knows he's the only one who can make things all right. He'll believe her. He'll support her. He'll tell the police it wasn't her fault.

She has to buy a plane ticket, but how? Mother froze her credit card as part of her grounding. The TransAsiatic Airlines VPN. She pulls it up. She knows it's illegal, but she's desperate. She uses the password-cracking program Julian left on her laptop. Julian told her no one would know. No one would care. This is an emergency. There's no time for second-guessing. Once she's in, she hacks herself a seat in coach for the flight taking off in two hours. If she leaves now, she can make it.

She raids her mother's emergency cash stash. Two

hundred in U.S. dollars, three hundred in euros. It's not a lot, but it will have to do. Then she calls a cab, waits for it impatiently on the main street outside the housing complex. When the chatty cabdriver asks her questions about America, she answers him in monosyllables. He soon gives up and puts in a CD of Bollywood hits.

At check-in Felicia realizes she brought her diplomatic passport instead of her tourist passport. She's sure Myanmar grants tourist visas at the border, but she's not so sure about diplomatic visas. It's another concern on a long list of them. At each step along the way—passport control, boarding, the fourteen-hour flight to Bangkok, and the transfer to the smaller plane that will take her to Yangon—Felicia fears being outed as a criminal. Can they hear her racing heartbeat? Smell her guilt? My shadow self, the one who knows the bitter climax of this story, can do nothing but let myself be pulled along.

It's upon us. The moment of truth. The immigration officer in the diplomatic line at Yangon airport scrutinizes Felicia's passport. He calls a colleague, and they confer in harsh tones, in a language Felicia has no hope of understanding. Minutes seem to stretch into infinity as she waits for a verdict to be handed down. Finally the officer tells her to follow him. He shuts her in a stifling hot, windowless room with two plastic chairs and a small table.

Hours, days, centuries later, the door opens again. A man enters. American embassy staff. Says his name is Logan and hands her a plastic cup of water. Felicia gulps it down, rivulets running down her face. She's in a lot of trouble. They've contacted her father. Her mother. They know about her dead friend. They're arranging transport back to Frankfurt.

Dad arrives. He's frantic with worry. He scoops her up in his arms and holds her so tight, she can't breathe. But when he lets go of her, she shivers. His face is twisted in disappointment and confusion. He begs her to tell him what the hell she was thinking coming here without telling anyone. Why didn't she call the police when she found Autumn? Doesn't she know running makes her look guilty? Doesn't she realize that misusing her diplomatic passport can get her mother in trouble with the Foreign Service? And how did she pay for her plane ticket? But Felicia finds she can't speak. Can't find the words to fix what she's done, to erase the last twenty-four hours and return to a world where her dad has never looked at her this way. Where he is still proud to call her his daughter.

A wave of regret washes over Felicia, over me, her shadow self. It is so powerful that for an agonizing moment I am reunited with her, with my body. And I feel the full weight of the hopelessness of my situation.

CHAPTER 19

I AM FORCIBLY RIPPED AWAY from the memory chamber by an ice-cold hand around my throat. I come face-to-face with a host of beings so terrifyingly beautiful, so infused with otherworldly light, I'm struck dumb. The Morati. "Felicia," they hiss. "We have been looking for you."

They suspend my body in midair, and my eyes dart back and forth through the crumbling hive, searching for Julian. For an escape. The Morati's alabaster skin shines so brightly, they blur around the edges, making it hard for me to look directly at them.

"Wondering where Julian is?" the Morati taunt. They speak together, one voice but delivered from each and every terrible mouth. Its booming is loud but intimate at the same time. "He is on our side. He called us here."

No, it can't be. The Morati are lying, attempting to confuse me. Julian may be far from perfect, but he'd never give me over to them. I examine them in short bursts, looking for weaknesses. They have willowy yet muscular builds, and each is six feet tall at least, some taller, with gleaming silver hair that falls to the shoulders, and large silvery wings. Androgynous in their simple white tunics and pants, they are so scarily alike, they bleed into one another. I concentrate on the hand holding me up, and imagine it opening and dropping me. It works. As soon as I fall, I push against my jailers with my mind, trying to clear a path.

But there are too many of them. For every individual Morati that I repel, another five sink their icy fingers through my clothes, straight into my flesh, burning me.

"Silly girl," they hiss, like a thousand snakes coiled for attack. And then they suck in a powerful breath and exhale a dustlike cloud that fills up every molecule of the hive. It's like being plunged into an ocean and getting ensnared and entangled by seaweed. My mind can no longer hold out.

I am dimly aware of being lifted by a group of hands and passed on, like the crowd surf after a stage dive, but the fight has been leeched out of me. It's so much easier to let go. I fall into a memory chamber pod, and the Morati fit my hands into the grooves and close a glass lid over me. As seven of them, like pallbearers, carry the pod through the hive door, I float into a memory.

Ward, Felicia. Memory #32777
Tags: Ohio, Neil, Confession
Number of Views: 57 (partial views)
Owner Rating: Not rated
User Rating: Not shared

Careful not to wake Neil, I slowly untangle my arms and legs from his embrace and lift my head from the pillow to check the time. The neon numbers of his bedside alarm clock glow 4:30 p.m., meaning his parents won't be home for at least another two hours. Neil fell asleep straightaway when we got here after school, but I've just been lying here, my head against his chest listening to the steady beating of his heart, and his deep, measured breathing.

Usually, if I can't sleep, it's because of the multitude of thoughts racing through my mind. But not today. Because today my mind is at peace, a huge weight lifted off my shoulders. After wrestling with myself for weeks, I've decided I'm going to confess my sins to Neil. To lay bare my soul so he can see everything, and judge the dark with the light. Because I want a future with him, and that future has to start with a clean slate. No secrets between us.

A rush of affection for Neil bubbles up inside me, for this boy who fought to save me when everyone else abandoned me. He deserves the best I can give him. And I deserve the chance to give him my best.

I'm ready. I untangle Sugar from the crook of Neil's leg, and she mews in protest. Petting her, I carry her to the hallway and shut her out. I sit down on the edge of the bed and slip out of my clothes, kicking them to the floor before I chicken out. My skin prickles, and despite the warm air of Neil's bedroom, goose bumps run rampant across my body.

I take a deep breath and lie on my side in front of Neil. He still hasn't stirred. My hand shaking, I lift my index finger to Neil's lips and trace them lightly. Without opening his eyes, he groggily pulls me into a hug, his hands sliding over my shoulders and back. The sensation of skin on skin feels so right, I forget myself. Desperate for more contact, I push up his T-shirt and help him pull it over his head. We press together, his lips finding mine. If he asked, I would give him everything.

While we kiss I let my fingers trail across his smooth chest, down his sides, over his flat stomach. The way his body trembles at my touch makes me dizzy. My heart races faster than it ever has before in my life, and I slip my hand under the waistband of his jeans.

Neil tenses up, as if finally realizing he's not dreaming. His eyes pop open and he scrambles away from me, throwing his T-shirt at me in a frantic attempt to cover me up. "What . . . what are you doing?" he chokes out, his eyes wild from not knowing where to look.

His reaction is so not what I expected; I start to have

second thoughts. Maybe this isn't the best way to go about my confession. But I press on. "I'm ready. I want to tell you what happened to me, because I want you to see me. All of me."

"But you don't have to be naked for that!" He closes his eyes tightly, scrunching up his face in the process.

I feel like I've been slapped. Why is Neil so freaked out by seeing me naked? "I'm sorry. I didn't mean to disgust you." I am deeply ashamed. But also so deeply horrified, I can't bring myself to retrieve my clothes.

He opens his eyes and looks at me, searching my face, seeing the pain of his rejection etched there. "Oh, God, no. . . . How can you say that?" he asks, risking a tentative once-over of my body, drinking me in. "You're beautiful."

"Then what is it?" I ask, confused.

He takes a deep breath. "It's just . . . and don't take this the wrong way . . . but I don't want you to think you need to get, you know . . . physically intimate . . . in order to get emotionally intimate." He sounds disturbingly like Pastor Joe, and at first I want to call him on it, but then he laughs. "And honestly, if you don't cover up, I promise I won't hear a word you say anyway."

Blushing but relieved, I laugh too. "I'll put my clothes back on." I whip his shirt at his chest, and as he puts it back on, he rolls over to give me privacy. I get dressed quickly.

I sit cross-legged on his bed, facing him, and he mirrors my posture. He takes my hands in his and squeezes them encouragingly. It's as if the highly embarrassing scene before never took place. "Tell me."

And so I do. It comes out in a rush. The nightmares, the sneaking around with Julian, the confrontation with Autumn, my overwhelming feelings of guilt, and all the events of the horrible day when Autumn died and I fled. He doesn't interrupt me, doesn't look away in condemnation. He takes it all in, and as I confess each and every misdeed, I feel cleaner—as if with its telling, each black spot unsticks itself from my soul and flutters away.

I tell him about the aftermath, how the military police in Frankfurt interrogated me about Autumn's death, how reproachful eyes followed me wherever I went. Because I left her there, and didn't call the police or them, Autumn's parents refused to talk to me, and broke off their long-standing friendship with my family. I was cleared of wrongdoing but reprimanded for fleeing the scene. They couldn't say for certain if it was suicide or murder, but they couldn't pin her death on me because my alibi was rock solid. I was miles away in class at the official time of death. The case is still open as far as I know.

As for the hacked plane ticket, the airline settled with us out of court, and just like that, my family's modest savings disappeared. Even worse, my parents were forced to take out a loan to cover the rest. The State Department revoked my diplomatic passport, and Mother had to make a choice between her job and me. And my father had to choose between his wife and his daughter. I can't blame either for their decisions.

Having told him everything, I fall silent. Neil pulls me up off the bed and into a hug. "I'm glad you finally decided to trust me," he says.

"Me too." And I do. I feel like an entire new world has opened up before me. So maybe I'll never live up to my mother's once high expectations, but there's so much else I can do. For the first time in a long time, I feel like I could have a future. And Neil will be beside me. Maybe forever. Maybe only for a while. But I'm no longer scared to live my life and find out.

Boom! The memory chamber pod the Morati plugged me into thuds to the floor, pulling me out of my memory and thrusting me back into my terrifying new reality. The Morati bore their oily eyes into me, and my whole body spasms uncontrollably. What will they do with me? Lock me in the isolation plains? Infect me with their rage virus? Torture me until my mind is a barren wasteland like Beckah's?

But when they push forward to help me from the travel pod, they are surprisingly gentle. "You wonder about our plans for you."

I can only stare. We're in a cavernous round room with walls as blindingly white as the rest of the Morati's dominion. Narrow passageways lead off in every direction, and the high domed ceiling is decorated with flecks of silver and gold. Is this their palace?

"We must plug you into our mainframe." There are so many of them now, their voices sound like a deep hum when they speak.

The mainframe? "But why?"

"Because," their voices pulsate, "your energy is the essential element in our plan."

CHAPTER 20

WHY IS MY ENERGY specifically so important to them? I stare in confusion until it dawns on me their words make a strange sort of sense. If my energy is essential, then that's probably why the hives have been deteriorating. Because I've spent less time plugged in. What was once a symbiotic relationship—I needed the drugs the net gave me, and the net needed my energy to function properly—became increasingly one-sided as I conquered my addiction and started reserving my energy for myself.

"So only my energy will do?"

One of the Morati steps forward and raises an arm in the air, as if it is about to conduct an orchestra. The others fall back against the far wall, leaving us alone, relatively speaking. As they retreat, the radiance of the leader's skin dims. I can see now he's a young man, with features as chiseled and cold as a marble statue of a Greek god.

"Do you remember the day before your thirteenth birthday?" he asks, his voice now singular but no less intimidating. He doesn't wait for my reply. He knows my answer is yes.

"It was the day we first attempted to leave this dimension. We caused a fissure to open up between here and Earth, and coincidentally at the exact same moment, your soul was straining to leave your body. But you didn't cross over, not fully. Your energy mingled with ours; our destinies fused together. We appropriated your technology, your understanding of the world, to create the net architecture we hope will propel us on to the next level. We reached within you and saw everything you were, and everything you'd become. When the fissure closed, leaving nothing but a window that followed your every move, we were disappointed we had not yet been able to travel. You returned to your body. Only, you were racked with visions of us, weren't you?"

My eyes widen in shock. "But in those visions, those nightmares . . . I saw Julian."

"Did you never suspect Julian's true nature?" The Morati leader emits a mirthless and hollow sound that might be his version of a laugh. "Julian is one of us. An angel. A Morati. We exploited your special bond. Once we had set up the net and siphoned enough power from humans, we sent him to Earth to bring you to us—so we could one day take advantage of the full range of your energy to break into heaven. In exchange we granted him his dearest wish. To live on Earth like a human."

What he is saying is too unbelievable to be true. Julian an angel? Julian a traitor? "That's impossible!"

He steps back. "You will see for yourself soon enough." The other Morati surge forward again to join their ambassador, and they surround me, picking me up as a group and carrying me through one of the narrow passageways into a great rectangular room. They set me in front of a mainframe computer so large, it takes up a wall the length of a city block.

In front of me is a sector that is flat except for a human-size indentation. It looks a bit like a giant-size muffin pan turned up on its end. When they press me into the indentation, I fit perfectly, like it was molded just for me. And I suppose it was.

I struggle against my captors, but it's no use. "Why didn't you shove me in here from the beginning?" I ask as they fit my hands into the master grooves.

"Too high profile." Their voices reverberate through the great hall. "Too easy for dissenters to find you before we were ready to use you." They fiddle with some buttons above my head, and a hologram screen lights up. "Quiet now."

My body spasms as bursts of energy and the fragmented memories of millions upon millions of people surge through me, fighting for dominance in my mind. But then I'm pulled under into a memory I recognize as my own.

Ward, Felicia. Memory #33017
Tags: none
Number of Views: 0
Owner Rating: Not rated
User Rating: Not shared

"What is that you're playing?" Grammy asks when I pause to shuffle the pages of the score in front of me.

I smile up at her. "It's the piano part for Dad's *Prancing Goat Symphony*. Came in the mail today. Isn't it gorgeous?" The way Dad has been able to capture the atmosphere of being there in those wild Turkish hills that morning blows me away. Playing his notes brings me back fully into the moment. I can feel the wind whipping through my hair, can taste the salty cheese on my tongue, can see the excitement in Dad's eyes as the goats began their performance. And it also brings me closer to him again. Even though we're an ocean apart, he made it clear on the phone last week that he's here for me. That he never stopped loving me.

Grammy blows on her steaming mug. "It's certainly . . . different. But then, your father's music isn't known for being accessible."

"No." I laugh, fingering the keys, itching to get back to the music.

"But it's nice to hear you play again. I wonder if we can attribute your recent good moods to a certain young man," she says, taking a small sip of her tea. There's a teasing twinkle in her eye that belies her gruff tone.

Blushing, I glance at the wall clock hanging in the foyer. Seventeen after one. "Speaking of which, Neil is picking me up in a few. His cousin is getting married." Well, technically it's more of a commitment ceremony, but they're calling it a wedding.

"Angela," Grammy states, a judgmental twinge creeping into her voice. "I haven't seen her since she stopped attending services."

"I've never met her, but Neil was pretty adamant about going to show his support," I say, not wanting to turn Angela and her alternative lifestyle into a discussion.

I stand up, stepping away from the piano bench so I can give the full skirt of my sundress some space while I spin. "How do I look?"

Grammy approaches me, using her free hand to smooth my hair and check for chips in my nail polish. I can tell she'd like to debate the appropriateness of bare shoulders, but surprisingly, she holds it in. "Yellow is a lovely color on you."

"Thank you, Grammy." I plant a kiss on her forehead and squeeze her shoulder gently. "For everything. I mean it."

Grammy nods curtly. "Have fun, dear." I think I might detect a ghost of a smile as she hobbles back toward the kitchen.

I use the few minutes I have before Neil's arrival to immerse myself in Dad's notes, letting my fingers fly across the keys as if they hadn't been away from the piano for months. I'm in the middle of the third movement when I hear a car horn blaring. Startled, I look up at the clock. Neil's late.

I close the lid of the piano, grab my purse, and rush to meet him.

"Happy Birthday, Felicia," Neil calls out to me across the lawn, opening the passenger door of his car as I skip out of the house, letting the screen door slam behind me. He's wearing pressed khakis and a summery blue-and-white-checked button-down shirt.

"It's not my birthday till tomorrow, silly," I say breathlessly as I throw my arms around his neck and tilt my head up, waiting for his lips to touch mine. He brushes them quickly and then takes my arm, twirling and depositing me in the passenger seat before firmly closing my door.

Not five seconds later he's beside me, gripping the steering wheel, his foot on the gas. "We're going to be so late."

"Well, better late than never, right?" I say as he peels out, squealing the tires, gunning it down the street. "And you'd better slow down. You've tempted fate by wishing me happy birthday early, you know."

He glances at me quickly, taking the corner at high speed, not even really pausing for the stop sign. "What do you mean?"

"It's just one of those German quirks. A superstition. They think if you wish someone happy birthday before the actual day, you are inviting death to swoop in and carry that person off."

Neil shakes his head. "That's crazy talk! I celebrate birthdays for at least a week, and I like to get a head start."

"Oooh . . . does that mean I get presents every day for seven days?" I say, teasing.

"I don't know, but you might want to check the glove compartment."

I squeal in delight and wrestle open the compartment.

Inside there's a small box, wrapped in silver paper with little silver bells hanging from a gold ribbon. I pull it out.

"You're not tricking me into opening Angela's wedding present, are you?" I ask.

He laughs. "No, but I did have both wrapped in the same paper."

I survey the backseat and then shoot him a wary look when I don't see any silver paper. "Where's Angela's?"

"In the trunk." He reaches over and pulls at the ribbon playfully. "C'mon. Stop stalling and open it!"

I disentangle the silver bells from the package and hang them over his rearview mirror. We've pulled onto an old country road, and the bells swing wildly whenever we hit the curves. "Aren't you driving a bit fast?" I ask.

Neil glances at the speedometer. "No more than seven over. Cops here don't pull you over for that."

I slide my finger under the tape, careful not to rip the paper, and unwrap a small white fabric-covered ring box. My heart skips a beat, and I freeze for a second. Did Neil buy me a ring?

I pull open the box, and the hinge makes a dull popping noise. It's not a ring. It's a charm. A charm in the shape of a skep. I exhale deeply, not exactly sure if I'm relieved or disappointed.

"Do you like it?" Neil asks, his voice wobbling slightly. "When I saw it, I thought of you. I know how much you like those vintage beehives."

I look at it in wonder. "No, it's perfect." I lean over to give him a kiss on the cheek, but as I do, he half turns his head, and I end up kissing him on the corner of his mouth.

"I love it. I mean, as long as you don't picture me in that bee suit every time I wear it."

"Aw, you were adorable in that big, plastic baggy suit," he says. "In fact, I think that might have been the moment I fell in love with you."

"Oh, please!" I shriek, whipping his arm with the ribbon.

He twists his arm away from me and scrunches up his shoulder as if to protect himself from my blows. "It's true! I swear!" I stop my assault, and he relaxes, turning to me with one of his trademark dimpled grins. "I really wish you'd wear it more often."

We're both laughing when we hear the sirens. The car jerks as Neil switches his foot from the gas to the brakes to round the next curve. I grip the handle on the door, suddenly alert.

When I see the police car coming straight at us, in our lane, I scream. Neil swerves. There's a terrible sound at impact. Metal upon metal. And as the cars spin together in a macabre dance, as glass shards come flying at my face, time slows to a crawl. The last frame of the film of my life, the last flash my eyes process before fading to black, is of the driver of the police car. Julian.

Lightning bolts tear through my body as the Morati flip the switch on me again, bringing me back with one terrible thought in my head. What the Morati said about Julian is true. He betrayed me. He caused the accident that killed me. I'm truly on my own. And then I black out.

CHAPTER 21

"WAKE UP, SWEET PEA!" Dad shakes my shoulders and pulls the thin sheet off me. "Mom wants to go out and pick up your birthday cake."

I grumble but wipe the sleep out of my eyes as I kick my legs over the side of the bed. One of my feet gets caught in the mosquito netting, and only then do I remember where I am. Kenya. Our second day. The late-afternoon sun trickles in through a window so reinforced with metal bars that I don't know why the builders even bothered to put in windows.

Dad hums in the hallway as I jam my feet into my red flip-flops. I grab my pink backpack from atop my suitcase. When I emerge from my room scratching a huge red bite on my arm, Dad hustles me down the stairs, out the door, and across the courtyard to the car.

Mother's already sitting in the driver's seat, and she puffs out short breaths when she sees me. "Why do you let her drag that infernal backpack everywhere we go? It's so stuffed full of crap, she can hardly carry it by herself."

Instead of answering, Dad calls shotgun. He gets into the front, ruffles my mother's hair, and plants a loud kiss on her forehead. She laughs.

I get into the backseat and slam the door behind me, hugging the backpack to my chest like a shield. It holds my favorite sweatshirt, a few books, a notepad with a book I'm writing with Autumn, and a glitter nail polish kit.

The guard that Mother hired this morning opens the gate for us, and we cruise through the narrow streets of the housing area until we reach a main avenue lined with stalls of all sorts. Venders hawk flowers, traditional African clothing, even furniture. Then I spy sleepy bundles of white glossy fur. Puppies!

"Can we get a dog, Dad? Look how cute they are. Please, please, please? For my birthday present?" I stick my head and torso out the window to get a closer look and squeal when a puppy with chocolate eyes lifts his head and whines at me.

"Sit back down!" Mother engages the automatic windows, and they close all the way. "Porter told me they drug those puppies to keep them docile. It's sickening."

Dad shakes his head. "Sorry, sweet pea. What else is on your wish list?"

Ugh! Why doesn't Dad ever stand up to her? "Nothing," I say sourly. I imagine taking home my chocolate-eyed puppy. I'll name him Hershey, and he'll always sit next to me on the bench when I practice piano.

At the end of the avenue, we enter a roundabout and then pull into the guarded parking lot of a fancy-looking mall. Whereas the rest of Nairobi has been dusty and rough, the shopping plaza is a sleek and pristine white. Several uniformed men rush over when we exit the car, and offer to watch it for us. And when we climb the wide stairs to enter the stately main building, we're greeted by at least a dozen armed guards.

"Well, if it isn't Evangeline Ward." A stiff man with a British accent approaches us and shakes Mother's hand vigorously. "What brings you here this fine evening?"

"Porter Huntley. Lovely to see you again." Mother smiles primly. "This is my husband, Elliot, and my daughter, Felicia."

"We're picking up my birthday cake," I blurt as Porter and Dad shake hands.

"Well, happy birthday to you, miss." Porter pats me on the head. "How old are you? Twelve?"

I stand straighter, gripping the straps of my backpack. "I'll be thirteen tomorrow."

But Porter has lost interest in me. He invites Mother for a ristretto. She says she'd love some and asks Dad to pick up my cake.

Dad tugs on my arm, but I dig in my heels and say I

want to wait by the fountain. He nods and tells me to stay there and not to move.

The fountain is round and relatively plain. It looks like a kiddie pool or a small pond, except for the fountain that protrudes from the center in a trumpet pattern. I sit on the low bench surrounding it and make tiny waves in the water with my fingertips. I think about my sweet puppy Hershey and how I could go visit him while my parents are otherwise occupied. It will only take me a few minutes to walk there, pet him, and then walk back. They'll never know I was gone.

I stride by the guards and enter the melee on the avenue. There are people and cars everywhere, and I have to push my way through the crowd. By the time I reach the puppies, my feet and bare shins are covered in grit. I'm sweaty, and the mosquito bite on my arm is driving me crazy. Hershey whimpers when I approach him, and the vendor, a scruffy, skinny man, holds him out to me. I scratch Hershey behind his ears and run my hands over his soft fur.

A car stops behind us, and a woman calls out, distracting the vendor. Hershey squirms out of his grasp and jumps away, weaving between people's legs as he makes his way toward an alley. I dash after him, my flip-flops thwacking against the ground and my heavy backpack banging against my tailbone. I'm close enough to reach out and grab the puppy, when I trip over my shoe and fall.

"Crap!" I've skinned my knee, and I wince as I pick myself up. How am I going to explain this to Dad? Hershey skitters around the corner, and long shadows spill around me. I look up to see the oranges and pinks of a spectacular sunset, and I realize with a sinking stomach that I'm alone in this alley. I shiver despite the heat.

Bummed about losing Hershey, I turn to head back to the shopping plaza, and run straight into two men. The larger of the two has a scar that runs the width of his forehead. The smaller one holds out a knife.

"Give your bag here and we won't hurt you," the smaller one growls. Instinctively I back away, and the bigger one lunges at me. He tears the backpack off me, lifting me into in the air in the process. I crash heavily to my hands and knees. I cough, trying to stand, but something slams into the back of my head and I go down.

There's a piercing light, a tunnel of sorts, and I blink furiously as I try to adjust to the brightness. When I squint, I can make out the shape of a boy a few years older than me. He's looking longingly into something shaped like a mirror, but the glass doesn't reflect his face. Instead it reveals a street scene. There's a police car, a mob of people crowded into a narrow alley. A man lifts a girl—is it me?—and cradles her to his chest. He's crying openly, inconsolable. She's limp in his arms, blood streams down her face, and a single red flip-flop dangles from one of her feet.

The boy spins around, and his wild, dark eyes bore into mine. "You!" he exclaims, glancing back and forth between me and his windowlike mirror. He leaps toward me, and I feel the icy stab of fear when he touches my arm. "Time to go."

I spin out of his grasp. I fall through darkness, and surface in my dad's arms. The boy in my nightmare is gone, and the pain in my head is unbearable. I let out a scream to rival the sirens reverberating through the alley. I squeeze my eyes shut.

After two heartbeats the pain is gone. Hard surfaces press into me from all sides, like a coffin. This is my new reality, and none of what I've experienced has been just a nightmare. Though that day in Nairobi is long past, I really am trapped in the Morati's palace, a pawn in their terrible plan.

Memories stream through me, and whether it's in the blink of an eye or in the passage of several millennia, I experience the lifetimes of millions. First steps, first kisses. Last days of school, last rites. The pure concentrated energy of these individual moments flows through my veins.

Sometimes a memory of a girl named Felicia will push through, imprint itself into my consciousness, and I'll think *That's me! I'm her!* But am I still me if only my shadow self remains, even if everything I am is eclipsed by the demands of the Morati, my new hosts?

Connected as I am to them, I feel the Morati's hubris. I can sense their movements, their gathering of an army of humans infected with the rage virus. The scanner drones relay positions of the enemy, and alarms blare as the rebels ambush the palace, trying to draw the Morati out. Through it all, the Morati's inner guard watches over me, and I have a front-row seat to the action, viewing it through their eyes.

I see Mira and Eli leading a charge of several thousand rebel troops against the Morati palace. The rebels are scarily efficient in dispatching the infected human army that makes up the front lines. These conscripts fall, and then fade away. The rebels' human recruits also disappear shortly after being cut down. One I recognize as Virginia. She fights valiantly, flipping and kicking like a ninja cheerleader, but a Morati arrow pierces her heart. I feel her energy as it swirls through the palace, heading off to begin her afterlife journey anew, to be resorted. She will forget all this, and forget me yet again. Nevertheless, she is still a friend.

After a few days, when the infected human army is annihilated, the rebels set their sights on the Morati. They don't generally shoot to kill, only to incapacitate. Eli shouts orders, and fallen Morati are bound and dragged away. But sometimes one of my Morati brethren is ripped away from the confines of this dimension, and I experience it as keenly as an amputation.

The battle rages on. Losses are high on both sides, but the Morati's inner guard stays put. They stick so close to me that their pollution coats my skin like a thick sheen of sweat.

Until one day a horn blasts, thundering through the palace. The Morati guards flow away from me like a retreating tide. My physical body has been left alone. My eyes see only what the Morati see: vicious fighting, the severing of wings. My ears are attuned to the deep silence of the hall. I call out, "I'm still here!" But no one answers.

Until someone does. "I am too," says a voice, reaching

for the shell of the girl who was. "I'm here to save you." He pulls at my hands, trying to disconnect them from their grooves in the Morati's mainframe, but they won't budge.

"It's too late," I say. "I know what you are. What you've done. How you gave me to the Morati."

"That wasn't me. You have to believe me," he says, his voice rising.

I don't answer. There is nothing to say.

"Yes, I was supposed to kill you that day in the police car," he admits, "but I didn't do it. I couldn't have—you know that. Because if I did, you would've skipped this level."

"You're the one who told me that. Likely another lie."

"I couldn't have killed you." He pauses then, as if he's taking a deep breath. "Because I love you."

"Prove it," I say. I know he can't. He doesn't even know what love really is.

"They took everything from me. They took away my chance to live on Earth. They took you. I was so happy to find you again here in Level Two . . . I would never turn you over to them."

"That's not proof."

"I can prove my intentions," he says.

I wait. Julian retreats. Time passes. I don't know how much, but the Morati guard does not return. They're still busy with their fight.

"I'm here. And I've brought him with me," says Julian.

"Who?"

"Neil."

At the mention of Neil I feel the essence of the girl who was once Felicia and how she yearns to break free. Perhaps she and I may rejoin after all.

"Felicia! It's really you!" The voice is pure love, adoration, gratitude. Pure Neil. He traces his fingers down the cheek of the body that stands before him. He peers into eyes that can't see him, because they're watching the Morati gain the upper hand again. Mira and Eli and the rest of the rebels are falling back, slumped over with exhaustion, their clothes in tatters.

I pull my attention away from the rebels' imminent defeat. I want to concentrate on Neil now, while I still can.

"How did you die?" I ask Neil. I feel a sob build within Felicia. She hates that his life was cut short, but she loves that he's so close, after all this time spent missing him.

He sounds shocked. "You don't know? I died with you."

So Julian lied about that, too.

"That doesn't matter now," Julian breaks in. "What matters is that there's a whole army out there fighting the Morati. We can beat them back, but only you can end this. Can't you see that everything you've been through, all your training, has been leading up to this moment? This choice? You have the chance to fight the Morati from the inside. Don't you see how big this is?"

"Don't you know you've already lost?" I ask.

"Felicia!" says Neil desperately. "Look at me!"

"I can't. I can't see you."

"Don't look with your eyes. Look with your soul," he

says. His voice is so near that when lips touch mine, I know they're Neil's.

The tingling sensation his kiss leaves and the confidence in his voice push me to pull together the little strength I have left. I reach deep into my shell. I struggle to set myself free. Finally I surge through veins clogged with the detritus of other souls, burst out, and reclaim my body.

Then I'm able to gaze upon the boy before me. The boy who never doubted me, even when I doubted myself. The way he's looking at me tells me he doesn't doubt me now. I smile at him, a single tear running down my cheek. "Thank you, Neil. Thank you for showing me what real love is."

As I take in the faces of Neil and Julian behind him, it becomes clear to me what I need to do. What my role is. The Morati stuck me in this machine because I'm a piece of their plan to break into heaven. But I don't have to let them use me. By sacrificing myself, I can take down the whole system, saving Neil and saving everyone else. At least I got to see Neil one last time.

Closing my eyes, I call up every shred of power I have within me. I must become part of the system in order to bring it down. What starts out as a low hum gets louder and louder until my body is shaking with energy as loud as a roar. My skin expands, begins to connect with the metal around it.

"Nooooooooo!"

I hear Julian's agonized scream at the same time I am

torn from the mainframe and thrown across the room. I force open my eyes, gritting my teeth through the pain, to see that Julian has taken my place. Because of our connection when I crossed over that day in Nairobi, I realize his energy is the only acceptable substitute for mine, and he must have known that too. As Julian's body fuses with the system, he looks directly at me. Light streams out of his every pore, but his intense gaze does not waver.

A powerful quake rocks the palace, and Neil is beside me, looking for a place to hold my body that is not ripped raw or cut. "We have to go!" he shouts into my ear, scooping me up into his arms. But I keep my eyes riveted on Julian, dazed by his sacrifice. Why did he do it?

A flash of light, more powerful than an atom bomb, blinds me, knocks us to the ground. For a long moment there is only white. And then it's over. Julian is gone. The palace is gone.

Neil and I are lying under a blue sky in a vast field of green grass, surrounded by wildflowers. There is not a single hive or sterile white surface to be seen.

He props himself up on his arm and surveys my body from head to toe. "Your injuries . . . they're gone," he says with wonder. "Am I dreaming? This all seems so surreal."

I laugh, pinching my skin, as fresh and pink as a baby's, and I smooth the folds of my yellow sundress. "It's real. We made it real."

And then he smiles the luminous and pure smile I've been waiting my whole death to see again. He fans my hair out around my shoulders, and I reach up and undo the top button of his blue-and-white-checked shirt. He presses against me, and when our lips meet, all the pent-up feelings inside me—the uncertainty, the longing, the joy, the sorrow—explode in my chest. Immersed in our kiss, we roll over until I am on top of him.

Neil breaks away first. "Uh . . . there's someone staring at us." I roll off him and look up. Mira. Glowing with a radiant inner light.

"You must be Neil!" She extends her hand to Neil, and when he shakes it, she pulls him up.

He looks at her in a daze. "Are you an angel?" I scramble up and stand beside him, now wondering the same thing.

"Why, yes. I am." She trills her bell-like laugh. She traces a circle above her head, and a halo appears. "Does this make it easier for you to tell?"

"And Eli?" I ask, flabbergasted. "Is he an angel too?"

"The head of the rebellion?" She smirks at me indulgently, shaking her head slightly. "Of course he is. Right now he's rounding up the rest of the Morati and locking them away until Judgment Day. We think God will be pleased. You'll put in a good word for us, won't you?"

"Maybe you could clear something up for me," I say. If I ever expect to get any answers, now is probably the best time to ask. "Do you know why Julian took my place? And if his energy was a substitute for mine, why didn't he sacrifice himself from the beginning? Why drag me into it?"

"Julian did try once to take down the system on his

own. He was angry that they broke their promise to him that he could stay on Earth. He wanted revenge. But the mainframe was molded for you. When your energy and the Morati's intermingled during the fissure, it opened a channel to your world and your technology—it was their access to your consciousness that allowed the Morati to create the mainframe at all. And that fusion was what made you so special here—such an active subject who could adapt relatively easily without the net. That was the reason we needed you just as badly. You were always the one who would have to start the process, either for the Morati or against them." She shrugs her shoulders. "Maybe he sacrificed himself because he was looking for redemption. Or maybe he had nothing left to lose."

"So that's it—he's gone?" Pressure builds in my chest when I think about how they had all known all along what I meant to the system. How they manipulated and used me. How Julian played me for a fool, over and over again.

Mira laughs again. "Not gone, my dear. His energy had to go somewhere. Question is, was he deemed worthy enough to ascend to the next level? I don't think you've seen the last of Julian."

I shudder. Because she's right—if anyone can find his way to me, it's Julian.

"But why did you pretend to be human recruits of the rebellion?" I ask. "Why couldn't you come out and tell me that you were angels?"

"That was all Julian's idea. He didn't want questions

hanging in the air that would be inconvenient for him to answer. And we agreed that it would be easier to get you to cooperate if you thought we were like you."

It does sound exactly like Julian, so I don't doubt for a second that he was behind it all.

"So what now?" I ask.

"Now the feast of saints can begin anew." She turns Neil and me so we are facing each other. "Here. Let me show you something." She lifts our hands and presses our palms together. Skin on skin, they become a conduit, sucking us both into our memories.

I see flashes of both our lives—together and apart. The two of us walking down the street, tucked into each other, in our own little world. Neil laughing with Andy as they throw firecrackers from atop a roof. Me, arms outstretched to the jungle canopy as I conquered the main temple of Tikal. Neil holding me tight in the wreck of his car until his life ebbed away.

Mira slides her hand between our palms to break us apart, and the memories stop.

"This was always how it was supposed to be," Mira says, and Neil and I stare at her, openmouthed. "Everyone sharing their memories, helping one another come to terms with them so they could move on. Maybe it's time for you to move on too." She pats me on the shoulder and glides away.

Since I didn't move on automatically when I faced the memory of my death, I must have some say in when I move on. How can she possibly think I'd want to now? I turn to Neil. "We're free."

Neil puts his arm around my waist, pulls me close. "It's unbelievable. All this. I feel like we've been given a second chance."

"Speaking of second chances, there's a particular memory of yours I'd like to access, if you'll let me." I look up at his face, taking in all his features. Committing them to memory.

"Really?" His eyes light up. "Which one?"

I want to be able to show him how much he means to me, how invested I am in him and his life. I long to feel him so deeply that he'll never be erased from my mind. No matter what. "I'm sorry I missed your performance in *Our Town*. I'd love to experience it through your eyes."

"Of course." Neil lifts his palm toward mine. When our skin connects, there's a hum of electricity, and a rush of images fills my mind. The transfer is nearly instantaneous, but I feel Neil's every bead of sweat that evening, how the bright stage lights cut him off from the audience, how he uttered every line as though he were really living the play.

We drop our hands to our sides.

"'*When you've been here longer, you'll see that our life here is to forget all that . . . and be ready for what's ahead*,'" I quote from the play. "Can we really just forget our lives? Do we need to?" It seems impossible to me that I could one day want to let go.

"Whatever happens, we have each other." Neil hugs me, and I lay my head on his shoulder.

It's pure bliss to be with Neil again. We spend time composing top ten lists of our favorite memories, diving in and out of our lives with ease. When he suffers symptoms of his withdrawal from the memory chambers, much less severe than mine but not magically cured with the collapse of the Morati architecture, I press my palm against his extra hard and give him some of my strength. People move on every day, and Mira tells us that if we don't find someone we're looking for, they've probably already found their peace and moved on. I know I won't see Autumn here, but I'm always on the lookout for Virginia.

But soon enough we find that despite our joy in each other, against the vivid backdrops of our memories, our lives here pale in comparison. Events fade into one another, details become fuzzy. Nothing is archived, so nothing can be retrieved or relived.

We both experience it, the gradual yearning for something more. And one day we know it's time to go. Maybe even to a place where we'll finally be able to get some sleep.

A door opens before us, a door into the great unknown. I take Neil's hand, and we step through it together.